SCARLET SISTER MARY

Scarlet Sister Mary

A NOVEL BY

JULIA PETERKIN

Foreword by A. J. Verdelle

BROWN THRASHER BOOKS

The University of Georgia Press

ATHENS AND LONDON

Published in 1998 as a Brown Thrasher Book
by the University of Georgia Press
Athens, Georgia 30602
© 1928 by The Bobbs-Merrill Company;
© 1956 by Julia Peterkin
Foreword to the Brown Thrasher Edition
© 1998 by A. J. Verdelle
All rights reserved
Printed and bound by McNaughton & Gunn, Inc.
The paper in this book meets the guidelines for
permanence and durability of the Committee on
Production Guidelines for Book Longevity of the
Council on Library Resources.

Printed in the United States of America

02 01 00 99 98   P   5 4 3 2 1

Library of Congress Cataloging in Publication Data
Peterkin, Julia Mood, 1880–1961.
    Scarlet Sister Mary : a novel / by Julia Peterkin ;
foreword by A. J. Verdelle.
      p.   cm.
    "Brown thrasher books."
    ISBN 0-8203-2377-2
    I. Title.
[PS3531.E77S37   1998]
813´ .54—dc21   97-28924

British Library Cataloging in Publication Data available

Scarlet Sister Mary was originally published in 1928
by The Bobbs-Merrill Company.

To

WILLIAM GEORGE PETERKIN

FOREWORD

A. J. Verdelle

LYRIC beauty must have been Julia Mood Peterkin's primary aim for her 1928 novel, *Scarlet Sister Mary*. Peterkin's Pulitzer Prize–winning novel has endured and was acclaimed because of the true literature of the book. Many aspects of *Scarlet Sister Mary* are worthy of note, including its canonical storyline—transposed into an African American context, Peterkin's approaches to writing narrative about black people, and the novel's reception among Peterkin's contemporaries. Peterkin's other works of fiction, *Green Thursday*, *Black April*, and *Bright Skin*, have survived also, but only *alongside* her master work, *Scarlet Sister Mary*.

Julia Mood Peterkin had a keen sense of concept, and she could turn a magic phrase. By writing about the enduring American subject—the "Negro question"—Peterkin places her novels squarely in the twentieth century's dialogic mainstream, a dialogue which continues as the century comes to an end.

In *Scarlet Sister Mary*, Peterkin presents a com-

munity of black fieldworkers on Blue Brook Plantation. The novel is set in the post-slavery low
country of South Carolina. For this community of
Negroes [1] to be the only characters in a novel was *in-
novative* for literature of Peterkin's day. At the time,
readers were amazed to encounter a community of
Negroes independent of the dramatic interference
of whites. Some readers were irritated, even threatened, that the oppression of black people does not
dominate Julia Peterkin's story. This was a new
notion, which one might imagine would inspire
relief. Observing the black community separately
highlighted its normalcy, its participation in the
emotional and developmental trajectories of the
larger human community. Without the low ceiling
of white denigration, the black characters in *Scarlet Sister Mary* exhibited both humanity and com-
plexity. Peterkin endowed the workers on the plantation in her novel with human psychology, human
emotion, human need.

Sister Mary—or "Si May-e" as she is called in
the novel—is a young woman, a strong and spirited character. Mary's primary work is fieldwork;
her way is the plantation way. Bound to a life of
planting, hoeing, and weeding, Mary harvests cotton by the hundreds of pounds. She is portrayed as
feeling better when she is sweating, when she is
swinging an ax. By magic of fiction and by jaundice

of time, Mary is happy with her lot—working in
the heat and living in a shack.

One could argue that *Scarlet Sister Mary* is
Hawthorne's *Scarlet Letter*, transposed into black.
Like the other scarlet novel, *Scarlet Sister Mary*
concerns itself with illegitimate children and the
moral conundrum that succumbing to the amorous
instinct can create. Sister Mary greets the narrative in the midst of her nubile, impressionable
youth. She is courted by several responsible men,
but Mary chooses her childhood sweetheart, the
feckless and charming July Pinesett, as her mate.
The early sections of the novel reverberate with
portents of the sorry choice she makes in wanting
July, but it is he she chooses—first to bed and then
to wed—and therein we have the central crisis of
the novel. When Mary's child is born some seven
months later, the "full ripe" baby reveals Mary's
sin, a condition that never ceases to be discussed
and referred to as Mary makes her journey through
to the novel's finish.

As a result of Mary's desire and fecundity, she
goes on to birth nine children. This brood links her
character to the kind of breeding slavery empha-
sized. But Mary's many children are sweet to her;
they represent nothing negative to her, and she is
proud of each one. Late in the story, when she is
faced with raising three infants at once, Mary re-

ports always wanting to have children "in a litter," which is how Peterkin presents Mary's multiple births.

Mary's commitment to her own right choices is necessary to keep her unrepentant, an emotional position that is central to the tension of the narrative. Mary's lack of trepidation about her sins only makes their commission worse, more glaring, more worthy of talk. And Mary's neighbors and fellow fieldhands do talk—gossiping if for nothing else but to ease their workload.

Mary's sins, the scarlet ones, are sex outside of marriage and the resulting illegitimate births of children. With almost a dozen babies and not one present husband, she is seen by most who know her as steeped and mired in sin. For most of the novel, Mary is unconcerned about her "sinfulness," the novel's central drama. Mary believes her life is all right. It is, after all, *her* life.

The novel does not date itself explicitly, but throughout the story, the characters leave and return to the plantation at will. This seems to place the novel temporally during Reconstruction, or during the subsequent sharecropping years. Some of the blacks presented in *Scarlet Sister Mary*, by virtue of their age and the past it suggests, could easily have been slaves on the very acres Peterkin "mistressed."

Notice how Peterkin romanticizes the cotton-picking gang and the cotton harvest time:

> She [Mary] went to the field to join the cotton pickers. . . . Bright-turbaned women, deep-chested, ample-hipped and strong, bent women with withered skin and trembling uncertain fingers, little gay chocolate-colored children who played as they worked, moved in a group up and down the long rows, laughing, talking, picking the white locks of cotton and putting them in the crocus sacks swung from neck or shoulder. . . . The picking is easy. Nimble fingers move quickly. Every boll is left clean. Eyes glance up to meet other eyes. Musical voices flow into one another. Cotton-picking time is the best of the year. Every work-day is a holiday. (pp. 59–60)

Peterkin seems to misunderstand, or at best, underestimate, the labor of fieldwork, of laundry, of bending, tending plantation crops. There is nothing romantic about picking cotton or leaning over a wash kettle all day, the heat from the sun and the heat from the flame surreal, a scorching sandwich. And Peterkin leans far too frequently into comparisons between African Americans and animals—a comparison that was not unusual for the 1920s and the decades before, but that has nonetheless been legitimately rejected, given the tides of time. The lens of our future has exposed Peterkin's kind of his-

toric and casual prejudices; her animal comparisons and romanticization of fieldwork are some of
the irritants we face in her work, today.[2]

The characters who populate *Scarlet Sister Mary*
have a clear past of slavery and a hazy future in the
vanishing, uncertain South. *Scarlet Sister Mary*,
however, is not written about Negroes on a cusp
of change. Peterkin's work is about *her* Negroes as
she saw them, lived with them, and cared for them
on the plantation in South Carolina that became
her own through marriage. One writer actually
referred to the characters in her books as "Julia
Peterkin's Negroes."[3] This reference is fascinating
in the way it makes a pun of ownership, in Peterkin's name. And, of course, it fits—Peterkin did
make up her own batch of Negroes, and let them
live out her southern ideologies and perceptions on
the page.

Scarlet Sister Mary was not, in its time, a historical novel, although there is a way that it is a
historical novel now. Nor was *Sister Mary* considered a slave novel in its time. But Peterkin's narrative and her characters are barely distinguish-
able from the stories of slaves; the actions of the
novel are hard to separate from what we know
of slavery time. Peterkin wrote about the Gullah
people—the same insular culture of African descendants depicted in the 1992 film, *Daughters of*

the Dust, by Julie Dash. Peterkin's themes, however, are not so anthropological but are more the grist of fiction: love, marriage, progeny and maturation, religion, personal systems of belief.

The novel's axis of event, crisis, and transformation, however, deviates from work and occupation— whether slavelike, or not. *Scarlet Sister Mary* is a love and marriage story, or in terminology more specific to Mary's caste and condition, *Scarlet Sister Mary* is a tale of love and breeding. That is to say, Julia Peterkin has written a stunning, beautiful, and memorable novel using images of African Americans that are now fatigued and timeworn. (In Peterkin's time, of course, the images seemed the vanguard—due primarily to Peterkin's humanizing pen.)

In constructing *Scarlet Sister Mary*, Julia Peterkin took away half the cast(e). The Blue Brook Plantation is artificial but absorbing with its complete absence of whites. This absence hangs heavily over the story and significantly affects the novel's drama. In the traditional slave narrative, with which *Scarlet Sister Mary* is reasonably compared, oppression is often embodied in white characters, who provide part of the slave narrative's dramatic opposition. The point/counterpoint of slave narratives includes the quest for freedom, which is often equated with resistance against enslaving whites. The counterpoint of this quest/resistance narrative line is the attainment of some forms of freedom, achieving some positive self-definition outside the oppressing rubric of white, southern, plantation society.

The dramatic or theatrical light of the novel, therefore, shone completely on the African American community—the erstwhile slaves, whom Peterkin knew from daily contact. Thus, the subject of her novel is the internal drama of the society of plantation Negroes. *Scarlet Sister Mary* is the story of those who stayed, that vast, partisan army of workers who did not, once freed, leave the South, but rather remained on the familiar estates, continuing to live in the slave shacks, continuing to work out among the crops.

Before Mary's wedding, early in the novel, Peterkin shows Mary contemplating her departure from the shack in which she lives. Although it is a romanticized description, Mary's thoughts reveal the poverty of the Quarters and indicate how these conditions come to cross generations:

> She loved every board in its weather-beaten sides, every shingle in its warped roof, every rusty nail that held it together. . . . The house where she and July would live at the other end of the Quarter street was exactly like it, for it was built at the same time, by the same people and by the same pattern.

Its roof was warped too, its rotted shingles were
edged with small green ferns, the wide-mouthed
chimney rising out of its ridge-pole took up a third
of the inside wall in the same way. It was an old
unpainted wooden cabin sitting low on the earth,
heavy with years, yet able and strong in its beams
and joists and rafters and sides, for it was built in
the old days when men took time to choose timbers
carefully and to lay them together with skill. Like
this old house, it had held many generations. Red
birth, black death, hate, sorrow and love had all
dwelt inside it, sheltered by its roof, shielded by its
walls. July's people had lived in it for generations,
but this was the home where she was born. Everything here was part of her life. She was born in this
same bed. The crippled table over in the corner,
heaped high with clean quilts, had been there ever
since she could remember. The cupboard where her
clothes stayed and the leaning shelf by the window
with the four sad-irons resting on it after their hard
week's work had never been out of their places since
they were put there by women who lived here before
Maum Hannah was born. When Maum Hannah
died they would all belong to Mary. (pp. 26–27)

Peterkin was impressed by the belief systems
and the religious practices of plantation blacks.
Peterkin observed, for example, that acquiescing

to or ascending the burdens one faced was central
to the beliefs of the community of Gullah people.
This is not news, of course: that one should bear
burdens was a major tenet of the Christian slave-
ocracy.[4] Peterkin used the concept of "burden bearing": she isolated it and translated it into the novel's action. Sister Mary's story, then, is full of acts
and visions, some of which are revelatory: Mary
carries many buckets with ease, Mary shoulders
many burdens sweetly. Mary's ability to carry—
her children, full buckets, her plantation provi-
sions—set the stage for her "triumph" in the narrative. Mary survives because she is a carrier
woman—she does not shrink from laundry, babies,
or her trials. Peterkin attached a tenet of religious
salvation to the actions of her protagonist; Mary
herself becomes a wavering argument about religious conversion. That is working a concept in fiction; that is writing near the bone.

Peterkin similarly writes in circles around black
mysticism, superstition, and folk wisdom—con-
cepts closely allied to religious practice for black
workers on the plantation. "Do Master, look down
and see what a rat is done!" Maum Hannah wails
in the prescient early pages of the novel. The rat,
of course, has created tragedy in the narrative.
In the middle of the crisis of the novel, Maum Hannah wisely advises Mary to "let old sorrows sleep."

This is a beautiful expression of a loving admonition; it is folk wisdom at its highest. Maum Hannah is the wise one, finding predictive truth in signs, speaking constantly and cogently on the order of the universe.

Sister Mary herself has also inherited and upheld superstitious notions, some of them wild. Peterkin renders Mary with both comedy and anxiety: "A screech owl began a mournful song. A bad-luck sound. Mary got up quickly and put the shovel in the fire to stop it. People have to rule owls."

Peterkin's arrangement of the narrative of Sister Mary is what is truly virtuosic. The story alternates between character scenes and plantation scenes, as if there may be some dialogue, internal to the novel, going on between them. It is a point/counterpoint within the structure of the novel. Mary, for instance, can ask a question, and the tepid night can answer.

Consider this: After Mary becomes visibly pregnant, and after she and July begin to talk about the baby—its gender, its coming, its future—Mary recalls July's antics with Cinder on the day of their wedding. Mary is happy because Cinder has gone away to town, via the riverboat that comes regularly to where Mary lives. She is full of thoughts of her baby, her marriage, July, Cinder, the town, July and Cinder's displayed attractions. She is on the edge of elation and worry; the reader knows this. Here is Peterkin's exterior, following Mary's repartee with July:

> The old roof was broken where some of the shingles had rotted, and every day the sun shone through the cracks and fell in bright streaks on the floor, reminding Mary that the roof ought to be mended before the cold winter rains would beat in. The old door sagged and the window-blinds creaked sadly on their hinges. Their time was out, and they ought to be replaced by strong new ones. (p. 62)

And there is more:

> By Christmas the tide of the year had ebbed very low. The earth lay silent. Buzzards floated aimlessly about in the high still air. Wild ducks filled the marshes with a confusion of quacking and splashing, but the song-birds hopped about sadly, hunting their food and the few notes they sang were low and cheerless. The winds gave the tides little peace but kept the water in the river and the rice-fields ruffled.
>
> Sometimes great, booming, wet gusts came in from the sea, making the trees bend and bow their heads. Icy gales shrieked and howled as they went rushing by, chilling and blighting everything they touched. The willows that bordered the river were

bare of leaves and the tall gums and cypresses
that towered over everything else in the swamp
were stark naked. Winter had come in dead earnest. (p. 63)

These passages are stupendous, speaking only to
the pitiful shack and to the weather outside. But
consider them in light of Mary's imminent aban-
donment: you can read it coming, just listening to
the out-of-doors.

The narrative lilts between interior and exterior
scenes: the emotional lives of the characters represent interiors, and the pastoral, bucolic settings
of the plantation are exteriors. The interiors are
rendered primarily in dialect—dialects of speech
or dialects of folk wisdom. This in itself is a mir-
acle of comedy, surprise, memory, timing, inter-
pretation. But the exteriors breathe and sigh and
pant and crackle, as if they too live. Within spit-
ting distance of any crisis, or sweep of action, or
wash of emotion, there is one of Peterkin's exteriors, ready to inform, soothe, comment, or change
the subject.

The narrative alternates interior, exterior, back
and forth; the strategy is not clumsy, there are
no visible missteps. There is an ongoing dialectic
not immediately perceived. The interior/exterior
construction "communicates" in the narrative. A

logic prevails, a dialogue transpires; the reader is only partially aware.

Peterkin demonstrates sublime competence as a writer. She shows shrewd clarity about choosing her subjects. Every good writer makes us wonder, as readers, how they did it, how they perceived it, how they they made us believe in what we find on the page. Peterkin writes so well, and so gracefully, that you wonder whether you've absorbed it all. You want to hear *all* the conversations: antiquated, vernacular, dialectic, folkloric, prejudiced, peculiar. You read, and read again.

Julia Peterkin articulated many characteristics of black plantation society . Peterkin created an environment with strong, hardworking, opinionated adults, each with a mind of his or her own, each with a place and a stake in the community. Of the many children within this community, almost a dozen were Sister Mary's. The children in the novel have a purpose—they are a help in the fields (not unlike during slavery times), and they are an antidote to Mary's despair after her husband abandons Mary and her first baby.

Peterkin positions Mary against the world—both the world of her compatriots, which is internal to the novel, and the larger world outside the novel, which judgmental whites control and other, no less judgmental, blacks inhabit. Peterkin positions herself (almost discreetly) as Mary's defender, or if not that, at least as Mary's more objective presenter, a person who can see through, or beyond, all her wanton, scarlet sin. The way the novel reads, not everyone is convinced of Mary's worthlessness. The rigid church, inside the novel, is softly put to shame for judging Mary so continuously, so harshly.

Peterkin relies on black folk religion and black mystery to accomplish "the world against Mary," narratively. Blame comes down hard on Mary in the novel. First there is Mary's gnawed wedding cake, which portends sad days ahead. July chooses another woman, Cinder, as a dance partner, on his and Mary's wedding night. (Mary's religious practice forbade her to dance.) But later that same evening, she deigns to dance alone. Mary dances to attract attention, to "show" July. This is her first public fall from grace.

After about one year and one baby, July abandons Mary, an event that is sandwiched between storms in the novel. Maum Hannah's directions about these storms is to sit quietly and listen, while the Lord does His work. Mary's subsequent trials of death and illness with her illegitimate brood of children are punctuated by her forays into potions and charms. Black magic is presented as another form of faith.

The poles of good and evil are everywhere plumb obvious in *Scarlet Sister Mary*. The church and the plantation are good; the town is bad. Children through marriage are acceptable, otherwise not. Living an instinctual life will send you to hell, living a holy life will permit you to sit at the front in church, will guarantee you a place with the lovely, gentle white "Jedus" in heaven. July is bad; twin brother June is good. Maum Hannah's life now is holy; Maum Hannah's life before now has its mysteries. There are the church and baptismal ceremonies of the saved, the dances and conjure charms of the sinners. The moral requirements and retributions in this community of black fieldworkers are many, extreme, fundamental, discussed, enforced.

Peterkin's views of the Negroes she employed do not stand up to time. She renders the black people that she knew as simple, primal and animal-like. And then, perhaps on another page, Peterkin presents her view of plantation blacks as mystical, mythical descendants of the Dark Continent. This too is an example of Peterkin's polarities: in this case, evil and then good.

Peterkin's overall approach is not of blunt polar opposites. She shows some consciousness of the universal scheme of things. Therein, the beast has redemptive qualities. There is redemption, also, in the idioms of mystery and myth.

In the midst of an early scene when July is marking his hogs, Mary and July mark themselves similarly, to exhibit their mutual belonging. This mutilation is undertaken while they are both young, in the full flush of a mutual childhood infatuation. July cuts Mary's ear first; it was his idea. Maum Hannah, the novel's matriarch, makes Mary perform the same affront on July. We can chalk up July's imitation of the hog-marking to childish unawareness, but there are many more examples in the novel that just plain prove Peterkin's distance from the race and its most problematic stereotypes.

When Mary's brother, Ben, for example, gets angry with July, it is said that he will wring July's neck, "same as a chicken." An animalism, and a violent tendency—stomached for humor's sake. A more troubling example shows Mary caught by surprise, having her first baby out on a road alone:

> She cried for help as loud as she could, but nobody was in hearing distance, and her child was born right there in the middle of the road. The poor little creature set up such a pitiful wailing that she had to forget her own troubles and pick him up and wrap him in her apron and hurry home to Maum Hannah. . . . She had done well in her first trial at birthing a child. A woman with plenty of experience could have done no better. God must have blessed

her with the same wisdom he gave to the beasts,
who know well when the time comes to birth their
young, and instead of complaining of God's ways, as
people do, go off alone without a word, and struggle
with their labor as best they can. (pp. 75–76)

Before Mary's bad-luck wedding, a rat eats a
hole through her carefully and lovingly constructed
wedding cake. This is certainly an act of graceful
fiction on Peterkin's part, but as a dramatic event, it
is loaded with a folk dialectic that a rat's behavior
can represent admonition, can speak for a larger
force—like the godhead or the universe or the
unseen master of things. All of Peterkin's animal
usages are not equally problematic—but they do
serve the antiquated and oxymoronic function of
positioning African Americans on a beastly con-
tinuum. Peterkin's gentle handling cannot soften
these biases of belief.

Since the whites are absent, one doesn't know
where they might fall in this schema. Although
one can imagine that whites might have their own
position in her logic—the people position.

If the word "seminal" can apply to works written
by women or to those works relied on by women
across generations, then *Scarlet Sister Mary* has
been a "seminal" book in my career as a writer. I
discovered the novel as a younger reader, when I

found it quietly waiting on a library shelf somewhere. As a youthful purveyor of novels, books about women or by women were my sole interest. I sought stories about black women as special "niche reading." *Scarlet Sister Mary* qualified on all counts. I did not incorporate *Scarlet Sister Mary* into my canonical texts until late, well after I completed reading for university courses. I had to rediscover the novel on my own; fortunately, I found it and studied it before I began to write myself. This University of Georgia Press reprint will undoubtedly change the way the book is discovered, bolster its availability, and make it easier for readers to know Peterkin's work.

Early in my experience of *Scarlet Sister Mary*, I presumed the book a slave novel because that's how it reads: the entire cast of characters is black, they live in the "Quarters" of a large plantation. They live in their own company—which is to say they seem segregated. Their lives revolve around their work, which is constant: washing, tending animals and livestock, planting, nurturing, harvesting and storing crops, birthing and raising babies. Their grasp of the larger world seems limited. Their expectations of life seem few. Their speech is rich in folk wisdom and short on standard syntax. Except for the absence of whites and the whip and the auction, the characters live like slaves.

As a story, *Scarlet Sister Mary* seemed so authentic, so true to its subject, that it was a mild shock to learn later that its author was white. This realization and the questions it provoked continue to bemuse me, even from the mine of my memory. Deep inside my own first novel, *The Good Negress*, Denise (my main character) discovers *Scarlet Sister Mary* and becomes infatuated with Julia Peterkin. In a wash of wry humor, Denise learns that Peterkin was white, and she too is amazed by this unsuspected truth. "The facts" about Peterkin became a private watershed in my own literary development, intimating early in my learning that character development can and should extend beyond identity—in writing and in life.

Julia Mood was born into a romantic name and pregnant expectations. Her father was a respected and influential South Carolina physician, who held both his daughters to high standards of achievement. Julia Mood completed Converse College—a women's college in South Carolina—at the precocious age of sixteen. She and her older sister went to college together. Dr. Mood made Julia stay and take a master's degree, to keep her from entering "the world" prematurely. Julia was born in 1880, in Laurens County, in the South Carolina piedmont. She was said to have been born with a caul.[5]

Julia's mother died giving birth to her. After her mother's death, a "Negro mammy," a Gullah woman from the low country, became Julia's surrogate mother. From her "Mauma," she learned the vocabulary, the speech patterns, and the value system of the Gullahs who populated the low country. Her early vocabulary incorporated Gullah dialect. For a time in her childhood, she considered that standard English was "good-behavior" English.[6]

Julia Mood Peterkin had three careers, which overlapped sometimes: the first—and shortest— was as a teacher, the second as a wife and mother and mistress of Lang Syne Plantation, and the third, as a writer. She was born on Halloween, which adds to her personal mystery. She had flame-red hair.

While working as a teacher in Fort Motte, South Carolina, Julia Mood married a midlands planter, W. G. Peterkin. The Peterkin family was prominent and well known for their wise management of their rich land holdings, which dated to before the American Revolution. Lang Syne Plantation, into which Julia Mood married, was the place where she raised her son, William G. Peterkin Jr., and managed several hundred blacks, *in times of freedom*. Peterkin wrote "Lang Syne Plantation" as her address at the upper right corner of a letter in 1937. This says much about how she thought of her place in the world.[7] She has been referred to as *the chatelaine of Lang Syne*.[8]

Julia Peterkin was frank about writing from experience. She admitted that she was looking, transcribing, observing for the text. As mistress of Lang Syne Plantation, she came to know and "administer" the several hundred blacks who worked the land. She drew explicitly from their lives. Peterkin acknowledged that her work "goes by the name of a novel but a large part of it is fact. . . . I have lived among the Negroes. I like them. They are my friends, and I have learned so much from them. The years on the plantation have given me plenty of material, my life has been rich, so why try to improve on the truth? . . . I shall never write of white people. Their lives are not so colorful."[9] Peterkin also wrote to H. L. Mencken in 1921: "These black friends of mine live more in one Saturday night than I do in five years. I envy them, and I guess as I cannot be them, I seek satisfaction in trying to record them."

Peterkin's work was considered fresh and new in her time. Many of her readers were encountering the lives of African Americans for the first time.[10] Following Harriet Beecher Stowe's 1852 radical treatise, with its own caste of blacks, Peterkin must have almost seemed a writer without a cause. After all, Peterkin did not openly *advocate* for blacks; she simply presented them dramatically, theatrically, as people. Her readership acknowledged an introduction to new subjects—Negroes living out their own tales of romance and livelihood within the sacrosanct pages of a white woman's novel.

Scarlet Sister Mary was hailed by reviewers as even better than Peterkin's first novel, *Black April*. *Scarlet Sister Mary*, according to the reviewer in *Saturday Review of Literature*, "firmly established [Peterkin] as an interpreter of Negro character." Robert Herrick, *New Republic* reviewer, had hailed Peterkin's *Black April*, as a "considerable work of art," which showed a "mastery of dialect."[11] He also wrote that *Scarlet Sister Mary* was "something more than a novel—the revelation of a race, which has lived with the whites for hundreds of years without becoming known beneath the skin."

Peterkin's innovation and celebrity endowed her with a kind of specialist status regarding Negroes. In 1927, Peterkin was invited to review Langston Hughes's second book of poems, *Fine Clothes to the Jew*. Like other reviewers, Peterkin praised both the book and the poet. In 1929, Amy Spingarn, who was a wealthy literary patron, wife of an NAACP leader, and a friend to Langston Hughes, hosted a tea for Julia Peterkin, at Spingarn's house in New York. At that tea, Peterkin extended an invitation to Hughes to visit her at Lang Syne Plantation, if he ever came to South Carolina. Her invitation was either casual or "the rules" at her house were absolute. In 1931, while Hughes was on one of his signature literary tours of the South, he went to Julia Peterkin's Lang Syne Plantation, and was neither announced nor admitted. Hughes's biographer reports that the eminent poet was dismissed at the door, "rudely turned away by a white man." [12]

In the face of the acclaim for *Scarlet Sister Mary*, Peterkin also found a need to defend herself. Public controversy arose from the Pulitzer committee's decision to award its prize for fiction to *Scarlet Sister Mary*, for doing so entailed a rejection of the fiction jury's first choice, John B. Oliver's *Victim and Victor*. The committee decided to change the qualifications for the prize in fiction in order to widen the range of competing books. The award had until then been presented to the book of fiction that "best present[ed] the wholesome atmosphere of American life and the highest standards of American manners and manhood." This clause was changed to read "preferably one which shall best present the whole atmosphere of American life." [13]

That year, the prize was awarded to the Pulitzer committee's choice and the fiction jury's second choice, Julia Peterkin's *Scarlet Sister Mary*. H. L. Mencken, who disliked the committee for its lack of "talent and ability," wired his friend Julia Peterkin, encouraging her to decline the award. Peterkin answered that she would consider refusing to be impolite. She accepted.

Peterkin also had personal detractors. The natural realist bent of her novels aroused disdain among her society peers. Her own grandmother was quoted as saying that no lady in polite society

would allow her name to be printed in the papers.
Her friends intimated that she might lose her social standing, while gaining notoriety. Her social
circle considered that Peterkin had forsaken the
domicile for controversy.[14] Peterkin's prominence
as the child of an important doctor and the wife of
a wealthy landowner brought these criticisms to
bear. It is an irony of history that Julia Mood Peterkin is, in posterity, responsible for the recognition
of the Peterkin name. The legacy she obtained was
neither ignominious nor tawdry. These are testa-
ments to her novel's brilliance, its staying power.

Scarlet Sister Mary sold well as a result of the
Pulitzer Prize and its controversy, and because of
other arguments the novel was embroiled in as
well. The novel became a best seller at the same
time that it was banned in Boston, and was ousted
from a library near Peterkin's home in South Carolina. H. L. Mencken, through his own battle being
fought over his *American Mercury*, had a hand in
precipitating the Boston ban. Mencken supported
Peterkin's work and had recognized her talent early
on; he helped to locate a major publisher for Peterkin's work. Alfred A. Knopf published Peterkin's
first work, *Green Thursday*, a book of short stories,
in part due to Mencken's support. *Scarlet Sister
Mary*, *Bright Skin*, and *Black April* were all originally published by the Bobbs-Merrill Company in
Indianapolis—a real irony when you consider that

Indiana was a hotbed of Klan activity—or anti-black activity—all through the twenties and thirties, when Peterkin's work was written and published.

The prize and the controversies proved excellent for sales. *Scarlet Sister Mary* sold more than one million copies in all editions (English and Spanish) and was the first American novel to be published as a "featherweight airplane edition," which was the precursor to the paperback books we now know and rely on.[15]

Scarlet Sister Mary is atmospheric, rich in context, full of twists and bends. The *Scarlet Sister Mary* story is about a novel *and* its author, about a tale and its time. Peterkin portrayed African Americans as people and was stuck nonetheless in the racism of her day. The Pulitzer Prize criteria adjustments had little to do with her. And she never answered the charge of forsaking the boudoir for the book. She wrote outside of her own identity, to which I say, hooray.

Of course, not every aspect of the novel is easy to take. This is not necessarily a failing of the novel, since the novelist does try to render life as best she can. And certainly, not everything in life is easily handled. But Peterkin has done tremendously well with the woven work of fiction. One of the primary tasks of fiction is to reflect what people find conceivable, or believable. Articulating belief in fiction is fundamental to good writing. To reflect the ideas of whatever time with both lyricism and grace—now that is the challenge, that is the work.

Julia Mood Peterkin's characters speak with folk wisdom and spunk about what we labor to say academically. In a grand example of the folk dialectic, Mary talks about her paramours: "I like to shoot de ducks as dey rise." Peterkin, I think, must have identified with that attitude. I can just see her, watching "her Negroes," trying to grasp a gesture or create an animalism or describe a crying human need, hoping to place it deftly in her fiction. *Scarlet Sister Mary* shows just how deft she was. Without Sister Mary, Peterkin may have survived, but more likely as a regionalist writer. All her books would have been collected and preserved, in a fine few specialized libraries, scattered witheringly far apart across the country. Because of *Scarlet Sister Mary*, Peterkin has a place in the American canon; she is read, referred to, revitalized, reprinted, discussed—on into the future, as it comes.

NOTES

1. The word Negro has certainly fallen out of favor in 1997, when this foreword is being written; "Negro" has

been retired in favor of the more contemporaneous "African American." This foreword is written with full cognizance of this transfer of terminology. As a nominative, however, "Negro" accurately applies to the period and to the community about which Peterkin writes. For some, it is difficult to understand that while "Negro" and "African American" are ostensibly equivalent—the difference between them is significant and relates explicitly to time. The easiest way to understand this, I think, is to consider whether there is such a thing as an unpaid African American plantation worker, one whose locus of control still resonates so substantially of slavery. Because of the simultaneous distance from slavery and temporal closeness to it, use of the term "Negro," which was the parlance of the time, makes more conceptual sense.

2. Certainly, there are many points to consider and discuss about Peterkin's constructions of black people in her novel(s), and the problems therein. To key into the larger concept of white fantasy about black culture in literature, see Toni Morrison's critical essay, *Playing in the Dark* (Cambridge: Harvard University Press, 1992).

3. Ann Shealy, *The Passionate Mind: Four Studies Including "Julia Peterkin: A Souvenir"* (Philadelphia: Dorrance & Company, 1976), 38.

4. It is unclear, historically, that Gullah people participated fully in this slave/Christian paradigm. However, the license of fiction does allow Peterkin to endow her characters with whatever religious orientation she perceived.

5. Shealy, 36.

6. Shealy, 32.

7. Mildred Flagg Papers at the Radcliffe College Schlesinger Library at Harvard University.

8. Thomas H. Landess, *Julia Peterkin* (Boston: Twayne Publishers, 1976), 16.

9. Grant Overton, *The Women Who Make Our Novels* (New York: Dodd, Mead & Company, 1928), 259–60.

10. Overton, 257.

11. Landess, 29–31.

12. Arnold Rampersad, *The Life of Langston Hughes* (New York: Oxford University Press, 1986), 227.

13. Landess, 32.

14. Landess, 23.

15. Landess, 32.

SCARLET SISTER MARY

CHAPTER I

THE black people who live in the Quarters at
Blue Brook Plantation believe they are far the
best black people living on the whole "Neck," as
they call that long, narrow, rich strip of land
lying between the sea on one side and the river
with its swamps and deserted rice-fields on the
other. They are no Guinea negroes with thick
lips and wide noses and low ways; or Dinkas with
squatty skulls and gray-tinged skin betraying
their mean blood; they are Gullahs with tall
straight bodies, and high heads filled with sense.

Since the first days of slavery they have been
the best of field workers. They make fine me-
chanics and body servants for their masters.
Their preachers and conjure doctors have always
known many things besides how to save men's
lives and souls.

The old owners of Blue Brook must have been
careful to buy slaves that were perfect, for they
built up a strain of intelligent, upstanding
human beings, just as they bred race-horses and

11

hunting dogs that could not be excelled. The slaves destined to be skilled laborers were sent across the sea to learn their trades from the best workmen in the world, and the house and body servants came into close contact with masters and mistresses who were ladies and gentlemen and not common white trash, or poor buckras. When the war between the states freed them and broke up the old plantation system, the black people lived on in the old plantation Quarters, shifting for themselves and eking out a living as best they could. The lack of roads and bridges afforded them little contact with the outside world, and so, instead of going away to seek new fortunes, new advantages, easier work and more money, they kept faithful to the old life, contented with old ways and beliefs, holding fast to old traditions and superstitions.

When their time is out and death takes their souls back to their Maker, their bodies are laid with those others lying so thick in the old graveyard that room can scarcely be found for another resting-place.

The world made by the old plantation is drawn to a simple pattern. The loamy red fields are bordered by quiet woodlands. A cluster of ancient cabins near the river is sheltered by a grove of giant moss-hung live oaks. A great empty

Big House, once the proud home of the plantation masters, is now an old crumbling shell with broken chimneys and a rotting roof. Ghosts can be heard at sunset rattling the closed window-blinds up-stairs, as they strive for a glimpse of the shining river that shows between the tall cedars and magnolias.

The earth's richness and the sun's warmth make living an easy thing. Years go by without leaving a mark or footprint. Sometimes black years come in determined to break the tranquil monotony. Earthquakes tumble down chimneys, storms break trees and houses, floods wash the earth so bare that its very bones are exposed, droughts burn up crops and weeds with impartial cruelty, but the old plantation is swift to hide every scar made by all this wickedness. New chimneys are quickly built and houses mended; trees thrust up young branches to fill empty spaces; new crops and weeds thrive under gentle rains and hot sunshine.

Life fills and enfolds everything here, never overlooking in the press of work to be done the smallest or most insignificant creature, and silently, with weariless patience and diligence, strange miracles are wrought as youth rises out of decay and death becomes only another beginning.

CHAPTER II

MARY had grown up in Maum Hannah's old house in the Quarters like a weed, and, although she could remember her mother faintly, Maum Hannah and Budda Ben were the only parents she knew. Maum Hannah was old and Budda Ben was crippled, but Mary had laughed and played through most of her fifteen years with clothes enough to wear and food enough to eat and pleasure enough to keep her happy. She worked almost every day in the fields, picking cotton, stripping fodder from the corn, planting or gathering potatoes and peas; never working too hard, for she could always stop and rest, or laugh and talk with the other field hands.

Fetching water up the hill from the spring was no burden for her lithe young body for as soon as she had grown big enough to toddle back and forth holding to Maum Hannah's apron, she had helped fetch water, first a tin can full, then a small bucket full, until at last she could come up the hill with three full-sized buckets, all filled to the brim, one balanced on her head and one in each hand.

Helping wash clothes every week was fun,
for all the Quarter women gathered together at
the spring on wash-day, and their cheerful bus-
tling about as they dipped up water and filled the
tubs and big iron pots, and cut wood to keep the
fires burning bright, made the work a frolic instead of drudgery.

At fifteen she was a slender, darting, high-
spirited girl, a leader of the young set, and all
ready to be married to July who was, perhaps,
the wildest young buck in the Quarters. The
girls Mary's age were much alike, with slender, well-shaped bodies, scarcely hidden by the
plain skimpy garments they wore. They went
barefooted all the week, but every Sunday morning, after undoing their black woolly hair and
rewrapping it into neat rolls with white ball
thread, they put on shoes and stockings and hats
and Sunday dresses and went to church.

Mary looked much like the others, who were
all her blood kin. But while most of them were
slender, she was thin. While the others were a
dark healthy brown, Mary's skin had a bluish
bloom. Instead of being round and merry,
Mary's eyes were long and keen, sometimes
challenging, sometimes serious, sometimes flashing with impudence under their straight black
brows, even when her mouth was laughing.

metaphor *what the diff?* *what* *the* *personification*

She had hardly known sorrow until lately. Three years ago, when she was twelve, Maum Hannah had made her seek God's pardon for her sins, and she had to go off by herself and pray for days without laughing or talking; but that was not so very hard, for whenever she got weary of praying she lay down flat on the warm pine straw in the shade of the tall thick trees and thought of pleasant things until she went to sleep. She was asleep when a vision told her all her sins were forgiven. Not that she had many sins, for here in the Quarters she seldom had a chance to sin.

She dreamed she was walking up a long steep hill toward sunrise side, carrying a pack of clothes on her head. The higher she climbed the heavier the pack grew until her neck fairly ached with the burden but just as she reached the top of the hill she saw a great white house, much like the Big House except that it stood in an open field in the sunshine. When she got right in front of it a tall man dressed in a long white robe came out of the door and without a word walked up to her and took the pack of clothes off her head. Then he said, in a deep solemn voice that sounded like Budda Ben's, "Go, my child, and sin no more." The words woke her up and her heart well-nigh burst with excitement as she ran to tell Maum Hannah. That night she told her dream before the deacons at prayer-meeting. After they asked her a few questions about it, and she gave her promise always to try to live as right as she could, never to dance again or sing reel songs, not to lie or steal or be mean or do anything low, they said she might be a candidate for baptism.

Maum Hannah made her a long white baptizing robe, and she was baptized the next first Sunday in the creek back of Heaven's Gate Church. She was terribly scared, for the water was cold and black and the tree roots along the bank looked like snakes, but Reverend Duncan was strong and she knew he would not let her fall. Her baptizing robe was put away in the bottom of the cupboard to be used for her shroud when she died, and her name was no longer Mary but Sister Mary.

She missed dancing, and whenever she heard the big drum beating and the accordion wailing she felt sad, but shouting at prayer-meeting was pleasure and the old hymns and spirituals were beautiful. When the people all sang them together in the fields while they worked, she joined in and felt so holy that cold chills ran up and down her spine.

This last year had been a bad-luck year.

Troubling things had happened, things she could not even talk over with Budda Ben, who was always kind to her no matter how cross he was with other people. But Budda was a cripple who knew nothing about love or pleasure.

When Budda was a tiny baby Maum Hannah fell with him in her arms and broke his body badly. He had been a cripple ever since. His legs were hamstrung and could not stand straight. He had to walk half-squatting with a stick, and sleep with his knees doubled up close to his chin. He had to work sitting down and most of the time he sat on the wood-pile cutting wood and fat lightwood splinters, or mending shoes worn out by strong firm feet.

He could not even stay a member of the church. He tried to pray, for God knows he needed help, but the children plagued him and called him names, until agony made him curse. Then he cursed everything: the children, his mother and God himself. His mother was to blame. She crippled him. She fell because she was afraid. Afraid her husband would see her going to meet another man, Budda Ben's own father. She was the one to suffer, not he. He had never done anything to God or man to bring such a misery on himself.

Budda Ben hated July. He declared July was

a wicked sinner, a crap-shooter, a poker-player, a gambler, a dancer who sang reels, and carried his "box" (guitar) everywhere he went playing wicked tunes for the sinners to dance by at birth-night suppers and parties and playing on Satur-day afternoon at the crossroads store for the boys and men who loafed there when the week's work was over. He sang songs with bad words and he was no fit company for Mary to keep. Budda Ben and Maum Hannah wanted her to marry June, July's twin brother, who had loved Mary all her life, and who was hurt to the heart now because she chose July instead of himself.

Mary prized June's devotion for he was steady and kind, a faithful friend, who helped her do all her tasks: bringing in the wood Budda Ben cut at the wood-pile, fetching water from the spring, or bringing broom-sedge out of the old fields for the winter's supply of brooms, setting out plants in the vegetable garden and hoeing the rows clean. June often helped her scour the floors Saturday morning when July went rabbit hunting. He was far more thoughtful than July and as much unlike him in looks as in disposi-tion. July was tall, lean, quick-spoken. June was short, big-chested, heavy, slow.

They fought all through their boyhood, for they were evenly matched, and to this day they would fight again at the drop of a hat, not with weak scuffles or wordy quarreling, but with terrible blows of clenched fists that brought blood.

Yet they loved each other, and to meddle with one of them meant to meddle with both.

When Mary told June she was going to marry July, he drew his thick black eyebrows together and his hands doubled up into hard fists. Something like surprise filled his eyes. "July?" he asked. "You is gwine to marry July?" Then he grunted and shrugged his big round shoulders. "July ever was a lucky boy. E ever was. I never had a luck in my life."

"Ain' you glad I'm gwine to be you sister, June?" she asked him.

"Not so glad, Si May-e." June smiled a wry smile and looked far away.

Maum Hannah called July a trifling time-waster and complained that he never stuck to any work; that he never saved a cent or stayed in one place long enough to take root; that he was always courting girls, then leaving them high and dry, and often in trouble. He would never stick to Mary. June would. June was honest and hard-working, strong as an ox, and he would make a fine husband even if he could not play a box like July.

Whenever July came to see her at night while

Budda Ben and Maum Hannah were both at meeting it made the old woman suspicious and unhappy. She'd sigh and say, "Company in de dark don' do, gal. Company in de dark don' do. When de kerosene is out and de moon don' shine and it's too hot for bright fire—just de dark and company—company in de dark don' do, gal."

Deep down in Mary's heart she knew this was true, but after she was married to July, she would help him to be steady and faithful. She would make him a home where he liked to stay. She would save his money, and teach him how to be a serious-minded man. He needed her to help him, for, in spite of his tall sinewy body and broad shoulders, July had a child's heart in his breast. He liked play better than work because something inside him had never grown up.

He liked to tease her and plague her in all sorts of ways. One spring day while she was seeking peace and July was helping June mark his pigs, cutting every one in an ear before it was carried over the river to roam in the pasture with its mother, so that he might be able to tell his own hogs the next fall, July came where she was, caught her by the arm and held her. She thought he was going to kiss her, but he took his knife out of his pocket and slit the lobe of her ear. "Now, you is marked for life," he said and laughed gaily. Mary wept with the hurt, but Maum Hannah called July and asked him why he had cut Mary's ear. He grinned sheepishly and said he had marked her with an underbit.

"Is dat you mark?"

"Yes'm," he answered boldly, adding that he had marked Mary so he could tell she was his when she grew up.

"Well, son, May-e's mark is a swallow-fork. Two cuts. You stand still while de gal cuts you ear. Lend em you knife. I ain' got a sharp one in de house."

July took out his knife and stood still while Mary cut his ear this way and that to make the swallow-fork. He was marked for life, too. His blood flowed fast, but he grinned good-naturedly and said nothing.

That very night he told her he loved her and was going to marry her when she grew up and she felt that she could walk on air, or fly like a bird, or blossom like a flower, when she heard his beautiful words.

Last summer he went away to find easier and better-paid work and her heart sickened in her breast so she could hardly eat or smile. But

[handwritten margin notes: "hes cruel", "she misses him a lot"]

now he was back, thin and bony, with new
lines in his face; his clothes were worn out and his
pockets empty, but his old happy grin was as
bright as ever. No matter what Budda Ben and
Maum Hannah said, July should never leave
her again.

All the money he made was gone and June
had to lend him some to go to town and buy his
wedding clothes. He used part of it to buy Mary
a present, a pair of hoop earrings to hide the cut
in her ear. The big shining gold circles were
wrapped up in a scarlet head-kerchief. When she
stood in front of Maum Hannah's looking-glass
and tied up her head with the kerchief as grown
women do, and slipped the earrings through the
holes which were bored in her ears long ago when
she was a tiny child, to make her eye-sight strong,
her fingers trembled with happiness. She had
longed for earrings ever since she could remember and she had carefully kept the bored holes
in her ears open with tiny straws so they could
not grow up. July remembered that. Bless his
heart!

"Who is dis all dressed up so fine," Budda Ben
asked from the doorway. "Wid earrings a-
danglin an' a head-kerchief makin' em look like
a grown 'oman? Who it is?"

Mary could hardly draw her eyes away from

the wavy glass where her image was fairly dazzling. "Does you tink dey fits me, Budda?
Does you like em, Auntie? Please stop a-frown-
in an' look at em, Budda Ben. I know you ain'
never seen prettier ones." She said it all in one
breath, then stopped to gaze in the looking-glass,
where her white teeth and black eyes flashed
bright as the earrings themselves.

CHAPTER III

Mary's wedding-day had dawned but instead
of being up at first fowl crow and running
around helping Maum Hannah get everything
ready, she lay still in her bed in the shed room,
thinking, pretending to sleep, watching the
streaks of light creep in through the cabin cracks,
while the old woman moved quietly about in the
big room, rousing the fire in the chimney,
filling the kettle with fresh water, stirring at the
pots on the hearth and pushing them up closer to
the fire so the breakfast victuals could cook
faster.

Mary was happy over her wedding. God knew
she had loved July all of her life; yet, when she
thought of leaving Maum Hannah and Budda
Ben and this kind old house where she had been
born and where she had spent most of her life,
something inside her breast ached.

She had no father and her mother had been
dead for years, but Maum Hannah had been
like a mother to her, Budda Ben, Maum Hannah's crippled son, had been both a father and a
brother, and this old tottering house was like a

dear friend. She loved every board in its weather-
beaten sides, every shingle in its warped roof,
every rusty nail that held it together.

The house where she and July would live at
the other end of the Quarter street was exactly
like it, for it was built at the same time, by the
same people and by the same pattern. Its roof
was warped too, its rotted shingles were edged
with small green ferns, the wide-mouthed
chimney rising out of its ridge-pole took up
a third of the inside wall in the same way.
It was an old unpainted wooden cabin sitting
low on the earth, heavy with years, yet able and
strong in its beam and joists and rafters and
sides, for it was built in the old days when men
took time to choose timbers carefully and to lay
them together with skill. Like this old house,
it had held many generations. Red birth, black
death, hate, sorrow and love had all dwelt inside
it, sheltered by its roof, shielded by its walls.
July's people had lived in it for generations,
but this was the home where she was born.
Everything here was part of her life. She was
born in this same bed. The crippled table over
in the corner, heaped high with clean quilts, had
been there ever since she could remember. The
cupboard where her clothes stayed and the leaning shelf by the window with the four sad-irons

resting on it after their hard week's work had
never been out of their places since they were
put there by women who lived here before Maum
Hannah was born. When Maum Hannah died
they would all belong to Mary. Crippled Budda
Ben was bound to die ahead of his mother who
prayed to God every day of her life to let her
outlive him, so that when he died she could see
that his box was made right. Budda's poor
legs must not be cramped when they were laid
away in the ground for their last long rest. She
knew how to pray and she would outlive
Budda Ben as sure as the world.

He was snoring peacefully in the shed room
next to Mary's as Maum Hannah went tripping
quietly about the big room so as not to wake him.
The shed-room door was open so Mary could see
the wedding-cakes standing in a long white row
in front of the jugs of wedding-wine. When
Maum Hannah began examining them and talking softly to herself Mary couldn't help smiling
to see how she peeped at one, then another,
turning each around, appraising them all, grunt-
ing with pride in so much beauty. "My jaws
pure leak water just to look at em," Maum
Hannah murmured. The neighbors had baked
and iced them all except the bride's cake which

stood like a tall steeple in the center of the row.
Maum Hannah made that one herself, and it was
the tallest and loveliest cake Mary had ever
seen: Its big bottom layer had been baked
in a dish-pan and the other layers grew
smaller as they rose higher and higher until
the last layer came, and that had to be baked in
a tomato can for no pan in the Quarters was
small enough to be right for it. When it was
all finished, iced white and dotted over with white
spots, Budda Ben hobbled to Grab-All, as the
crossroads store was called because it got every
cent everybody ever had, and bought pink and
white candies that looked like rice grains and
sprinkled these all over the whole cake. Then
it became too beautiful to eat. Maum Hannah
said that the candy rice would bring good luck
to the bride. Rice always does. Until yesterday,
Mary thought rice brought luck to brides because after a woman marries she must cook
rice for her husband every day, but Maum
Hannah told her that rice sprinkled over brides
and bride cakes brings many children and that
Budda Ben's rice candy would bring many children to her.

It had taken many an egg and many a pound
of sugar and flour to make so many cakes, but
everybody on the whole plantation could have a

good hunk to eat to-day. Maum Hannah had been saving eggs since early fall; and every scuppernong grape and bullace that could be picked and squeezed was made into wedding-wine.

Mary had worked hard all the week and now she lay still with half-closed eyes until all of a sudden Maum Hannah threw up her hands and groaned, "Do, Master, look down and see what a rat is done!"

Mary's heart flew up into her mouth. Cold chills ran over her as she ran to see what had happened. There it was, a great hole gnawed deep into the bride's cake's tender meat. Candy rice and rich yellow cake crumbs sprinkled the shelf and the floor. She wanted to cry out, to scream, but her voice froze in her throat and she fell into bitter dumb sobs. Maum Hannah's head shook gloomily from side to side. Such bad luck was hard to face. But her hand reached out and gave Mary's shoulder a comforting pat. "Don't fret so hard, honey. You eyes will get all red an' ugly. Wipe de water out em on you gown-tail an' go get me some eggs an' sugar out de safe. I aim to make some new icin an' mend dis cake so nobody won' never know it was hurt exceptin you an' me an' Gawd an' Satan. We won' even tell Ben. Satan is de one sent dat rat here to kill we joy an' make we

have sin to-day. But I'll show em, e can' rule me.
I done fought wid em too many times in my life
to let em get de best o me now. Now, you go
on back to bed an' get warm, whilst I whips up de
icin. Gawd'll help me fix dis cake. He wouldn'
have de heart to let Satan ruin a lil mudderless
bride's cake on de weddin-day. No. Gawd promised to be a mudder to the mudderless, honey.
You run jump in de bed an' get warm. I'll call
you when I'm done."

Mary shivered with misery as she crawled back
under the quilts. Maum Hannah whipped
the egg whites stiff with sugar, and with many
sighs and grunts and prayers, filled the ugly hole
full, patted the icing smooth and neat, and stuck
some of the wasted candy rice over it. Then she
came to Mary's door and called softly so as not
to let Budda Ben hear her, "De cake is good as
new, honey. Get down on you knees an' thank
Gawd."

The cake was mended. Nobody would ever
guess it had been hurt. Mary was so happy
she gave Maum Hannah a tight hug, then
stepped out on the floor and started cutting a
pigeon wing while she hummed the tune of
"Black Annie, Black Annie Moore——" But
Maum Hannah stopped her sternly. "Is you
gone crazy, gal? Is you forgot you is a church-

member? I told you to kneel down an' thank
God an' here you is singin a reel song an' crossin
you feets. Dat's a sin, gal, a pure sin."

Mary grinned and gave the old soul another
great hug and hurried back to the shed room to
dress. But the morning was chilly, and Maum
Hannah was thoughtful.

"You better fetch you clothes in here an' dress
by the fire. It's mighty airish to-day. Come eat
a tater first to hotten up you insides so you can
move fast. Budda Ben put a lot o nice yams in
de ashes when he banked de fire last night. Dey's
all good an' done. A nice soft one'll do you belly
all de good. A full belly makes a brave heart,
an' you'll need a brave heart to-day."

The floor felt cold to Mary's feet, the big room
was drafty, with its chairs and tables pushed back
against the wall to make room for the wedding-
guests. It looked almost as large as a church.
She stood close to the great yellow fire, warming,
but Maum Hannah jerked her farther away with
a warning. "Mind, gal, dis fire's mean. Gawd
knows e's old enough to have better sense, but
e would just as soon catch you an' burn you as
not. I done had enough worry-ation dis mornin
to last me a long time."

"Fire couldn' catch me to-day, Auntie. Not
me," Mary said, but she stood farther back and

ate her potato slowly while she looked around
at all the things she had done to make the room
attractive. Every board in the floor had been
scrubbed white with lye and sand, her hands were
still sore with the lye cuts. The walls were fresh
covered with newspapers bought from Grab-All
with eggs; circles of fringed papers sewed to
barrel hoops and tied to the rafters looked
like big lanterns as they swung gently overhead in the cold drafts of morning air which
fell through the broken shingles in the roof. The
wide rock hearth was newly reddened with clay,
and the mantel-shelf had a newspaper cover
which she had carefully scalloped and cut with
holes to make blossoms and stars. That was
lovely. She tried hard to get one more paper to
fix a cover like it for the water-shelf where the
cake and wine stood, but not another paper was
to be had for eggs or peanuts or anything else.
June whitewashed the shelf with the white clay
that fell in lumps out of the side of the duck
dam gully and it matched the whitened front
door and window-blinds, and looked clean and
nice enough.

Maum Hannah's bed in the corner of the
room was freshly made up with clean things
and the wedding-dress lay spread out on it,
waiting to be worn. The wide white muslin

skirt trimmed half-way up with narrow frills and the tucked waist trimmed with lace at the neck and sleeves made a garment that matched the wedding-cake in looks. Budda Ben had dug up all his buried savings to buy the cloth and to get the best seamstress on the plantation to make it, but it was worth every cent he paid out. He said so himself when Mary tried it on to let him see how well it fitted.

She carefully licked off the sweet potato bits that stuck to her fingers, then squatted on the hearth close to the fire to warm good through and through before she put on her clothes. One good yawn, one good stretch, then she would dress fast and fetch the water and finish up whatever had to be done yet this morning. "You ever was like a cat, Si May-e; always stretchin. But after to-day, you ain' gwine have time to be gapin an' warmin, an' pleasurin youself in de mornins. You'll see."

Sister Mary stood up and slipped out of her night-gown, which dropped near to the pot Maum Hannah was stirring. The old woman looked up with a merry twinkle in her eyes. "Is you crazy, gal? Look how you duh fan ashes in de victuals. Fo Gawd's sake put on some clothes. You ain' to stand up buck naked like dat. You's a grown 'oman now. Is you forgot?"

Mary laughed and stretched out her long slim body until every muscle was taut. What did she care if Maum Hannah saw her buck naked now when she had seen her so a thousand times? But Maum Hannah's laugh had cut off and she was leaning forward with her eyes blinking and gazing as if they could not see quite clearly. They were searching Mary's body from head to foot, marking each line, each curve, as if something astonished and distressed them. Mary crouched down and, picking up a garment, hurriedly put it on, but Maum Hannah's eyes were wise and keen. There was no use to be covering up now.

"What de matter ail you, Auntie? How-come you duh gaze at me so hard, like you ain' never seen me naked befo?" Mary tried to sound cool and guiltless, but she could not look Maum Hannah in the face.

"May-e,—honey, I can' hardly b'lieve my own eyes. What you been doin, gal?" Her piercing eyes cut into Mary's heart.

It was no use to lie, or to try to deceive them. Nothing could escape them when they shone like that.

"Honey,—May-e,—look at me——"

"Yes'm—I'm a-lookin——" Something quivered in Mary's throat.

"Honey,——" It was the third time Maum

Hannah said the word, as if she could get no further. It fell so sorrowfully, with such pity, that Mary hung her head low.

"May-e, you an' July is been a-havin sin, enty?"

Mary wanted to deny it, but to save her life her lips could not raise a sound. She could not even say, "Yes."

"Enty?" Maum Hannah asked again, softly, gently. "I raised you to know right from wrong, enty? An' you went an' let July make you have sin?" Maum Hannah sighed deep. "Lawd, dat July is a case. A heavy case in dis world."

Mary wanted to say that July was not all to blame, but her breath fluttered and spilled the words.

"I see now why Satan sent dat rat to gnaw a hole in you weddin-cake. Satan knowed you b'longed to him an' not to Jedus. Oh, honey, I'm dat sorry, I could cry. What you done pure cuts my heart-strings. I wouldn' a thought you had de heart to fool me so. No."

"Wha dat I done so awful bad, Auntie? Me an' July is gwine marry to-day." She tried to speak calmly, but her throat went dry and the words fell into a husky whisper.

Maum Hannah shook her head gloomily. "Don' ax me, gal. Looka you bosom, a-struttin, a-tellin de bad news an' you body a-swellin an' a-braggin. Why couldn' you wait for de preacher to read out de book over you an' make you July's lawful wife? Lawd, gal, I'm dat sorry, I could pure cry like a baby. I could, fo-true. Some sin is black, an' some ain' so black, but dis sin you had is pure scarlet."

Cold misery made Mary sick. Frightened tears began streaming down her cheeks. She slipped down on her knees.

"But you love me, enty, Auntie?"

Maum Hannah sighed, "Sho, I love you, I couldn' stop lovin you. I'll never stop, not till I'm dead. I love de sinner, but I hate de sin. Yes, Jedus. A scarlet sin is a awful bad sin."

A sudden hope sprang in Mary's heart. May-be if she denied the sin, Maum Hannah might think her eyes had not seen right.

"I ain' had sin, Auntie—I'm just a-growin. I'm just fat by I eat so much victuals lately." Mary ventured it timidly, but Maum Hannah's eyes flashed fire and her voice grew sharp and stinging.

"Shut you mout', gal, befo Gawd strikes you dead wid a lie on you tongue. You might could fool some people, but you can' fool me! Neither Gawd. Gawd's eye stays on you, all de time, day an' night. A-seein all you do same like dat lookin-glass on de wall sees dis room. Evy time you have sin, a big white angel up in Heaven writes it down in a book. All dat what you an' July done, is wrote down. On de day o judgment, dat same angel'll stand up an' read em out for de whole world to hear. De livin an' de dead'll know, same like I know right now, how you an' July let Satan fool you. If you don' repent, yunnuh'll go to torment when you die too."

Mary sat on the floor speechless. Here, on her wedding-morning, all the joy in the world was gone. She wanted to be good. She tried to be kind, never to hurt anything or anybody; yet she had become a sinner because she loved July so much. And the worst of it was that Maum Hannah had found it out.

The old woman leaned over the pots, stirring them, tasting them, talking mournfully to herself. "I ever did say—company in de dark don' do for gals. No. Company in de dark don' do. Company's right wid light, but in de dark—company don' do."

The wavy looking-glass hanging in its square wooden frame beside the fireplace stared at the room, its wrinkled face making everything it reflected look more twisted than ever. The fire, rushing straight up the chimney full of sparks and light, looked wavy and foolish in the glass.

Maum Hannah's eyes knew too much. They must be wise as God's.

Everybody had been saying lately how fast she was growing. Her old clothes were too tight and too short, her skimpy skirts left her bare legs looking very long and lean, but her body was almost as slim as ever except that her breasts had budded up. But she was almost sixteen and a grown-up woman to be married to a husband to-day, thank God.

"Auntie, you wouldn' tell nobody on me, would you?" she whispered, and Maum Hannah shook her head. She would not tell. People would find out soon enough. A sin like Mary's tells on itself. A scarlet sin is a blab-mouth thing.

"Will dey turn me out de church, Auntie?" The thought of such deep disgrace made her shiver. Maum Hannah nodded sadly that they would. The deacons have to keep clean right-eous people on the church roll. Not sinners.

Budda Ben was up, bumping around in the shed room. He would soon be coming out to get his breakfast. Mary wiped her eyes. She must go to the spring for water before he saw her.

"Eat some breakfast, befo you go, honey. De

mush is done now, an' de fry-meat is brown."

"I rather eat when I come back, Auntie. Le me fetch de water first, I want to eat breakfast wid Budda dis last time." At the door, she paused. "You wouldn' tell Budda Ben, would you, Auntie?"

Maum Hannah threw up her hands. "Who? Me? Great Gawd, gal, Budda would choke July to deat'. E would wring July's neck same like a chicken."

As Mary hurried along with her three empty buckets, walking quickly between the long rows of houses on each side of the rain-rutted road, gay greetings were called to her from the open doors and windows.

"Hey, Si May-e, how you feel dis mornin?"

"You sho got a fine weddin-day!"

"Looka how de sun is a-shinin on you, gal!"

"July's a lucky boy fo-true."

Mary laughed and called back merry, good-mannered answers to them all, holding her small head high, and hoping that nobody saw that her eyes were red.

The fresh morning air was filled with delicious scents: ripe leaves, fragrant weeds, late cotton blossoms, and the breath of the dark red earth itself. Summer was over. The birds were singing restlessly; their nestlings were all full feathered and ready for mating.

Katydids and crickets creaked a few faint words over and over, speaking sadly to each other before frost came and silenced them for the winter. Morning-glory vines sprawled everywhere, on the hedge rows, on the old rail fence, around the stalks of corn in the field, holding up white-throated blossoms to the light, patiently striving to make all the seed they could before their time was out.

The path dwindled as it dropped down sidewise between the shoulders of two hills, running over gnarled tree roots and rocks that jutted up out of the clay on to a hollow where the clear little spring bubbled out.

Tall poplars and sweet-gums clutched at the dark earth with black crooked roots, but they flaunted purple and scarlet and yellow heads up in the face of the sky. With every stir of air a shower of gay leaves fell, some to lie still on the ground while others, alighting on the tiny stream, floated away, slowly at first, then faster and faster as the bright current hurried to reach the great yellow river.

Mary sat down on a rock and watched the water trickle out of the shining pool. She was so still the shy birds grew bold and came to drink where the water was new and sweet. A gray fox came stealing out through the broom-sedge and frost-bleached grass and after stopping to size up Mary, he crept closer and began lapping the water daintily. He was heavy with food. This very morning Maum Hannah's hens had cackled loud and cried for help. Budda Ben had got up and cursed the varmint that disturbed them, but Maum Hannah shamed him; she said God made foxes and hawks and owls so they had to eat flesh to live. They were not to blame. Ben must have patience with them and ask God to protect the hens.

Mary had always been afraid of God. He and Death were the two most fearsome things in the world. If she were to die, now, in her sin, God would put her in Hell and burn her for ever and ever. But if God knew everything, then He knew that July was not mild and easy-going like June, and that she loved him so much she had lacked the strength to rule him.

"May—e—e! May—e—e!"

Lord, how Maum Hannah could call.

"Yes,—Aunt—ee! I'm—a—com—in!" Mary sent back her answer as loud as she could, but it was weak beside Maum Hannah's clear trumpeting. That old voice had grown strong with long years of use. Many a time Mary

had stood beside Maum Hannah in the door
while it announced the news of the plantation to the whole world: births, deaths, fires,
accidents, each thing shaping its own wail.
Now, Maum Hannah's persistent calling
meant that her childhood was over. No more
romping and laughing with the little children who were left at Maum Hannah's cabin
while their mothers worked in the fields. No
more playing with the funny little dolls she made
for them out of peanuts and bits of cloth. She'd
soon have a baby of her own to sew for. July's
baby.

"May—e—e! Si May—e—e!" Maum Hannah called again.

Taking the three empty buckets, Mary filled
them to the brim, one by one, then carefully putting one on top of her head, and taking the other
two, one in each hand, she stepped quickly into
the foot-worn path and walked up the hill toward
home, as if she had no load at all.

At the top of the hill she turned to look back
at the hazy blue world lying so far away over
the river. July had been out there and had
overcome all kinds of danger and seen all kinds
of places, all kinds of women. He had been in
great towns with long streets filled with big
white houses, standing at the end of long ave-

nues. He had seen box-bordered gardens full of sweet-smelling flowers like the gardens of the plantation Big House. Many girls out there had tried to get him to stay, but he had come back to her. He wanted her who had never been more than five miles from home for his lawful wedded wife. Thank God. She would never, never do anything wrong again.

The sun was climbing up the sky, the morning's haziness was going, taking with it the glistening dew. The Quarter street was full of noise, everybody was awake, talking, laughing, tramping up and down the street, going back and forth, helping Maum Hannah get everything in order for the wedding.

CHAPTER IV

As THE wedding-time drew near, the house and yard were jammed with people. July came, all clean shaved, with a fresh hair-cut, dressed up in the fine new clothes June's money bought him. Mary's heart began beating faster, but July was calm as could be, laughing and talking with the people, answering their banter, joking with the bridesmaids and groomsmen, even joking with old Brer Dee whose shaggy white eyebrows stuck out farther than ever.

July's full black eyes were shining under brows that ran in a straight line from temple to temple. His fine new suit looked very grand, though not quite long enough for his arms and legs. Nobody ever looked better than July looked now. No man on earth ever had a handsomer body or one so supple and straight and strong. Mary's second cousin, Cinder, had tried hard to get him, but she was not the bride, thank God. She might as well go along and sweet-talk June and leave the groom alone.

Reverend Duncan held up the holy black Book to let the people know that the time had come.

They must all go outside in the front yard
and give the bridal procession a chance to form.

As they hurried out, choking the door, pushing
one another, laughing and shouting happily,
Maum Hannah put her arms around Mary and
gave her a tight hug. "Gawd bless you, Si
May-e," she whispered, and Mary felt a wet
old cheek pressed against her own until July
stepped up and took her from Maum Hannah,
and began hugging her himself, "Lord, gal, you
pure look good enough to eat." He put a kiss
right on her mouth, then drew her arm through
his. "Come on, honey. De preacher's ready to
make you my lawful lady."

"You gwine mash Si May-e's dress, July,"
Maum Hannah cried out, and July laughed
gaily, but for all his big-doings talk, Mary felt
his heart thumping fast under her arm.

Reverend Duncan, a great, fat old man,
marched out first with Brer Dee, the oldest deacon of the church, then turned to face them under
the big oak tree. The "waiters" marched out next,
a couple at a time, ten couples in all. They
walked round and round so everybody could see
them well, then formed a gay half-circle. The
girls wore beautiful bright-colored dresses
and had ribbons and flowers in their hair.
Twelve little flower girls dressed in white fol-

lowed the waiters. They walked slowly two by two, holding hands and making funny little mincing steps, for most of them were wearing shoes and stockings for the first time in their lives. Their white teeth gleamed with happy grins as they darted quick looks all around them.

Mary could find only eleven little girls the same size, so Andrew let his little Big Boy take a flower girl's part in the wedding. Big Boy wore a little, full-skirted, white frock too, and a bow of white ribbon was tied to his short kinky hair.

When the waiters and flower girls finished marching around Mary and July came arm in arm together down the rickety steps out into the sun-bright air, past the red rose-bush, down the violet-bordered path, with Maum Hannah following close behind them. On they went by short slow paces through a narrow aisle made by the crowd. A soft wind stirred and the old hackberry tree scattered bright yellow leaves over them, and Mary's full skirts billowed around her. Her shiny new shoes squeaked proudly with every step, while grunts and exclamations of approval sounded on every side.

"Lawd, de bride do look sweet, fo-true!" somebody shouted happily.

"Like a fresh blossom."

"E weddin-dress fits em same like a green shuck fits a young ear o corn."

"Si May-e must a been melted an' poured in em." The laughter that followed each comment was hushed by the preacher's deep-booming words beginning the solemn marriage service.

Mary's voice was low and husky when she answered, "I will," but July spoke clear and loud and ahead of time. Everybody laughed when Reverend Duncan gave Mary a sudden smacking kiss. The ceremony was over and July was her lawful wedded husband, until Death came to part them.

All the people surged forward to kiss the bride and the groom; to wish them joy, a gal and a boy; to hope they would live together like Isaac and Rebecca. The fine earrings bobbed about in Mary's ears and the wreath of white flowers on her head had to be straightened now and then when so much kissing pushed it out of place.

When Brer Dee took his place beside a long table under the hackberry tree at the side of the house and began bawling in a high-keyed voice, "Come on up, brudders an' sisters! Put you presents on de table, so you can get you cake an' wine. Don' stand back," Maum Hannah smiled kindly and encouraged him.

"Hurry em up, son, tell em plenty o cake an'

wine is a-waitin for em right inside my house."

The presents were brought up one by one, and each was held up and announced by Brer Dee until the table was brimming full, then everybody came forward and crowded around to look at the presents while the old tree scattered its bright yellow leaves among the plates and cups and saucers, the pots and pans, water glasses, forks and spoons; no knives, for knives are bad-luck things.   Pieces of money were heaped up in the middle, and chickens tied firmly by the feet lay patiently under the table, dozing or blinking bright eyes at everything.

"Now, all o yunnuh git you cake an' wine!" Brer Dee shouted the announcement so every one could hear, then drew a fine red handkerchief out of his pocket and wiped the sweat from his head.

The soft warm wind hummed a low tune, then blew a thin cloud over the sun, darkening the faces of the people but it passed quickly aside, making the day seem brighter than ever.

Before sundown, Mary was weary.   She had kissed everybody there and answered every greeting with some pleasant word.   Her feet, unaccustomed to shoes, had begun to ache, but the crowd was thinning out.   Most of the people were going down the street to "Foolishness," a leaning old house where the sinners had their dances. The big drum was beating and calling everybody to come on to a dance and hot supper which Cinder was having there.

July loved to dance and pleasure himself, and even on his wedding-day he hated to miss any fun. Mary felt she ought to go with him. This was no time to be thinking of hurting feet or weariness. She was a church-member and she could not dance, but she could eat rice and hash and drink some of the sweetened water.

"Good-by, Auntie; good-by, Budda Ben." Mary kissed and hugged them both, but Maum Hannah shook a warning finger. "Mind, honey, don' forget an' shake you foot to-night. Foolishness ain' no place for a child o God. I'm sorry to see you gwine in de company of all dem sinners. Yunnuh ought to go straight on home."

July's face fell for a second, then he quickly smiled again and answered blithely, "We ain' gwine to stay wid de sinners long, Auntie. I's gwine to take my wife home early dis night."

CHAPTER V

NIGHT had fallen; trees, houses, roads, fields were all melted into one darkness with a clear starlit sky far above them. The house where sinners went for pleasure was flooded with blood-red light from the great fire in the front yard. The place seethed with life, for crowds of people were weaving back and forth from the yard where great pots full of victuals were cooking, to the room where the dance was going on. Some of them were singing, some clapping their hands as they marked time to the tune which one lone fiddle squeaked out gaily to the booming beat of the big bass drum. The dance room was packed full, the door jammed with onlookers. "Hop light, ladies, take a drink o' wine," came a high shrill chant from many treble voices, so loud that the dim kerosene lamplight flickered.

"Hop light, ladies, whilst de stars duh shine," answered the men's deeper notes. July sang too as he pushed his way into the room, but Mary was a member of the church and she stayed silent. The drumsticks clattered, the fiddle squeaked, Cinder's eyes glittered bright.

Every corner was packed tight and the walls were lined with onlookers, but a place was quickly made for the bride and groom. Cinder came up and murmured something to July who smiled brightly at her, then said to Mary, "I'll be right back, honey, as soon as I lead off dis set wid Cinder. You wait here till I come."

Mary was surprised, but she tried to smile as July settled his hat more firmly on his head, stepped out into the middle of the floor and stamped so sharply that the board under him shook with the blow; then, clicking his heels together, he seized Cinder in his arms and whirled her round and round. The dancers joined them, but Mary looked away out of the window. Outside in the yard where the great fire gave plenty of light the people were laughing, talking, running on with much gay banter as they bought Cinder's rice and hog meat, her store-bought white bread soaked in brown liver-hash, the sweetened water, and hot toddy made of molasses and white corn liquor. They were celebrating Mary's wedding by buying Cinder's food. Cinder would get rich to-night with so many hungry guests.

Instead of leading the dance off and then stepping right back to stand beside Mary, July danced on. He must have forgotten what he was doing for he wheeled and glided back and forth; Cinder's skirts whirled swiftly about his feet as he whisked her on through the figure, swaying, swinging, turning, now and then pausing to beat the floor with a heel. Once, he spun her so fast, Cinder stopped and cried out, she was pure dizzy, but she clung to July, and her small eyes were sparkling as she glanced sidewise at Mary. Cinder was shameless to keep July dancing when his lawful wife had to stand by the wall.

Cinder cared nothing for what anybody thought of her. She was showing Mary she could make July pleasure himself even on his wedding-night. Mary ached to stop her, to tell her what she thought, but shyness kept her silent. The fiddle sang out with all its might and main, the drum beat faster and louder, the racket became so deafening with the dancing and singing that Mary gave up trying to hear the things that were shouted at her. She felt left out and lonely, almost sorry she was a church-member. If she were a sinner Cinder would not be July's partner.

Her knees trembled, her lips twitched, her heart thumped. That same Cinder was a devil. She had always wanted July, and she had not given up hope of him yet. She was ugly and black and skinny, but she knew how to snatch men away from their women as brazenly as foxes snatch hens from their mates in the fig trees. July was so taken up with showing off some of the new steps he had learned away from home, he could not see how Cinder's eyes shone with wickedness, or how sharp her white teeth showed between her thin black lips. With every heart-beat, Mary's anger and jealousy grew. July's promises were not cold on his lips and yet there he was, cavorting about with that wicked, man-stealing Cinder, and holding her tight in his arms before everybody's eyes.

Mary tried to fix her gaze on his so he would see her and stop, but no, he was bending down a little to hear something Cinder was whispering to him. On he went, his fine new hat cocked jauntily on one side, forgetting everything but the measure of the music and the steps which Cinder followed so closely.

It was too much. Mary could stand it no longer. Following the wall, she pushed through the crowd and went out through the door into the night. Her heart was full of gall, although the people gathered thick around her, joking her, praising her looks, offering to treat her to food or drink, making her many fine wishes. She could hardly smile, or give back civil answers, or laugh over their sly predictions about her.

She had not seen June until she felt a hot hand on her shoulder, and he whispered in her ear, "Come on, Si May-e, dance a set wid me. Le's show de people how you an' me can take all de shine off o July an' Cinder." July's guitar was slung over June's shoulder and he was already taking it off and putting it into the hands of a bystander to be free for dancing with Mary.

She shook her head. "No, June, if I was to dance to-night, de deacons would turn me out o de church next Sunday. Dat would hurt Auntie too awful bad. July'll come for me toreckly. I'll wait."

The fiddle whined out a high sad note and the big drum rolled and growled. Mary hesitated and June plead. "You ain' to stand out here by yousef an' let July dance in yonder an' you a bride." His arm slipped from her shoulder and went clear around her, "Come on, Si May-e. I'm a sinner an' July is one, you may as well be one too."

She could feel her body yielding while the two minds inside her considered what was best to do. One mind said, "No," and the other mind answered, "You are the best dancer here. Show the people that Cinder has no time with you," and before she knew it, she heard her lips saying:

"Get de box, June, and play me a tune. I rather dance by myself out here in de yard."

June's fingers fell light on the strings at first, as he plucked out a low chord, but soon a clear swinging tune rang out above a strange syncopated rhythm. July could have played no better.

Mary listened, then she placed her hands on her hips and with a laugh stepped out into the firelight. At first she bent and swayed without stepping out of her tracks. Her feet felt heavy as if they were loath to shake off her soul's salvation, but as the music went faster, they began moving with it until they hardly touched the ground at all. With her eyes half closed and her blood tingling hot, she whirled and twisted, dancing less for joy than for the wish to triumph over Cinder and to show July that she cared nothing for the slight which had stung her heart down to the quick.

Some of the merrymakers outside had been stepping around and jumping to the steady beat of the drum, cutting pigeon wings or buzzard lopes, or chasing one another out into the black darkness which cut them off completely. Now, they all stood in a circle around Mary.

The fire leaped higher, quick shadows ran over the ground, Mary's breath came faster and faster. The earth seemed to rock, the trees to be unsteady, but never had she danced so well. June's box had gone crazy, its soft wailing had changed into chords that twanged out hot and wild.

The music stopped suddenly, and a dead silence fell. The people looked blurred. Across the fire from her Mary saw July standing by himself with his arms folded and his eyes watching her with a look in them that she had never seen before. Instead of smiling at him, she leaned over and wiped her wet face with her petticoat, then took the cup of sweetened water June offered her and sipped it slowly, one small taste at a time.

Without looking up she knew that all the people were staring at her watching every move she made. Some of them were grinning and rolling their eyes, others were pursing up their lips. All of them were marveling that she had fallen into sin on her wedding-night. July leaned against a tree without turning his head. His black frown sent a shiver, then a pang of fear through Mary's heart, but she made herself laugh and talk gaily as she thanked the people for the praise they gave her.

"Great Gawd, Si May-e, you sho is outdanced evybody dis night!"

"Gal, you pure outdanced yousef, and dat's de Gawd's truth."

"Lawd, child, you is light on you feet as a duck's breast feather."

"Brer Dee is gwine to mark you name off de church book befo daylight, gal."

But Mary answered up cheerfully, "Shucks! If July is gwine to Hell, I may as well go long wid em, enty?" Then the air hummed with laughter and July came forward and took her by the arm and smiled down into her eyes. What a splendid fellow he was. So tall. So well-made. His teeth were as white as a hound's.

Two pans full of rice and pork were handed them, but Mary could not eat. Her heart was too full, the rice stuck in her throat, but July swallowed the victuals down by great spoonfuls, smacking his lips with enjoyment. Everybody talked, nobody listened, pans and cups were emptied and filled over and over again. The great black iron rice pot began a hoarse clanging as its bottom was scraped to get the last white grain. The couple's health and happiness were drunk over and over until July complained that his head was swimming round and round. He was ready to go home. Then the crowd seized Mary and held her fast, but July fought for her bravely until he had her tight in his arms, and gathering her up off her feet, cleared a way through the jam of people and hurried down the street through the darkness. He soon had her home with the door shut and barred behind them.

CHAPTER VI

THE mild autumn days streamed swiftly past, some warm, some cool, most of them fair. All of them were busy for Mary, who went to the cotton-field almost every day and picked a fair weight of cotton, besides keeping house and making a cozy comfortable home for July. Every morning she got up at first fowl crow, cooked his breakfast and fixed his dinner in a bucket for him to take, before she woke him to get up and dress and eat. The early mornings were chilly, but the shining stars made them beautiful, and the cold dew made the earth smell damp and sweet.

When July had eaten and gone she milked the cow and staked her out to graze, fed the chickens and the fattening shoat in the pen and straightened up the house before she went to the field to join the cotton pickers.

Bright-turbaned women, deep-chested, ample-hipped and strong, bent women with withered skin and trembling uncertain fingers, little gay chocolate-colored children who played as they worked, moved in a group up and down the long

rows, laughing, talking, picking the white locks
of cotton and putting them in the crocus sacks
swung from neck or shoulder.

The picking is easy. Nimble fingers move
quickly. Every boll is left clean. Eyes glance
up to meet other eyes. Musical voices flow into
one another. Cotton-picking time is the best of
the year. Every work-day is a holiday.

Maum Hannah is old and bending over long
makes her painful, but as she works she tells wonderful stories.

She knows all about Africa, that far country
over the water. Old Paupa July, her grandfather, and Mudder Charity, her grandmother,
were children of chiefs there. They talked a different talk from the people here and they were
very wise. They knew signs and how to cast
spells and how to take off spells which doctors
put on people.

The days ran swiftly and happily. When the
afternoon turned, and the sun began to drop,
Mary hurried home to fetch water from the
spring and get wood for a rousing fire so the
cabin would be bright and supper done by
the time July came at first dark. July's coming home was the best time of the whole day
even when he came in weary and dirty with river
mud and sweat. As soon as his feet were washed

clean and cocked up on a chair to rest and Mary
had put a pan full of good victuals in his lap,
she sat on the floor beside him, happy to watch
every spoonful he put in his mouth.

Just outside their closed door, the Quarter
street might ring with merriment, as the people
went to dances or prayer-meetings or hot
suppers, but Mary had no interest in any of them
so long as July would sit by the fire with her
talking, or silent, or nodding with sleepiness.
Just to have him in reach, to know he was hers,
was enough.

They spent many a happy evening together
in front of the fire whose pleasant gleam was
bright enough to let them see each other. Mary
had been turned out of the church, but when
July praised her housekeeping she could hardly
have been happier, for July's smiles meant more
to her than God or Jesus or any hope of Heaven.
The year had been a good one, the crop abun-
dant; they had a barrel of peas picked and dried
in the shed room, waiting to be eaten this winter;
strings of onions and red peppers hung on the
wall; a big bank of sweet potatoes sat in a
corner of the vegetable garden where no hog
could root into it; the small barn held a nice pile
of corn in the shucks, to make meal and food for
the cow and pig. She had earned some money

picking cotton, and she had carefully buried every extra coin in a secret place under the house to stay until hard times came. She had every reason on earth to rejoice. Blessings were on every side. Her waist was certainly bulging before its time. If she had not danced she would have been turned out when her child was born.

July laughed when he noticed her growth, and warned her to have a boy-child. No girl-child for him. He had a lot of projects to carry out when he got a little money ahead, and he would need a son to help him. Mary laughed back and promised, and happiness filled her heart.

Cinder had gone away to town on the river-boat, not very long after the wedding. A good thing. Not that July would ever look at Cinder again or at any other woman on earth but Mary.

The old roof was broken where some of the shingles had rotted, and every day the sun shone through the cracks and fell in bright streaks on the floor, reminding Mary that the roof ought to be mended before the cold winter rains would beat in. The old door sagged and the window-blinds creaked sadly on their hinges. Their time was out, and they ought to be replaced by strong new ones. But July was busy all the week, and when Saturday came he had to pleasure himself after five days of hard work. Sundays were rest days, and to mend a house then would be the unluckiest thing in the world. June offered to fix it, but Mary would not let him at first. She could wait. The old house would shelter them well enough until the days were longer and July's work lighter.

By Christmas the tide of the year had ebbed very low. The earth lay silent. Buzzards floated aimlessly about in the high still air. Wild ducks filled the marshes with a confusion of quacking and splashing, but the song-birds hopped about sadly, hunting their food and the few notes they sang were low and cheerless. The winds gave the tides little peace but kept the water in the river and the rice-fields ruffled.

Sometimes great, booming, wet gusts came in from the sea, making the trees bend and bow their heads. Icy gales shrieked and howled as they went rushing by, chilling and blighting everything they touched. The willows that bordered the river were bare of leaves and the tall gums and cypresses that towered over everything else in the swamp were stark naked. Winter had come in dead earnest. Mary's fattening pig was taken out of the pen and killed. June did it. July said the sight of so much blood made him sick, and the smell of the raw meat always killed his appetite for the good sausages and hams.

June made quick work of it, then he mended the roof of the house so no drop of rain could beat through.

Mary was heavy, but many tasks to be done kept her days filled from morning until night. A woman who is about to bear a child has a strangely good hand for planting seed; something magic in her touch makes the seed sprout quickly and grow fast and mature in half the regular time. Everybody in the Quarters who planted a winter vegetable garden wanted Mary to drop the seed.

Medicines brewed by a woman at such a time have more strength to cure ailments, and her hearth was kept full of pots holding herbs and roots for remedies, the Quarter people kept always on hand. Even Daddy Cudjoe, the old conjure doctor, brought some of his root teas for her to stir.

July did some things that were hard to under-stand, but he made a good husband, for she never trusted any woman with him. Not one. The sweet-mouthed ones, the very ones whose mouths would not melt butter, were the very ones July liked best. Mary told him a lot he did not know. One thing was not to trust kind-talking, oily-worded women.

It wasn't that she herself suspected July of

wrong-doing, but it did vex her to think he would want to spend his money or break his night's rest for the hussies that were always watching for a chance to get a hold on any man.

She begged him not to eat anywhere but at home. It would be so easy for some women to trick him or to cast a spell on him by giving him something to eat. She had always heard that the least little thing works with a man. Once Brer Dee's wise old dog left home and followed July because July laid a strip of bacon inside the heel of his shoe, yet that dog had sense. Men are strange things. The best and the strongest are weak as water when a charm gets to working on them.

But July was satisfied to stay at home most nights and he seemed to care less about pleasuring himself. Thank God, he thought more of work than of women now.

CHAPTER VII

Christmas Eve was the gayest in years, for the crops had been good, the price of cotton high and money more plentiful than usual. All day the sky had been overcast, but at sunset a keen wind rose from the west and brought out the stars and swept the crisp brown leaves from the cotton stalks down the long straight rows of the field to mix with the leaves that were falling from the trees in the Quarters. Some of them skipped gaily about on pointed tips until they found quiet spots to rest, while others joined small whirling groups and kept going from place to place.

All the doors and windows on the north side of the Quarter houses were shut tight to keep out the cold, but every cabin was brightened by a great fire roaring up its chimney. At one end of the street where a great bonfire gleamed, crowds of little children dressed up in their Sunday clothes were playing, munching apples, sucking sticks of red and white peppermint candy, pulling roasted sweet potatoes out of the hot ashes and slyly slipping in fire-crackers to see

how the old folks jumped and laughed and cried
out threats with every small explosion. "Better
mind! Santy Claw ain' gwine fetch you a Gawd's
ting if you don' stop you crazy doins."

Every gust of wind fanned out sparks from
the flames and a smell of oak smoke that
was flavored with powder from fire-crackers
or from the occasional Roman candles and sky-
rockets that flared clear up among the stars.

From Mary's doorway she could see a ring of
people, men and women, children, all ages, all
sizes, holding hands to make a big ring, moving
round and round the big fire, singing as they
circled, and keeping step to the song while a
blindfolded girl outside the ring sang answers
to their questions:

"Aun' Katie dead?" the chorus chimed.

"Yes, ma'am," came a girl's voice in answer.

"Is you been to de buryin?" chimed again.

"Yes, ma'am," fell promptly, clearly.

"Did you git some cake?"

The circle stepped faster.

"Yes, ma'am," keeping quickened time.

"Did you git some coffee?" faster still.

"Yes, ma'am."

"Did you git some tea?"

"Yes, ma'am."

"Den, shoo, ducky, shoo, don't come by me!"

Shouts of laughter followed as the blindfolded girl tried to catch somebody in the ring, to take her place. If July were at home, Mary would join them, but he had taken his box and gone to the crossroads store to pleasure himself with his friends there.

The merry musical voices were as crisp as if the frost had touched them, and the steps were light and quick.

Nobody would sleep to-night. The cattle and the sheep would get on their knees and pray like people when midnight came. The all-night watch meeting would be held at Maum Hannah's house, and most of the people, sinners and Christians, would be gathered there, but some of the sinner men would go off to the woods and build up a fire and shoot craps until dawn.

The old cow-bell was ringing. Meeting-time had come, and the cabin doors were flung open filling the dark street with ruddy light, while people poured out of them, laughing, talking, greeting one another. When Christmas comes people have to pray as well as play. July had taken his box and gone off to pleasure himself, so Mary went to meeting with June, sitting near the door and watching the people crowd in. They came in groups, laughing and talking until

they reached the door, then they all grew sober
and silent and came in quietly, sitting close together so as to make all the room they could.
The old meeting benches stayed under the house
except at prayer-meeting time on Sunday and
Wednesday nights, and again on Christmas Eve
and New Year's Eve when the people spent the
whole night singing and shouting and praying
to God.

All the members in good standing took places
up in front, close to the fire, but the sinners had
to sit wherever they could find room, back against
the wall or on the steps outside. Mary sat back
with the sinners.

When the room was packed and the steps full
to the very bottom one, the service began with
a hymn which Brer Dee read out of a book two
lines at a time:

"Whilst shep-herds watched dere flocks by night,
All seated on de ground."

There was a deep hush while the old man raised
the tune, then every one joined in with such deep
feeling that Mary was thrilled to her very heart.
Christmas was a wonderful time. When the
hymn was ended and Brer Dee said, "Let us
pray," she got down on her knees and closed her

eyes and prayed for herself and July and for
their little unborn child who would be almost big
enough to hang up his stocking by the time
Christmas came again.

Brer Dee read out of the Book how Mary
and Joseph went all the way to Bethlehem
to pay taxes, and how, because there was no room
for them in the Inn, Mary's son, little Jesus, was
born in a manger. Only three wise men on earth
knew who the child was and they came from a far
country to see him and bring him gifts, but the
angels in Heaven knew him well, and they sang
all night in the sky, while a great star shone to
give them light. Hallelujahs and shouts of Glory
to God rose all about over the room, Mary herself could hardly keep back her tears, so moved
was she with the story. Her joy would have
been complete if only July were with her, singing to God and asking humbly for His blessing
during the coming year. But July was as likely
as not already in a crap game, and since it was
Christmas Eve, he would hardly be home until
morning. But she was not lonely or unhappy,
here with so many kind friends thick all around
her, singing and praying and hearing the story
of that other Mary who was the mother of God's
own son.

CHAPTER VIII

The short winter passed quickly and before Mary knew it spring had come. The old black plum tree beside her door hid its knotty black branches with soft white blossoms, which became thicker and sweeter hour by hour as the sunshine gathered strength, and when honey-bees climbed in and out of them showers of fragrant petals were scattered around the old tree's foot. The crab-apple thickets were masses of soft pink. The birds which had gone away for the winter had come home and were picking out nesting-places. Tender green leaves screened a brown nest in the fig tree where a mocking-bird laid its eggs. The woods and hedgerows were alive with bird chatter. Woodpeckers and jays and redbirds scolded and fussed among themselves noisily. Humming-birds fluttered in and out of the red woodbine. A wren chose her last year's home in the knot-hole at one side of Mary's door. A blue-bird used her same nesting-place in the corner post of the garden fence. Larks hopped about the fields and in the roads; doves mourned tenderly; squirrels chased each other up and down trees.

Hens cackled up and down the length of the
street telling of new-laid eggs, and cocks cackled
back in loud encouragement. Yellow jessamines
in full blossom made treetops gay and fragrant
as new leaves pushed the old ones off the boughs
and the wind scattered them in brown showers
over the new grass. The old oaks tasseled out;
pines sowed their winged seed. The whole earth
was full of birthing and growth.

Men and teams, oxen, mules bent at their
work, plowing, hauling and getting the fields
ready for planting. The women cleared out the
cabins, washed and sunned clothing, bed-cover-
ings and beds; they scoured the floors, planted
the gardens, set the hens, raked fresh pine straw
to put in the stables, which were cleaned out to
enrich the land.

Medicine men were going the rounds selling
their brews to each household; they offered
strong bitter stuff for the grown men; milder
concoctions for the youths and women; gentle
doses for the children.

Rabbits played in the gardens by the bright
white moonlight and nibbled many buds off the
peas and cabbages.

The clear sunshine was burning hot, but the
cool moonlit nights were too bright for sleeping. Mocking-birds and whippoorwills left no

silence. Roses and honeysuckles took up all the air with their fragrance. All through the noon hours people lay flat on the warm earth, resting, turning up the soles of their lazy feet to the sun, that great friend of man, who not only gives light and food, but healing.

In Mary's house, fat flies swam about in circles all day long, droning the same tunes over and over. Dusk brought swarms of hungry mosquitoes out of the woods to pester men and beasts until rags were set afire and the smoke smothered to make a stench that drove them away. Crickets sang, frogs called, lightning-bugs sparkled in the dusk. The sky came close to the earth, and a soft haze veiled the fields as a thin green tide of life spread and deepened over the world. Dawns grew pinker, noons brighter, afternoons long and yellow. Short fierce storms boomed up out of the west, growling and thundering, drenching the earth with clean cool rain, then passed on, leaving a rainbow behind them. Open windows let tattered curtains stream out gaily in the breeze. Fires in the old chimneys were neglected and left to burn low. Skillets and spiders and pots sat cold and dumb on the hearths. Thank God, winter was gone. Mary could feel the spring growing in herself warming her blood, mixing strength with her weakness.

Every fair morning she went to the field with her skirts tied up short with a string around her hips to keep them out of the dew. Field work was no hardship to her. All her people before her had been field hands. Hoeing cotton was no more than a game. The hoe in her hands became a sharp seeing edge that slipped in between the tender stalks and carefully cut out hiding grass blades. She could guide it without thinking or with her thoughts on something else.

On rainy days she sewed at home, and the needle in her fingers became a shining eye that ran ahead, leading the strong blind thread behind it, sewing cloth into garments for her child.

Her time to go down was not far off. The next change in the moon might bring it, and yet she was still light-footed and deft-fingered, thank God.

One morning while she was hurrying home from Grab-All, where she had been to buy a few more lengths of cloth to finish some of her baby's clothes, a terrible spasm of pain seized her body. It scarcely passed before it came back and seized her again, tearing her bones and sinews apart, fairly cutting at her very heart-strings. Lord, how scared she was. She cried for help as loud as she could, but nobody was in hearing distance, and her child was born

right there in the middle of the road. The poor
little creature set up such a pitiful wailing that
she had to forget her own troubles and pick him
up and wrap him in her apron and hurry home
to Maum Hannah.

The old woman shook her head and looked
very stern. "Dis child ain' no seven months' child.
Look at de hair on his head. E got toe-nails an'
finger-nails good as my own. You might could
fool de people, but you can' fool me, gal, an'
you can' fool God. All two o we can tell a full
ripe baby from one what comes too soon. You
know I'll forgive you quick, but I don' know
how God feels. You better confess you sin, gal,
an' beg de Master to forgive you.

"It's a bad sign to drop a child in de Big Road.
Dis is gwine to be a far-roamin child. You'll see,
too. His legs is awful long. Just like July's own.
E ain' gwine to be no mild-mannered man what
stays round home all de time."

Maum Hannah's words were scolding words,
but they were spoken between chuckles for her
old eyes beamed with pleasure as her deft old
hands washed and dressed Mary's and July's
fine, strong, new-born son.

When all the neighbors came hurrying to see
Mary's son, tears trickled down her cheeks as
they declared that Mary had a brave heart.

She had done well in her first trial at birthing a child. A woman with plenty of experience could have done no better. God must
have blessed her with the same wisdom he gave
to the beasts, who know well when the time comes
to birth their young, and instead of complaining
of God's ways, as people do, go off alone without a word, and struggle with their labor as best
they can. So many women who are made in the
image of God himself, lie down helpless, full of
groans and bitter words, quickened by fear as
much as by the pain itself. Mary had a brave
heart, and she had come through well. God had
blessed her.

The neighbors said many fine words agreeing
with Maum Hannah, but they looked to the
child's hair and tiny nails and could hardly wait
to get outside of Mary's door before they began
whispering behind their hands that Mary's child
was not a too-soon one. He was full ripe,
come to full time. Mary was a sinner. Mary
knew exactly what they were saying. But what
if she had been married only half a year? What
difference did it make? July was her lawful,
wedded husband now, and her baby's father.
What more could they ask?

July was as pleased as he could be. He hurried
to Grab-All for the castor-oil Maum Hannah

said Mary must have, and he not only brought back a jug of whisky for everybody to take a drink, but a piece of fine cloth for a dress for Mary. He named his son Unexpected. Mary had never heard that name before, but July explained to her that it meant coming as a great surprise. The baby had done that very thing. They would call him Unex for short; a nice name, a pleasant-sounding name.

Blessed little Unex, a better baby never came into the world. Happiness filled Mary's heart. Life was full of joy. She could have asked for nothing more in the world.

CHAPTER IX

On a fine afternoon in the late summer, Mary stayed at home to wash the clothes and to cook a fine fat possum July had caught the night before for supper.

The Quarter street was quiet, except for the children playing around Maum Hannah's door, while their mothers were in the field picking the first cotton that was opening. The stillness was peaceful except when merry laughter drifted in from the cotton-pickers. Contentment filled the world as Mary went about her tasks, humming low to herself so as not to wake the baby, stopping now and then to look at him as he slept.

Sunshine fell on the floor through the open window making the room look cheerful and bright. Outside in the yard, the clean clothes were hanging on the line, drying. Inside, all the pots on the hearth steamed merrily, the possum was roasting, new potatoes were softening in the ashes. When the rooster hopped up on the door-step, flapped his wings three times and crowed, Mary stopped to listen, for that rooster had

sense. He always knew when somebody was
coming and gave her notice. He crowed every
hour in the day to tell the time, then at midnight
and again at dawn. No clock could have been
better, but whenever he came up to the door and
flapped his wings three times and crowed, Mary
might as well stop and get ready for company.
Her clothes were wet through with sweat, and
she must change them before she got caught
looking like a fright.

She had hardly put a fresh white apron on
over her clean dress when who should walk in
but Cinder. A surprise indeed. That rooster
was wise. Yet, in spite of all the warning he
had given, Mary felt upset and disturbed. A
cloud passed over the sun and dimmed the day
and gave the air a queer greenish light. Why
had Cinder come back?

"Is I scared you?" Cinder asked with a dry
little laugh. "You jumped all over when you
seed me."

"No,—no,—you just make me feel surprise. I
didn' know you was home an' when my eyes first
fell on you, I thought right at first, you might
be a sperit."

"No, gal, I sho ain' no sperit. Dis is de same
old mean Cinder a-walkin in de flesh."

As they shook hands slowly, Mary noticed

that Cinder's hand was as hot as fever, so she
said as kindly as she could, "Come set down whe
de air is cool here by de window, an' tell me how
you do an' whe you been." Mary tried her
best to sound pleased and cordial as she placed
the chair beside the window.

Cinder sat down carefully, spreading out the
fine rustling cloth of her black silk skirt. She
was dressed in the finest of clothes. Gold was
in her front teeth, and her cheeks were covered
with a dust of white powder which made her look
pale and strange. She was nervish too. Her
hands acted tremblish and her face had a twist-
mouth look.

Talk was hard to make. "How's July?" Cinder asked and Mary answered, "July's well,"
then a silence lay heavy between them again.

"You is mighty dressed up and it a Friday."
Cinder smoothed out her skirts again.

Mary answered as politely as she could that
the rooster had flapped his wings and crowed
three times at the door, so she knew somebody
was coming. She had changed her clothes to look
decent to meet her visitor.

A sudden gust of wind came down the chimney
and blew ashes over the hearth and a smell of
food rose in the room. Cinder sniffed and gave
a short laugh.

"Jedus, Gawd, is dat possum I smell? I ever was raven about possum. Do, for Gawd's sake, le me taste em."

She spoke with her old bold ease, and asked for the possum as if she had a perfect right to it.

Mary got up and filled two pans, one for Cinder and one for herself, for she had not stopped to eat any food since early breakfast. Cinder took up her spoon and began eating slowly and looking around the room. "You house looks nice and clean, Si May-e," she praised. "You ever was a good scourer. But how-come you ain' got no chimney on you lamp?"

Mary swallowed a mouthful before she answered. "De chimney got broke, but de fire gives plenty of light. Me an' July don' set up late."

Cinder's round eyes narrowed a little.

"It's awful bad luck for a lamp chimney to break, enty?"

"I don' know, I never did hear so."

"You didn'? Great Gawd, gal, I been knowin dat ever since I was knee high. It's de worst sign ever was when a lamp chimney breaks in you house."

Mary looked straight and hard into Cinder's eyes, but they turned away and gazed out of the window where a dark cloud was banked in the west. What was the use to dispute?

"Fire makes a house awful hot in de summertime, enty?　Look like you'd a heap rather be out in de field in de coolness.　But it's gwine to rain, enty?"

"I like de hotness," Mary answered quickly, "I like to sweat a plenty. I can work in de field any time I get ready."

Cinder smiled steadily, but she looked older. Her eyes were deeper set and her skin had lost its shiny blackness.　She had a string of red beads around her neck, gold earrings in her ears, and a gold ring on one finger.　In spite of the scent of cooking food, the whole room smelled sweet from something about her; not Hoyt's German Cologne or essence of lemon or any of the perfumes Mary knew, but a strange new scent, that was delicate as the breath of crab-apple blossoms. Just as likely as not it came from some new charm Cinder got yonder in town to put a spell on the men here. She always knew some way to make the men take to her, although she was skinny and dry, and had a fox chin and squirrel teeth and a sly stepping walk like a cat.

A sudden flash of lightning made Cinder jump, and Mary looked straight at her mouth. "I'd be 'fraid so much gold an' silver would draw lightnin," she remarked.

But Cinder grinned and one thin shoulder
lifted with her old scornful shrug. She wore gold
all the time. She was not afraid it would draw
lightning. People in town always wore plenty
of rings and bracelets and necklaces, and lightning never struck them. She had many more
things in her trunk besides these bracelets and
beads and rings. At one store yonder in town,
you could buy a fine diamond ring for a quarter.
Town stores were not like Grab-All.

"Whyn't you stay in town if fine tings is so
cheap dere? Why you come back here?"

Cinder looked up at her quickly.

"You talk like you ain' so glad I come. Dat's
a pity. But July'll be glad to see me."

Cinder's pan was empty and she got up to go.
But she paused at the door. "I hear-say you got
a baby, Si May-e."

"I sho is, de finest lil boy-chile ever was. De
pure spit o July too. E's a-sleepin right yonder
on de bed in de shed room."

"I hear-say you had em too soon, an' de deacons turned you out de church. Is dat so?"

"No, it ain' so. You know good as me it ain'
so. I ain' been a church-member, not since I
danced at Foolishness on de night o my weddin."

A flash of lightning made Cinder's eyes glit-
ter, but a smile fluttered over her thin lips as

she moistened them with the tip of her pointed red tongue.

"I ain' meant a bit o harm by axin. You is my own second cousin, an' I was a waiter at you weddin. I ever did think a lot o July. I come mighty nigh marryin him mysef one time. E use to beg me so, but I'm glad now I didn' done it."

Thunder was rolling and the clothes were on the line in the yard, but Mary had forgotten them.

"You say July begged you to marry em? July? Great Gawd! Dat's de biggest lie ever was! Gal, you ain' shame to talk such a talk? You like to a popped you gizzard-string a-tryin to get July. Evybody in dis Quarter knows dat. You'd jump up an' crack you heels wid joy evy day Gawd sends, if you could a caught him. You know dat too, good as me."

The words were hardly off Mary's lips when a shadow darkened the doorway and July walked in. His eyes blinked when they fell on Cinder, as if he were trying to make her out.

"De Great I Am! Whe'd you come from, Cinder?" he asked in glad astonishment. "I didn' know you was home. How you do, gal."

His big rough shoes were covered with dust from the road and caked with river mud that made ugly tracks on the clean floor, but he was too taken up with Cinder to notice.

"Do scrape off you feets, July," Mary bade him, but he didn't hear for Cinder was holding his hand, laughing up into his face, gazing at him with shining eager eyes, answering his questions with trembling lips. A flame of hot jealousy flared up in Mary's heart. Cinder had forgotten that July's lawful wedded wife was looking straight at her, watching every move she made, seeing how she held July's eyes, and how her sweet-mouthed talk pleased him. Mary's ears tingled as they heard Cinder's words, but Unex woke with a loud wail and she had to go get the child, who had slept a long time and needed food. A bad dream must have scared him to make him cry so hard.

The shed room was stifling hot although the sun was under a heavy cloud and in spite of the lightning Mary sat close to the open window.

"You look better'n I ever seed you in my life," July declared, as free and easy as if he were a single man.

"You look good, yousef." Cinder answered him in a voice that was husky with pleasure. Lightning lit their faces and a long mutter of thunder rumbled, but Cinder, heeding none of it, stood sweet-talking July, pretending that she

was the only person in the world who knew how
fine and handsome and smart he was; and July,
with all the sense he had, stood looking down at
her, his ears drinking up every deceitful word,
his eyes swallowing in all her silly town airs. Cinder was as tricky as a fox, no wonder her chin
was pointed, but she had no more sense than a
sparrow except when it came to making eyes at
men.

"July," Mary called sharply, "go fetch in de
clothes. It's gwine to rain." A gust of wind
lifted a cloud of dust off the ground and sent it
into the house. A clap of thunder cracked overhead.

"Good-by, Si May-e," Cinder called out sweetly, and out of the door she went, leaving a cloud
of that sweet smell behind her.

July followed her out, but he soon came back
with his arms full of clothes which he laid on
the bed. "You want me to do anything else?"
he asked quietly. The trees were rustling loudly
as the wind bent their branches low. Pans flew
off the shelf and the papered wall crackled.

Mary was almost ready to cry with im-
patience. Where were July's senses that he
stood asking her what to do when a rain was
almost on them. He soon had the cabin closed
tight, but it was filled with an awkward silence

that marked the heavy rolling thunder. Mary wanted to say many things but she remembered Maum Hannah's training; when the thunder rolls, people must sit down quiet and listen while Up-Yonder, the Great I Am, the Maker of all things, talks.

Instead of helping himself out of the pots, July fixed himself a cup of sweetened water and swallowed it down, thirstily.

Mary could keep silent no longer even if the clouds were shouting.

"What de matter ail you, July? How-come you don' eat some possum?"

"I got de headache. I ain' hungry."

"How-come you got de headache?"

"I dunno, lessen so much sun-hot to-day done it."

That was a poor excuse. Sun-hot could not make July's head ache when shade covered the whole swamp where he worked. Sun-hot does not make people sick. July must have headache for some other reason. His eyes looked like corn-liquor eyes.

"Come lay down on de bed. Le me put a wet rag on you head, July. Dat'll make you feel more better. When de rain stops I'll get a collard leaf an' tie on em. Dat'll make you well."

Men are like children when things go wrong.

July was as helpless as Unex now. Mary pushed the rough-dried clothes aside and made him lie down on the bed, and soon he was sound asleep, in spite of the storm outside.

Lightning cracked sharp whips overhead and ran crooked white fingers through the cracks of the house. Mary shivered at the crashes of thunder and held Unex closer, but July lay still and snored. The muddy boots were still on his feet, ruining the clean bed, soiling the clean clothes. He was no more than a child after all. She had to look after him the same as she looked after Unex. Putting the baby on a quilt on the floor, she gently, quietly, began untying the string that fastened the shoes, and slipped them off his feet carefully, slowly, so he would not wake. Sleep would cure his head.

A wild wind whined around the house corners, rain poured on the roof and beat at the door and windows, trying to get in. The trees creaked painfully as the storm wrenched their limbs, darkness blotted out the day. Then the storm slackened, and July woke.

He sat up and stretched, buttoned up his shirt at the neck, got up and opened the door to look out. He felt better. His head was clear now, after his nap.

Lord, how good and clean the fresh air smelled

after the cabin's hot lack of breath. He went into the shed room and changed his clothes and stepped out into the yard to see if any damage had been done by the storm, and to breathe the fresh pleasant air.

Evening had come with a crimson sky and a clear thin wishing moon hung in the west. Bull bats darted about catching gnats and mosquitoes; squirrels chittered and scurried from one tree to another; frogs croaked noisily; grasshoppers, crickets, katydids, glad to be alive, made a whir of loud clear chirping. Partridges whistled "Bob White, peas ripe," asking, answering, over and over again. The street, washed clean except for boughs and green leaves torn from the trees by the fierce wind and puddles left in low places by the streams of rain-water that gurgled away toward the river, was full of women and children, carrying in wood for the night, going to get the cows and milk them, calling up their fowls and scattering grain around the different doorways, to show each flock which was home.

Distant thunder boomed far away over the river where the storm had gone and the air grew chilly, but July was restless. Instead of sitting down quietly, or offering to help fix the ash-cake for supper, or to fetch a bucket of fresh water

from the spring, he went into the shed room,
tarried there a minute and came out buttoning
up his shirt at the neck.

"Whe you gwine?" Mary asked him timidly.

He waited a minute; then he asked, "How-
come you got to know evywhe I go, here lately?
I'm gwine whe I'm gwine. Dat's whe I'm
gwine." His words ripped through the quiet.

The room was hot. Its close air was full of
the smell of steam from the pots and smoke
from July's pipe. There was scarcely a
sound except Mary's sniffles. July walked to
the fireplace and stirred among the ashes, selecting a small live coal which he dropped into his
pipe bowl. Her back was turned to him, but
she knew how his lips were drawn, how his pipe
stem was gripped between his set teeth, how his
chin was pushed forward, how his lean young
face had grown hard and set.

"How-come you duh cry?"

How could she tell him when he stood there
smoking, gazing down at the sticks of wood,
jerking out his words so vexedly.

Instead of going to fetch the cow home, for
it was past milking time, he walked out, his heavy
brows frowning, his wide lips tightened. Mary
watched him from the window as far as she could
see him walking to the very end of the street.

Cinder was still on his mind. He was going to
see her, and leave all the evening work for
Mary to do alone. Tall, slim, dark as the tree-
trunks, he moved quickly through the twilight,
then disappeared.

Mary listened at his feet splashing through a
pool left by the rain. His overalls would have
to be washed again, but that troubled her less
than the vague uneasiness that gnawed at her
heart. July was not himself. He had gone off
and left her with supper to cook, all the things
to feed and the cow to milk.

Night fell and the baby had gone back
to sleep but July had not come home. Mary
drew the pots a little farther away from the fire
so the food they held would not scorch or become
dry, then she went to the door and looked up
and down the street for sign of him.

Children were playing games in the dusk,
shouting, singing, screaming out when the one
who was "booger-man" ran out from a hiding-
place to catch somebody, but Mary's mind
was too full of something else to notice
them. July loved his home, he loved her
and Unex; what made him stay so long? The
little new moon slowly fell behind the black trees,
a multitude of cold white stars crowded the sky,
twinkling, sparkling, now and then one of them

dropping toward the earth, marking a path for somebody's soul. The fire dwindled and almost went out for lack of a stick of wood, but Mary sat on the door-step, alone, and an aching uneasiness had her flesh trembling and all her bones weak.

One by one the houses grew dark and silent, tears rolled out of her eyes and fell in her lap. July had forgotten her.

The dawn brought him. A puff of cool air pushed in with him when he opened the door. Mary sniffed it softly for a faint scent of Cinder's perfume came with it on July's clothes.

"You needn' walk so easy, I'm wake, July. I ain' shut my eyes all night long. I'm sick as I only can be. Worry-ation kills me. Whyn' you tell me you was gwine off an' not a-comin home?"

July gave her no answer, but with his jaws locked he sank into a chair and began putting on his boots to go to his work in the swamp. Mary could not tell if he heard her or not for he made no sign that he did. Then anger stirred her.

"Whyn' you answer me, July? Whe you been? What de matter ail you?"

Then he straightened up. "Nuttin' ain' de matter ail me. I been in de woods shootin' a

little crap, dat's all. You ought not to quarrel if
I pleasure mysef a lil."

"I can smell de stench o Cinder's scent
on you, so you needn' lie to me. I ain' no fool. I
got some sense—some sense——"

July shrugged. "If you got so much sense,
whyn' you bank de fire last night? E's dead as a
wedge. Now I got to go borrow a piece from
somebody to hotten me some victuals to eat."

He knelt on the hearth, muttering and stirring
among the ashes, moving blackened chunks of
wood, trying to find a live ember. When he found
one he laid a fat splinter on it and blew it into a
blaze. Mary wept quietly for she could think
of no words to tell July how hurt she was, how
utterly grieved at the way he was doing her now.
She'd forgive him if he would only come sit on
the bed beside her and hold her hand and ask
her pardon. She was even willing to get up and
go to him and beg his pardon for being vexed,
if he would only look at her. But he didn't.
He ate some food and left her without saying
good-by.

CHAPTER X

MAUM HANNAH kept Unex while Mary picked cotton all the week until Saturday, when she washed the clothes early and ironed them all before noon. She was starting to the spring to fetch water to scour before night when Doll, July's sister, came by. When she saw Mary still working she burst out laughing, "How-come you duh scour when evybody else is pleasurin? How-come so?"

Mary began trying to explain: July didn't like her to be roaming around and trapesing up and down the road. He liked to find her at home whenever he came in.

Doll laughed. Being July's sister, she could say things about him nobody else could say. "Lawd, gal," she began seriously, "if you pay 'tention to July, you would pure work yousef to death. Put down dat scourin brush. Come on go to Grab-All wid me. Some fine new dress cloth come on de boat yesdiddy. You need some new clothes, well as me."

Mary was afraid to do it at first, for July had

94

not come home for dinner yet, and he liked his victuals to be nice and hot. But Doll insisted, so she put up the scouring brush and changed her dress, put on a clean white apron and her fine hoop earrings and went to the store with Doll.

The dress cloth was beautiful, but she had no money to buy a single yard. June treated Doll and herself to a bag of candy and a bottle of soda-water and after they had laughed and talked a while, he bought them each a string of beads and a can of salmon, then they came on home.

July was standing in the door when they walked up. His face was frowning and he had little to say to any of them. Doll had prepared Mary for that very thing. Doll warned her that if July started any short talk, just to outtalk him; if he said anything rough, to answer him back still rougher. That was the way to manage men. July was spoiled. He was used to having his own way with everybody. He needed a wife who would rule him instead of one who was soft and gave in to all his spoiled ways.

Mary went in the house and started to feed Unex, and when she saw the black frown on July's face she put on one that was blacker. As soon as she laid Unex down on the bed July reached out a hand and took her by the arm. His eyes cut deep into her face, and his voice rumbled out, "Whe you been?"

"I been to Grab-All."

"How-come you gone off an' ain' told me whe you was gwine?"

"But I fetched you a nice can o salmon. You ought to be glad stead o cross as two sticks." July grabbed the salmon off the table and threw it on the floor so hard the can bent in.

"You better behave yousef, July." She tried to sound brave but her heart knocked clean up in her wind-pipe, for July's eyes were sparkling.

"I don' like you to take de baby out in de night air. Don' do dat not no more. It's you business to stay home. A married 'oman ain' to trapes de Big Road. It don' look nice. An' don' be spendin' my good money for no salmon, neither. I can' stand de smell of em, much less de taste."

"I didn' spend you good money. June bought de salmon an' gi em to me."

"You went wid June? Well, you stay home lessen I take you to Grab-All."

There was no use to fuss with him, so she stirred around and cooked him a nice hot ash-cake and some bacon.

"Whe'd you git dem beads round you neck?"

"June gi em to me."

"June? When did you and June git so thick?"

"We ain' thick."

"Well, take em off."

She hesitated, he had no right to order her around like a dog. Then the necklace seemed suddenly hateful. She unhooked it and started to throw it into the fire but July stopped her. "Go put em in de trunk and keep em in de trunk lessen I tell you to take em out. Is you hear me?"

If July would only have sat still long enough for her to talk to him, she could have made up with him, but as soon as he ate, he got his hat and left the house. Later on, when he came in and went to bed, she tried to talk but he pretended he was asleep.

Sunday morning he seemed more like himself, and then she tried to tell him she was still young, and liked to go somewhere now and then, to meeting or to a birth-night supper, or to Grab-All, just for a little pleasure. He ought to be glad for her to go. As soon as she began to talk, he shut up as tight as a clam, and in a little while he got his hat and left.

When night fell Doll came by on her way to meeting and Mary wrapped the baby up and went with her. She was not spying on July for he had disappeared down the street going toward

Cinder's house while she went in the other direction. No harm was in that. But when he came in late that night, with his eyes all hot and bloodshot, he ground his teeth together and asked, "Didn' I told you to stay home to-night?"

She made herself stand up straight and look him in the eyes.

"Looka here, July. No man livin can' boss me around dis way an' work me to death." She spoke out boldly and tried to jerk herself loose from his grasp.

"Yuh duh back-jaw me?" He pressed her. "Tell me dat?" His head was bent so close his eyes were near to her face.

"Sho, I'll back-jaw you much as I please. Who is you to be so big-doins anyhow?"

The words were hardly off her lips when he gave her face a slap that laid her flat on the floor. She jumped up like a cat and hit him back, but she might as well have used her fist on iron. July's sinews were too tough to feel her blow.

She reached up and tried to scratch his face, but he held her up off the floor with one hand and with the other he laid licks on her that knocked the breath out of her and blistered her skin. She didn't know a man's hand could fall so heavy. Lord, those were awful licks. She

saw stars, and she couldn't suck in enough breath
to yell for help. She had to think fast, for, vexed
as July was, he might kill her. Her body was
stunned, but her wits were strangely sharpened.
She lay flat on the floor without moving, and
when she saw him looking down to see if she
really was hurt very much, she began to cry.
Not a loud grown-woman's crying, but a poor
little pitiful whining like a young baby too sick
to live much longer.

"Git up off dat floor, May-e," July shouted,
and she pretended to do her best, then fell back
down like something hamstrung, crying weakly
all the time.

"What de matter ail you?" he stormed.

"My back's broke," she whispered, "broke in
two—you done killed me, July."

He jerked her up roughly and tried to make
her stand on her feet, but her bones melted and
fear shook her like a palsy.

"Stand up! May-e!" He tried to compel her,
but she fell up against him, and with her arms
around his neck, she sobbed against his breast.
She could feel the blood beating in his heart and
his breath was heaving hard, but his big arms
went softly around her and he picked her up and
carried her to the shed room and laid her on the
bed. She shut her eyes and held her breath so

July would think she had gone off in a trance.

"May-e! Gal!" He called her and felt for the pulse in her wrist.

She waited a little before she answered feebly, "Is you call me, July?" and put a blind hand out to feel for him. "My eyes is gone blind, July. Dey can' see a bit. You done ruined me fo good."

"Great Gawd, gal. I didn't mean to hurt you so bad. Le' me go for Auntie." But she begged him not to leave her. She wanted him to stay by her. And he did, pleading with her to forgive him, promising her he would never do such a thing again; he was worried and fretted, so he forgot himself. After she was quiet and ready to sleep he sat by the fire a long time, staring at it and studying. Cinder had him conjured, poor fellow. That was his trouble. Cinder's black hand had him all but out of his mind.

For three days Mary made like she was nearly dead. She stayed in bed, while July waited on her and cooked for her and washed her face and tended to her as though she were a baby. He thought she was crippled, and he could not bear for anybody to know he had done it. Once he wept with grief and shame, but Mary had learned her lesson too. A strong man's hand can fall heavy, and the best way to deal with strength is to be weak and helpless. She was not able to fight with July. It was better to knuckle to him any day.

Maybe she could get Daddy Cudjoe to put a black hand on Cinder that would get the wicked slut out of July's way. Mary felt that she would be willing to kill her if it came to the worst. There were ways, plenty of ways. Poison roots and herbs grew in the woods; pleasant-tasting teas could be made out of them. Cinder would drink a swallow or two and then shrivel up and die and nobody but Mary would know why. Still, teas are dangerous and hard to manage. Sometimes the wrong person drinks them.

Mary had strong sharp teeth, set in blue gums. If she could bite Cinder one time, one lone time, that would settle things. But Cinder had gums as blue as her own; Cinder's teeth were just as sharp; Cinder's sinews were like wire; and as quick as a whip-lash. Mary's mind milled one plan after another, over and over. None was easy enough to try. Misery was gnawing a hole deep down in her heart, making a dark place where her thoughts stayed most of the time. Her blood got thin, her body weak and her skin grew ashy and pale.

CHAPTER XI

SUMMER's time was out, yet it tarried stubbornly on the plantation. The deceitful season had fooled everything into striving for the utmost growth and fruitfulness and now, when harvest-time had come and cooler nights and paler days would bring a gentle ripening, summer hung on, ruining everything it had wrought. The cotton leaves were wilted and hanging limp, no longer able to hide the tight-packed bolls or to shade the tender new squares and late blossoms from the scorching sun. The pleasant rustling of corn blades had changed to a harsh complaining crackling, as the fodder was slowly withered. The roads cast up sullen clouds of red-hot dust to hang between them and the sky, and quiet little shady paths puffed up breaths of dry mold if the lightest footstep were laid on them. Instead of scratching for worms and hunting tender seeds to fatten themselves for the fall laying season, the fowls sprawled under the houses, panting through open beaks, holding their wing feathers far out from the down on their breasts. The birds left the high trees and went to stay

near the water streams, singing blithely enough
in the dawns but leaving the days silent after
the sun swallowed up the dew.

The sky lifted high and far away. The tall
pines stood still against it, every needle shining
in the sun, and moaning softly with the slightest
stir of the hot air. The old oaks shielding the
cabins' roofs from the burning sun must have
sunk their roots deep in the ground to reach
moisture, for their leaves stayed glossy and
green, and the long moss hanging from their
branches kept its fresh grayness.

The people in the Quarters gave up sleeping
in beds and spread quilts on the floors beside open
doors and windows. Even if snakes and bugs
and spirits walked in the darkness, the risk must
be faced to get whatever coolness the night
brought.

The river was shrunken, the lakes were dry,
the clouds moved overhead white and empty.
The water in the rice-fields lay as smooth as ice
and as silent as death as the tides kept it rising
and falling. The air drifted in heavy-scented
with withered cotton blossoms, shriveled figs and
grapes falling off the vines to waste.

Mary was unhappy, restless, disturbed, uncertain what to do. She must make up her mind
to something for she could not go on any longer

pretending she did not feel things that were breaking her heart. Even the plantation seemed different. Those hot fields, spread out before her eyes, looked silent and cruel. They offered her no hope for better things, no way of escaping sorrow.

She had been married less than a year, yet cold fear made her heart shiver when she thought of July and the change that had come over him this summer. As soon as first dark came he would go, leaving her alone, sleepless, wretched, to spend the long lagging nights as best she could. Misery dimmed the sunshine, blackened the shade, blighted her pleasure in the flowers and trees and in all the things she loved best.

To-day, instead of being noisy and gay with fun, the plantation Quarters was silent as on Sunday. Everybody who could raise the price of a round-trip ticket had gone to town, on the Saturday excursion. Men, women, old, young, saints, sinners, all had got up before dawn and walked the long miles to the landing where the excursion boat stopped to take them aboard.

The only people left in the Quarters were too sick, or too young, or too old, and these were seeking shade from the sun-hot which beat down strong, burning up the smells of pig-pen and goats and cattle raised by the damp morning.

Mary sat alone by her cabin window, looking out across the fields where the cotton, only half gathered, hung dripping from the bolls. The long red road bordered with tall blooming weeds and seeded grass-heads was empty. The trees stood motionless, their dark green heads stretching upward toward the dry white sky, where the sun plowed a fiery furrow.

To-day, instead of staying at home with her and the baby, July had gone on the excursion and left them behind, all by themselves. He could have taken them along and found them no trouble for the baby was as good as gold. But he said women and babies were better off at home, that they had no business gallivanting around on excursions.

The baby, Unex, was six months old to-day, yet he was able to creep across the floor and say things that sounded like words. He had more teeth than he was due to have and his head was covered with crinky little wool. A blessed baby. A joy. He had only one fault in the world. He put things in his mouth if Mary did not watch him, and wretched pain twisted his little middle if he swallowed nothing more than a straw or a stick. Food was the only thing his precious insides could stand.

Thank God, food agreed with him. Any kind

of food. She had trained him from the very
start to eat some of everything she ate. She took
him right in her lap when she sat down with her
victuals and held his mouth close to her pan.
When she took a big bite she gave him a tiny
taste. When she ate collard greens he had a sip
of the pot licker. When she ate peas and rice he
had a spoonful of the good blue gravy. When
she all but bit her fingers over catfish stew, he
smacked his baby lips over a thread of the tender
white meat, or sucked at a knot of the salt bacon.
He never had colic from her breast milk or her
food, for his insides were taught and trained to
deal with strong things, with good full-flavored
man rations.

Maum Hannah had warned her at the very
beginning of his life not to coddle and weaken
him with sugar rags and sweetened water and hot
milk tea, but to make him a real man and raise
him hard, strong, tough, so he could grow up
able and hot with life.

When he first began crawling and went near
the door-step, she did not say a word, but let
him fall down the steps and bump his head hard.
He remembered it and next time watched out
and was careful. The first time he crawled near
the hearth where the old fire burned day and
night, sometimes slowly with a dull blue light,

sometimes fast and bright, she left him alone and let him burn his hand. He learned for certain that fire is hot and wicked, a bad thing for babies to play with. People learn best by experience, whether they are babies or grown-ups, and Unex had sense like people already, although he was only half of a short year old. She could leave him at home, alone on the bed, or on the floor, and he could take care of himself.

He was raven about his daddy. His baby eyes fairly danced whenever July came near him, and July's funny motions and talk made him shriek out with pleasure. Unex had manners too. At night, when he woke up in the dark, he cooed softly and patted Mary to wake her instead of bawling and disturbing July's sleep.

But now, in spite of Unex's nice ways, July had gone off on the excursion and left them behind, and Mary was down-hearted and weary. She never had any pleasure. She did not mind work, for she was raised to work and she was never happier than when she was jerking a hoe, or cooking, or washing clothes. To sweat made her feel better; to swing an ax and cut wood limbered up her muscles; to spread black manure in the field cleared out her lungs and gave her breath a good clean feeling. She liked work when her mind was free and her heart light, but she needed some pleasure too.

Now, her heart lay like a rock in her breast and the same thoughts walked back and forth through her mind; her head well-nigh had a hole worn in it with studying about what was best to do. July did not love her, that was his trouble, and her love for him had become so bitter with jealousy it was a sickness, a weakening ailment.

When the preacher read out of the holy Book over them last fall, July promised to take her for better or worse, for richer or poorer. He swore to God he would love and cherish her until death parted them. He meant every word of the promise then. He spoke out so brave and loud that all the people laughed and even the preacher smiled. But he had forgotten the promises he made that day. He thought only of himself, now. He made money, but he spent it to pleasure himself, and expected her to be satisfied if she had food and clothes and shelter. He thought less and less of her, and more and more of other people. The excursion round-trip tickets cost three dollars apiece. Three dollars would have bought many things that she and Unex needed.

The people in the Quarters were careful what they said when she was around, but she was not blind or deaf. She knew more than they thought, more than July thought. She was no fool.

June always praised the way she managed things. The last time he brought her a piece of cloth and she cut it out and sewed it with strong, tight stitches into a dress, between supper and time to go to bed, June declared that no other woman in the Quarters could have done it. June praised her cooking too. He liked the way she seasoned things. He bragged that she kept the cleanest house in the Quarters, or on the whole plantation for that matter. But July was so taken up with his own life that he had forgotten Mary had any rights at all. He ate the food she cooked for him, slept in the bed she sunned and aired and made up for him, wore the clothes she washed and patched and darned for him, but he seldom noticed they were mended. When she was weary and down-hearted, July took what she gave him then went his way to find some more cheerful woman to go pleasuring with. She had no hat, no decent shoes. She told him so last night. The protracted meeting would begin next week too, but July laughed and said if a woman wanted to save her soul she must mind her husband and treat him right.

She tried to do that. This morning she was up ahead of the morning star, fixing hot coffee and bread for July before he went off with the crowd. But he swallowed it down and hurried off with hardly as much as, "Thank you."

After he had gone she worked on to keep from thinking about her troubles, but now she was hot and tired, her clothes were wet with sweat. The hands in her lap were skinny and hard, the skin on them was shriveled, her body was worn out, ready to drop to pieces like her faded dress, which was thin from so much washing and wearing.

When she married July everybody said she was the prettiest bride that ever stepped in the Quarters. Now she was withered and ugly with no way to stop being so. Trouble had caught her as a cat catches a mouse and she could not get loose. She would as soon be dead as not, except for baby Unex, who could not be left alone in the world for July would never bother with him; July, who was on his way to town now, laughing, talking, singing gay songs, eating bananas, drinking bottled soda-water, having pleasure in the cool breeze on the river, while she was here, lonesome and down-hearted and weary enough to die in this old empty tumble-down home, where every noise sounded hollow and strange.

May Satan wring Cinder's stringy neck and

break her back in two before he drops her into his bottomless pit! July would have stayed at home and been a good husband if Cinder had never come back to the plantation.

Mary heard a hen's anxious clucking and baby chickens crying, then Maum Hannah's voice asked softly, "Honey—is you sleepin?"

She sat up quickly. She had heard no step, and she felt confused and guilty that Maum Hannah who believed in loving everybody had caught her crying and wishing bitter curses on Cinder.

"No'm, I ain' sleep. I just got de headache. I was a-leanin out de window by it's so awful hot to-day. Seems like I can' hardly catch enough air."

"We must be tanksful we is able to feel de hotness, honey. Be tanksful, gal. Tank Gawd for life, den come look at de present I brought you. My lil blue hen stole a nest in de chimney corner and hatched dese beedies, all blue like dey mammy, an' spry as can be. A blue hen's chickens is lucky, so I fetched em to you for seed. But don' feed em, not yet. Let em sleep in de basket until to-morrow."

Maum Hannah put them down in a dark corner of the room and carefully covered them up; then she sat down, took her pipe out of her apron pocket and filled its small bowl with plug-cut tobacco. "Git a coal, daughter, an' light my pipe. I feel de need o a good cool smoke. Dat blue hen sho made me sweat befo I could put em an' all e chillen in dat basket. You wouldn' believe it to see how quiet e is now."

Maum Hannah had come to say something else and she was uncertain just how to begin, but presently she asked between puffs of smoke, "Whe is July, Si May-e?"

"Gone to town on de boat."

"On de excussion?"

"Yes'm."

"Is Cinder gone wid em?"

"I don' know, Auntie."

Maum Hannah smoked in silence, then she took her pipe out of her mouth and pressed the burning tobacco down tighter.

"Budda Ben's been a-talkin about how July goes off an' leaves you all de time whilst e's a-spendin money on dat Cinder."

Maum Hannah's eyes sent sidelong looks at Mary to see how these words were being taken. Mary hung her head at first, ashamed that they were so and she could not deny a single word.

"Budda Ben talked it all over last night, an' we done agree dat you don' need to stay here wid July lessen you want to. You got a home

right yonder wid me an' Budda de same as you
had befo de preacher ever read out de Book over
you an' July an' made yunnuh man an' wife. If
you want to come home, den you come. Me an'
Budda will divide de last crust o' bread we got
wid you an' lil Unex, long as we live. You don'
have to stand mistreatment a day longer'n you
want to. Not a day. You just say de word, an'
we will help you move all you things right now."

Mary's heart thumped with hollow sickening
licks. "Thank you kindly, Auntie, but I can'
leave July. I know you an' Budda Ben would
take me an' de baby an' do for we de same as you
done for me, but July couldn' get on widout me.
July is a fine man. E's raven about me an' about
de baby too. Cinder has been a-tryin to get em
off de right track by runnin after em so much all
de time, but I'll get em straight befo long. July
don' never mistreat me. E has a short patience,
fo-true. Sometimes e misses an' talks kind o'
short, but I don' mind dat. Budda Ben used to
talk de same way. Me an' July gets on good
most o de time. You an' Budda Ben mustn'
fret about me. No."

Once she had started defending her husband,
Mary's words flowed on and on. Sometimes
they rose loud and jerked and broke, then they
slackened and started all over, saying the same

things, as if repeating them made them true.
Declaring to Maum Hannah that July was good
and kind and free-handed brought easement to
her heart, somehow.

Maum Hannah smoked slowly and listened
without a word until Mary finally stopped.

"You ever did have a brave heart, gal. I'm
glad to hear you got such a good husband. But
if I was you I'd go to see old Daddy Cudjoe an'
get me a good strong charm to keep him a good
one. Times is changed. Women ain' like dey
used to be. When I was young, a married man
was a married man an' nobody didn' bother em.
But dese days, it don' matter if a man is married
or single, de womens don' let em rest. No.
Gawd knows what de world is a-comin to." She
sighed deep to think of how slack the ways of the
women were.

"You take my advice an' go see Daddy Cudjoe
an' get em to fix you a charm to keep July home.
Daddy is a wise man. E knows black magic as
well as white. E could gi you a charm so strong
July never could leave you no more. Not long
as e lives. Daddy's wise."

Mary sat thinking, listening while Maum
Hannah told of the many ways in which Daddy
Cudjoe had helped her. Once she had a pot that
would not boil, and she took the contrary thing

to Daddy Cudjoe. He gave it a good frailing
with a stout hickory stick and the pot had been
the quickest one on her hearth to boil ever since.
Once, when Budda Ben's ax refused to cut
straight, Daddy Cudjoe taught it to behave itself right. Everything gets out of order and
gives trouble sometimes; men and women and
pots and pans and axes; everything needs to be
ruled. The river flowed quietly and kindly now,
but sometimes it got mean too, and overflowed
and drowned out the crops and swallowed up
men and their boats. Instead of giving rain to
water the earth, the clouds held every drop so
tight, not one can leak out. Sometimes they get
cross and send down hail that breaks everything,
and lightning to strike trees and houses and kill
men and beasts.

In the old days, all the people trusted to magic
to rule the river and clouds and seasons as well
as their tools and each other, but times have
changed. Only Daddy Cudjoe, of all the old
people left, knew any of the old secret ways. But
he knew them well. He could fix July too.

Mary admitted she had thought of going to
Daddy Cudjoe, but she wondered if he could help
her now since Cinder had him conjured. Maum
Hannah declared that every ailment on earth
has its cure and sometimes the simplest things,

such as river mud, or the scale of a fish, or the eye of a snake, or the skin of a frog, even a hair or a toe-nail can work wonders. Daddy had always been kind to the most useless things and befriended them. In return they worked for him. They told him where lost things were, what the past was, what things were to come; they trusted him, and taught him all their own wisdom.

He could fix Mary something that would not only keep July safe from Cinder and all other women, but would bind him to her for ever. It would pay her to go and see the old man and tell him about her troubles.

If she had stayed a good Christian girl, as she started out to be, then God might have listened to her prayers. But she sinned. She was a fallen member. She would have to depend on magic now, the only power that will work as well for a sinner as it does for a Christian.

When Daddy Cudjoe did give her a charm, she must be mighty careful with it. Charms are strong things. Sometimes they miss and start up troubles of their own that are worse than the ones they are meant to cure.

Daddy Cudjoe made a bad mistake one time himself, when he fixed some kind of a root medicine to help his shortness of breath. Lord!

That was a funny thing! Maum Hannah laughed
so she could hardly tell how the old man came to
her house late in the night one cold night last
winter and tapped softly on the door. She
jumped up quickly for she thought some poor
sick somebody had sent for her. But there stood
old Daddy Cudjoe, shivering with cold but with
his eyes hot and shining. He began whispering
to her so easy she could hardly make out what he
said. He wanted to come in and spend the night
with her. Think of that! Poor Daddy Cudjoe,
already so old he could hardly walk, and all upset by a root tea he had made for himself.

He almost cried when she told him to go on
back home and sleep his misery off. Poor Daddy
Cudjoe! He swore he had not thought on a
woman for twenty years, but that root medicine
he took for his shortness of breath was so awful
strong. One dose had made him too restless to
stay home. He had come all this way to ask
her to do him a favor.

She told the joke on him the next day, but
Daddy did not seem to mind. Some men would
have got vexed, but not Daddy Cudjoe. He
laughed about it himself, and said he thought he
would have to get himself a wife, he was getting
so young and spry. Didn't apple trees bloom in
the fall sometimes? And didn't the Book tell

about an old woman named Sarah who bloomed in her old age? Maybe such things were not so uncommon after all.

Charms and roots and teas are dangerous things if people don't use them exactly right. Mary would have to be careful when she got a charm or it might do herself harm too.

Mary's heart was so heavy she could hardly get up to go. If Cinder had July conjured what good could any charm do?

Sadness filled the world. The sunlight was pale. The trees sighed as the soft wind fluttered their leaves and stirred the hot grass-blades. A rabbit peeped out from a briar patch with his scared eyes staring, and his nostrils twitching. He must not cross the road in front of her now. Mary clapped her hands and shouted, "Git back," as loud as she could. Everything was against her; even the field rabbit which hurried across the path, added more bad luck to what she already had.

CHAPTER XII

THE road leaving the Quarters ran straight
to the river which was the plantation's main high-
way out into the world, the faithful carrier which
took away its bales of cotton and brought back all
its luxuries. The road's deep ruts cut by slow-
moving wagon-wheels ran side by side past
cotton-fields, through woods where last year's
fallen leaves and brown pine-needles made them
dim and where every grass-blade or leaf budding
up above the ground was crushed back into the
earth by the cloven feet of patient oxen or small,
round, quicker-stepping mule hoofs.

As the road reached the brow of the hill, it
slackened its gait and sent a small fork off to
one side. Mary followed this as it crept cautious-
ly and with painstaking curves through thickets,
under low-hanging trees whose roots clutched the
earth, until the cabin where Old Daddy Cudjoe
lived came in sight. Small, dilapidated, paint-
less, lonely, it squatted low on the ground in the
midst of a confusion of little rickety outbuild-
ings. A crape-myrtle tree beside it was gorgeous
with leaves that the heat had dyed in every shade

of crimson and yellow. Frosty blueberries filled
the tall cedar that rose behind it and a giant
hickory scattered golden leaves over the cabin's
sagging roof every time a breeze came up from
the river and stirred the air.

Daddy Cudjoe's cabin sat on a hill just above
the river bank, its weathered roof green with
moss, its old cracked sides the color of the deep
shadows cast around it by the twisted live-oak
trees. Chickens scratched around the door. A
mother hog lying under a tree fed her babies and,
when Mary passed, she blinked and grunted but
did not move. An old horse munched eagerly at
a dry grass patch, and one of his eyes was white
with blindness.

Daddy Cudjoe, shriveled, old, crooked-legged,
white-bearded man, came hobbling up from the
spring with a bucket of water, and his face
beamed as he spied Mary. His stumbling old
feet hurried faster until he reached her, then
putting his bucket on the ground, he took off his
tattered old hat, and plucking at a white forelock
with his crumpled fingers, he pulled a foot back
and made a fine bow.

His words were broken into bits by stammering, but Mary understood them; he was glad
to see her; she looked as sweet and pretty as a
flower garden in the springtime; she must come

in and sit down and have a cup of newly steeped
life-elastic tea that he had just finished brewing;
it would do her good. Nothing is better in the
fall than life-elastic tea.

Daddy Cudjoe was used to having people
come to him for advice, and he knew how to make
them feel at home. Mary had never been here
before, but when she was a child, whenever she
saw the old, white-haired, bent man passing the
house, or in the woods digging roots, she always
ran from him, and he would stop and laugh and
shake his fist and cackle out, "You better run! If
I catch you, I'll conjure you!" and he looked so
strange, with his black eyes shining under thick,
white, bushy brows, she believed he would.

His cabin's two rooms ran the length of the
house with a low board wall between them, one
for Daddy Cudjoe to sleep in and the other for
him to work in. Mary sat down by the fireplace,
whose hearth was filled with steaming pots.
Strange smells rose. Medicine, charms, love-
and hate-potions all mixed their breaths together
as they brewed side by side on the red coals.

"De sight o you face makes my eyeballs feel
pure rich," Daddy Cudjoe greeted Mary.

He poured her the drink, then he rubbed his
knotted hands together, and with a kind smile
asked, "What you want, daughter?"

There was no use to hesitate, she might as well talk right out.

"I want a charm for July, Daddy Cudjoe. July's got a side-gal."

Daddy looked grave.

"How long you been married, honey?"

"Me an' him ain' been married a year yet."

"Who is de side-gal, daughter?"

"Cinder."

At this answer he puckered up his lips and puffed out his cheeks. "Cinder? Why, Cinder's de very one what come here last month and got a love-charm to catch em a beau. You don' mean dat gal is used em on you husband? Jedus have mercy. You womens is someting else." He threw back his head and cackled long and loud.

"Now, de beau's lawful lady is come for someting to get e husband back. Well, I declare. I got to make a charm to fight a charm. Black hand is got to squeeze black hand. Dat ain' no easy ting, gal. I got to study a minute."

Then Mary told him July was not the only thing giving her trouble. Cinder had put a hand on everything in her house. The fire was conjured so it muttered and popped red coals out on the bare floor scorching black spots in the clean boards around the hearth. Food stuck to the pots. Water would hardly boil in the kettle.

Wind flew down the chimney in hard gusts driving smoke into the room and fanning up the ashes, scattering them in the victuals. Her baby was in mortal danger too, for he cried out in his sleep, frightened by evil things he saw in his dreams.

"I'd like to kill Cinder, Daddy—kill em dead. If you'll gi me a pizen I'll feed it to em till e is stone dead."

Daddy shook his head kindly. "No, honey, you wrong. Pizen ain' to be trusted. Sometimes, it works backwards as well as forwards, you might be de one to dead. Hatin ain' good for you, neither. It'll pizen you breast milk an' make you baby sick. It's better to go easy wid conjure. You must stop frettin an' bein scared. Keep you belly full o victuals, make you mouth smile, laugh an' be merry if you can. Don' never let people see you down-hearted, or a-hangin you head, an' lookin sorrowful. Dat ain' de way. No. Mens don' crave a sorrowful, sad-lookin 'oman. Don' never let a man feel sorry for you if you want em to stick to you."

He got up and went out of the door into the yard and Mary could hear him puttering around, scratching in the earth as if he were digging up something. Presently he came back smiling and poured her out a cup of tea from another one of the several pots boiling on the hearth.

"Drink dis, honey. It'll do you all de good whilst I fix you someting to try. If July ain' conjured too bad already e won' never get shet o' de spell we'll work on em. I ain' never seen no man get loose from a 'oman what wears dis mixtry. It's de powerful-est one I knows."

Daddy took a needle and stuck the little finger on her right hand and took a drop of her blood on a wisp of cotton. "You right hand is de strong hand, honey," he said. "It's de hand what catches an' holds."

Then he took a bit of skin from her left heel. "Dis is de foot what walks fastest, honey."

A bit of toe-nail from a toe on her left foot was added to one hair plucked from her left arm-pit as near to her heart as she could get it. These were all mixed with some sort of conjure root and tied into a tiny scrap of white cloth with a string long enough to go around her neck. Daddy Cudjoe was excited. His eyes shone and sweat ran down off his forehead as he handed the bag to her with a high crackling laugh.

"Put em on, gal. Wear em day an' night. If e don' work, den I'll quit makin' love-charms for de rest o' my life. Dat charm is a man. Great Gawd, yes. E's a mans o monkeys, honey."

As Mary took it her heart began beating violently. Lord, yes, she could feel it was strong!
Now she'd hurry home with it for July might by
some chance come back on the regular boat this
afternoon instead of waiting for the excursion
boat to-night.

"How much I owe you, Daddy?"

"Honey, you don' owe me a Gawd's ting but
a sweet smile. An' I wish you all de luck in dis
world. I hope you will get you husband back an'
keep em de rest o you life."

The old man really seemed grateful to her for
coming to him. Perhaps he was lonely, living
so far off by himself.

"Come see me sometimes, Daddy."

"Gawd bless you, chile, I'll do it. But befo
you go let me get you some fresh eggs to take
home. When you eat em, hang de shells side de
mantelpiece so de fire'll keep em warm. Dey'll
make you hens lay good. Come look at some
fine new layin stock shut up in a pen."

He hobbled ahead of her toward the back of
the cabin where a rickety hand-split clapboard
fence enclosed a small yard. Taking down the
props of the hingeless gate, he showed Mary six
straw-necked pullets and a young cockerel.

"Dey's fine, Daddy," Mary praised.

"Is you like em?" he asked with pride. "I sent

all de way 'cross de river an' got em. Le me know when you got a hen settin an' I'll gi you a clutch o eggs for seed."

A tall black rooster on the outside walked up close to the open gate, and stretching up his neck gave a long shrill crow. The smile left Daddy Cudjoe's face.

He picked out a stick and threw it violently, stammering and spluttering and shaking his fist threateningly at the offending fowl, declaring that any rooster old as that ought to know how to settle down and behave himself. He had ten grown hens running loose outside with him in the open yard; all he could say grace over, to save his life; yet, instead of attending to his own business and helping those hens scratch and find worms for themselves and for the children they had for him, there he was, running up and down by that fence, peeping through the cracks at those pullets, calling them and making a big to-do, telling them to come see what a fine thing he had found for them to eat, talking all kinds of sweet-mouthed talk to them, until the fools had their combs all bloody from reaching their heads through the fence. They believed every word the scoundrel said. They had no sense at all.

The rooster stood eying Daddy Cudjoe from

a safe distance. When he flopped his wings and stretched his neck and gave a bold crow, Daddy laughed, "I hear you, son. I hear how you sass me. But you better mind, or you'll be a-stewin in a pot befo you know it." His words were threatening but his eyes were twinkling; he said people and fowls were much alike. That same rooster was just like a man.

A man may have the finest wife in the world, but just let a strange woman come around and smile at him a little, and he turns to a fool right away. He will start lying and doing everything he can to fool the strange woman into loving him, but as soon as she does he will leave her and go trying to find some other new woman to fool. It is a hard thing to keep a man satisfied. A hard thing. If it wasn't for love-charms and conjures to help women keep their lawful husbands at home and out of devilment, only God knows what would become of the world.

"Whe is you husband, to-day, daughter?"

Mary shook her head. July was gone on the excursion and Cinder was with him.

Daddy Cudjoe turned away and gazed at the rice-fields that lay sunlit and still under a circle of soft blue sky. "Po lil gal," he pitied. "I'm too sorry to see you a-frettin. But remember dis: as much good fish is in de river as ever was caught out. July ain' de onliest man in de world. No. Gawd made plenty just as good as him. Just as good. Don' forget dat."

A wild plum thicket full of reddening leaves stood close at the old man's elbow, and when he put out a hand to pat Mary's shoulder and emphasize what he was telling her, one of the slim thorny switches reached out and caught his sleeve. He jerked quickly away from it. "What you mean by pickin at me?" he asked it gruffly. "I know what I'm a-tellin dis gal." Then he snapped the branch off with his short knotted fingers and twisted it between them until all its red leaves were gone, and its sharp thorns were left stark naked.

"I'm a-tellin you what Gawd loves, daughter; de truth, de pure truth. Gawd made plenty o' men besides July. If dat charm don' fetch you husband back to you, you use it on somebody else."

"But I don' want nobody else, Daddy. Not nobody but July."

Then Daddy cackled out merrily again, "You's young, honey. You ain' got much sense, but you'll learn better. Sho. I got good hopes o you. Good hopes. Some o dese days you'll learn better." Daddy Cudjoe laughed, then wiped the

tears out of his eyes. "You can' nebber blongst
to nobody, honey, an' nobody can' blongst to
you. But Ki! Dat ain' reason fo cry! You
breath come an' go mighty sweet when e free,
but you strive fo hold em. Den e bitter!"

CHAPTER XIII

SATURDAY passed, then Sunday. All the excursion people were back home except July and Cinder and nobody knew what had become of them or where they had gone. Mary was so miserable she scarcely knew what to do. She could not sleep all night for listening and hoping and praying to God for her July's return. Maybe he got left and would get a boat from somebody and manage to row home up the river. Her eyes burned with gazing so hard and so long out of the window, scanning the road, the fields, the whole countryside, looking for him, for some message from him. But none came.

All day long she had fidgeted about the house, then outside in the yard; feeding the chickens, watering the cow and staking her in a fresh place to graze, carrying a pail of meal mixed with water to the hog in the pen, trying to make the dragging hours go by. The heart in her breast felt dead and cold, and she moved about with slow heavy steps. Her eyes would do nothing but drain out water, drop after drop.

Everybody else was stirring around talking

about the trip to town yesterday, except herself and Budda Ben who sat out on the wood-pile in the late afternoon sunshine, resting his chin in his hand, staring at the ground, thinking, and thinking. His face was so solemn it scared her away after she went close enough to speak to him. Budda Ben had begged her not to marry July. He said June or Andrew or anybody else would make her a better husband. He had ranted and raved when he heard how July danced with Cinder on the night of her wedding, but now, when she went near him, he paid no more attention to her than if she were a shadow. He behaved like a rank stranger who knew nothing of what was going on, and she needed him so. He let her cut her own wood, not offering her as much as a splinter. But he knew. He could not fool her about that. He knew that July had gone off with Cinder and left her and Unex all by themselves.

The fire on the hearth had almost gone out, the room was dim and she must get some wood to last for the night. Putting her apron over her head, she hurried across the yard to the wood-pile.

"Budda," she called him low, "Budda, please, cut me a lil wood for my fire. I ain' got a stick yonder home."

She turned her head away to hide the tears that gushed out of her eyes.

"Whe is July?" he growled furiously.

"Gawd knows. July went off yesterday on de excursion an' e ain' never come home, not till yet." Grief melted all her pride and she sobbed out loud.

"Is cryin gwine to fetch em back?" he asked presently in a gruff tone. "I told you to leave dat no-count rascal alone, enty? You wouldn' listen at nobody. Not nobody. You's made a hard bed for yousef, now you got to lie in it."

With each word he waxed crosser. "Budda," she plead meekly, "please, Budda, don' holler at me now. You an' Auntie an' de baby is all I got left in de world."

"You would have you way, enty? Now, you want evybody to be sorry fo you. You ought to be shame. A-blubberin' like a baby, stead o bein glad to be shet o dat low-lived scoundrel. What did you want wid em, anyhow? Didn' e disgrace you befo e married you? Tell me dat?"

He paused for Mary's answer, but she had become wordless. Her one thought was to get home before she fell dead of misery there on the wood-pile, for the merciless words went clean through her heart, cutting off her breath, her strength, her courage, all her hope.

The great crimson sun dropped behind the trees, black shadows came out from under the houses and stayed.

Night was falling, red firelight twinkled out through the open doors and windows of the cabins up and down the street, but Mary's house was almost dark. She sat alone by the hearth where only a few embers glowed, bewildered, filled with unspeakable loneliness and grief. Maum Hannah was off with some sick person, Unex slept and she had no friend left to comfort her. A few people had come by to speak to her this morning, but she knew they had come to see how she took July's going and she didn't encourage them to stay and talk. If she had the heart, she would go away and leave everything, everybody. She could find work of some kind in the town, and yet, this was home. She had known no other place in her life. The very earth here was a part of herself, and it held her so fast she could never leave it, no matter what came. She must stay and face everything the best she could, as well as her misery would let her.

The old cow-bell began ringing for meeting-time. Voices and footsteps passed her door. A sudden stumbling on the steps startled her. "Budda Ben? Is dat you?" she cried, fear jerking the words out of her mouth.

"I cut you some nice wood, Si May-e. Come, fetch it in befo de dew has it wet." He spoke gently, kindly, as if he had never said a harsh word to her in his life.

"Budda—Budda—I'm so glad to see you— I'm lonesome, I'm most dead——"

She was not angry with him, for deep in her heart she knew Budda was her faithful friend. Puffing and groaning with the effort to mount the steps, Budda came inside. Sobs choked Mary, and her brain whirled dizzily.

"Go get de wood, gal. Le me mend you fire. Whe de baby is?"

"Yonder on de bed—a-sleepin." She stood still in bewilderment as much a helpless baby as Unex himself.

"I'll stay wid em till you get you wood. Hurry, befo somebody else takes em. Dem chillen is tricky devils. You can' leave nothin' a-lyin around."

Budda hobbled to where Unex lay sound asleep. "Such a fine lil boy," he murmured.

Mary went and hurried back with an armful of wood, then another. Budda built up the fire, and when it blazed up bright, he said this was meeting night. Mary had better come go.

Mary's heavy heart throbbed in her breast, and a sob shook her as she leaned over the bed where

Unex was. If she went to meeting she'd
have to take him. He couldn't stay by himself
in the dark, even asleep. She had been by herself
all day, she might feel better to go where some
people were.

Wrapping a warm shawl around him very
gently, so as not to rouse him, she eased him up
into her arms. Then holding him carefully, she
closed the front door behind her and stepped out
into the warm dark. All the red light the sunset
had poured over the land and sky had died out.
Night had crept out from under all the houses
and rose up over the fields, chasing every shadow
of daylight away. The afterglow had left the
sky. The stars were appearing one by one, white
stars first, then red ones and blue ones, all marching slowly toward sunset.

Where was July now?

Maum Hannah's cabin, where meeting was
held every Wednesday and Sunday night, stood
at the other end of the street, as the washed-out,
dilapidated road running between the two rows
of weather-beaten cabins was called. Not many
people would be there yet. Only the old people,
the good earnest Christians, cared to be on time
for the beginning of the prayer-meeting. The
young and the sinful preferred to linger on the
door-steps chatting, laughing, smoking, talking

over the pleasures of yesterday's excursion to town.

As Mary passed them she called out as cheerfully and pleasantly as she could, "How yunnuh do?" but she knew that her lively tone fooled nobody.

The answers came back at once, clear, warm, but pitying, "I well, Si May-e, how you?" with an undercurrent of murmurs, "Poor child." "E's frettin right now." "July ought not to do em so." "No." "July is a case, a heavy case." Then the kindly voices fell back into talk about the excursion to town.

The same talk had run steadily through the whole day. That excursion yesterday was the best excursion ever run. The most orderly. Not a soul had been shot. Nobody got cut with a razor. The one man bent on starting a row got pushed clean off the boat. A good thing, too. Lord, town had a fine restaurant. The fish there tasted too good. A pity all the day had to be spent going and coming. Still, it was sweet-riding. Yes, Lord. Such a pity July stayed in town with that black devil of a Cinder. But if he had come back, there would have been trouble. July always started a row or quarrel. A shower of hushes fell, for Mary was not yet out of hearing, and nobody would wilfully hurt her.

Maum Hannah's big room was ready, waiting for the people. A great yellow pine fire leaped high up the chimney, fanned by drafts from the wide-open door and windows. The same draft fluttered the swinging circles of fringed newspapers that were fastened on barrel-hoops and hung overhead to the old time-stained rafters, which they completely hid, making a cool, light adornment for the room. The side walls were covered with newspapers, soiled, smoky, yellow, for they were put up before Christmas and this was September. The small pine table, bare except for a small glass kerosene lamp and a worn Testament, stood a few feet from the hearth. Around this the wooden benches, which lived all the week in a pile under the house, were placed in orderly fashion clear back to the very walls. These old benches, each one a narrow board with four stout legs and no back, were sturdy and strong, able to hold up all the weight put on them.

Mary chose a seat near the door, for only members in good standing were entitled to sit near the front. Sinners were required to take the back seats. But she liked to sit where she could see everybody who came in the door, or who stood outside in the yard. July might get home to-night. He may have been left by mistake somehow. He'd find some way to get home. Cinder could not fool him off and make him forget all about her and Unex. Never. He knew Cinder and her tricky ways too well for that.

Some of the old sisters sitting near the lamp and the Bible, opened their eyes from praying and peered at Mary when she tipped in. "Good-evenin," they all said with a bow.

"Good-evenin," she answered softly.

Maum Hannah looked up again and cleared her throat, "How-come you is settin so far back, honey? You could come up nigher to de table. Unex could sit on de front bench."

Mary thought hard for an answer. "De fire is most too hot for Unex, Auntie. I'm 'faid e might would catch cold." It was a good excuse, and Maum Hannah folded her arms again, and closed her eyes and went back to her praying.

The yellow pine fire blazed higher and brighter, sending its hungry tongues in and out through the logs, hunting the tender rich spots, eating them first. By twos and threes the people came in, sometimes by whole families, father, mother, children like steps. The benches were all filled and those coming too late to get seats had to stand beside the walls, or stay outside in the yard, where their low talking hummed as if bees were swarming out there in the darkness.

The firelight beamed on the women's Sunday hats and dresses, on the men's close-clipped heads, but the yellow lamplight stayed on the table, for its work was to show Brer Dee, the leader, how to read the fine print in the Testament, and to help him line out the hymns for the people to sing, two lines at a time.

Brer Dee stood with his back to the fire, and found a place in the Testament by holding it right up to the lamp's dim eye, then, laying that book down, with its open face on the table, he took up the hymn-book and searched its leaves until he came to what he wanted.

He straightened up, looked the crowd over, scratched his bony head, stroked his beard and began in a rumbling voice:

"Yunnuh listen, chillen, whilst I line out de hymn for all o we to sing to de praise o God."

A deep silence fell. Even the tiny babies in their mothers' arms, and the little children holding to grown people's knees, gazed at him with round eyes while he rolled out the musical words:

"Guide me, Oh Thou great Jehovah!
Pilgrim through this barren land."

Brer Dee himself raised the tune, and all the people joined in singing to God, asking help of

His mighty strength for their own weakness.

As Mary sang tears streamed out of her eyes and fell on the shawl around Unex. She patted him softly, gently while he slept peacefully through the great full-throated waves of sound.

Where was her July now? Mary's heart ached bitterly. It lay heavy and slow-beating in her breast, weighing her whole body down.

Brer Dee lined out the next two lines of the hymn:

"I am weak, but Thou art mighty,
Hold me with Thy powerful hand."

Mary sobbed as she sang. Sorrow had her weakened so her knees quivered with little Unex's weight. She who had been so strong a year ago, even a month ago, had become feeble and trembling in one short day and night of misery.

God had forgotten her. Maybe He was vexed because she loved July too much. And to punish her He had let Cinder take July away. He is a jealous God, with the power to give and take anything and everything. Maum Hannah said so.

He could even take babies out of their mothers' arms. This idea pierced her with a sharp pang, and her arms tightened on Unex's soft yielding body, until he wriggled and squirmed, and fretted out loud with discomfort. Mary patted him and rocked her body from side to side putting him back to sleep. Maybe God held another thing against her. God knew she got Unex before she was married, but He knew too that July was the only man in the world for her, and if he had refused to marry her she would have been faithful to him just the same.

She had prayed for pardon, over and over, but God must not have forgiven her sin. He might be punishing her for it now. She thought over all this while the hymn was still being sung:

"Death of death and Hell's destruction
Land me safe on Canaan's side."

Those were solemn words, and shivers ran down her spine. She had never really repented about Unex, and to have July back as in those happy first days when she had been everything to him, she'd give up all her hopes of Heaven and choose Hell's destruction with July rather than have the safety of Canaan's side without him. She was never afraid of anything when July was with her, for he had no fear.

"Let us pray," Brer Dee called out, and Mary knelt down with the others.

Maum Hannah said prayers were answered. God listened to people and gave them the things they asked for, provided they plead with Him long and hard enough. Maybe praying now would bring July home. She began whispering, silently, earnestly, "Please, God, do, little kind Jedus, send July back home to me. Do don' let that wicked woman, Cinder, keep him. She is a sinner. One man is the same as another to her, so long as they are young an' strong an' have money jingling in their pockets." Mary's prayer was filled with telling God about Cinder's sins. She forgot all about praying for the forgiveness of her own sin, that old scarlet sin she and July had sinned together before they ever married.

She had never even confessed it to Brer Dee and the deacons, who turned her straight out of the church for dancing. Kind old Brer Dee had no pity where sin was concerned. He would turn his own child out of the church as quickly as he'd turn out a stranger.

He opened the worn Bible, and, although the lamp was dim and smoky and blurred and his eyes were not sharp and his lips stumbled badly over some of the long hard words they tried to say, he still made enough of them plain to tell the story of Moses and Pharaoh, the wicked, powerful, heathen king who held the children of Israel in bondage. Cinder was a lot like King Pharaoh, who was stiff-necked and hard-hearted and mean.

Brer Dee took as the theme of his talk the command given to Pharaoh by the Lord God: "Let my people go." He shouted as loud as he could, over and over the earnest, high-pitched, half-sung words, "Let my people go!"

The rhythm of the sentence, "Let my people go" shifted in Mary's ears into a call to Cinder away off in town, "Let my July go!" A human voice could not go so far, but Brer Dee said the Holy Spirit was all-powerful. Time and distance were nothing to it, and it could reach to the ends of the earth.

If that were true the Holy Spirit might take her prayers right now, through the night, across all those miles of swamps and river and fields and forests clear to town to make Cinder let July go and to fetch him home to Unex and her. Tears trickled down Mary's face as she tried to plead with God to send the Holy Spirit for July, but Brer Dee suddenly closed the Book with a snap and called on Andrew, the blacksmith, to pray, since his own voice was too hoarse to say another word. The strain of trying to move sinful hearts to prayer and repentance had him spent and breathless, and the hot fire back of him had him wet with sweat.

Although Andrew was little older than July, he had already been married twice, the first time to Mary's cousin who died and left one little boy named Big Boy, then soon after her death he married Doll, July's sister, a woman some years older than Mary, who already had a house full of children. When Andrew first became a widower he courted Mary, and Budda Ben urged her to marry him, for Andrew would make a fine husband, but Mary had argued that while no man on the plantation was more able than Andrew, who was a solemn deacon, she loved July best because he laughed and joked and sang as he worked and was fresh and ready for frolic when night came.

Andrew was now the faithful husband of Doll, her own sister-in-law. And Doll was shaking and patting Andrew's colicky baby, hushing its cries while its father prayed to God, and July, her July, was God only knew where. Still, if she had it to do all over again, she'd choose July before any man in the world. Nobody else knew how to be so tender, or so gay, or so bold in loving.

Everybody stood up and sang the last hymn, slowly, solemnly, following the words **Brer Dee** lined out of the book.

"My soul be on thy guard
Ten thousand foes arise,"

The weight of dismay in Mary's heart made her knees shaky. Tears burned her eyelids.

"The hosts of sin are pressing hard
To draw thee from the skies."

Prayer-meeting was over and the shouting was about to start. The middle of the room was cleared quickly as the benches were carried out into the yard and put back under the house where they would stay until next meeting night. All the Christian men who had strong singing voices grouped themselves in one corner, and after a few minutes' talk decided on the spiritual *Jubalee*. Andrew raised it, his deep voice ringing out full, his great throat swelling with the song.

"Dis is de year of Juba-lee.
Shout you, mo'ners, you done free."

The others marked the beat of the words with a slow hand-clapping and a quiet knee-bending, singing low until the whole congregation joined in with a hearty fervor. Men, women, children sang with faithful reverence, waiting for the spirit to move the people's hearts and make shouts ring out with pure joy.

The smoky lamp on the high mantel-shelf shed its dim yellow rays on the men's bare, close-clipped heads and the women's hats. Some were old with broken brims and others were new and trimmed with gay ribbons; lack of proper apparel kept nobody home from meeting. God expects people to dress as decently as they can when they gathered to worship Him, but **He** knows all their needs and what they lack, and while men must always pray with bared heads, women must have their heads covered somehow.

Everybody sang with utmost strength. The room could hardly hold so much sound. Hearts swelled fuller and fuller as feet beat time and hands patted sharply, palm against palm.

"Juba-lee, Oh, yes. Juba-lee——Juba-lee."

Maum Lou, the weakest frailest soul in the room, had begun the shouting. With short, shuffling, rocking steps she eased into the center of the room. Her arms were bent at the elbow, her veined old hands hung limp from her stiff wrists, "Juba-lee" her old lips quivered. Tears shone in her eyes, her joy was keen as grief.

One by one the women joined her, forming an

ever-moving circle that widened steadily, while
the men sang louder, faster, bending their legs
deeper, popping their palms together in deafening claps:

"Shout! Oh, Christian, you done free!
Dis is de year of Juba-lee!
Juba-lee, Oh, yes. Juba-lee—Juba-lee."

Doll gave her fretful baby to Maum Hannah
to hold while she joined the shouters and her
little stepson, Big Boy, came and stood beside
Mary, holding to her skirt. Doll's feet beat the
floor with stiff thuds. The fringed paper circles
swayed and rustled overhead, the lamp flickered
in its socket, the fire settled low in the chimney.
Jubalee was done, and singers and shouters had
to catch breath and wipe the sweat off their
dripping faces.

"Better tell Doll not to stomp so hard. E's
gwine kill eself if e don' mind," Andrew called
out to Maum Hannah, loud enough for everybody to hear, but Maum Hannah smiled and
shook her head. Andrew need not worry. Doll
would not hurt herself. She was strong as an ox,
and besides, God never lets a woman suffer from
shouting His praises.

"Looka Lou," Maum Hannah said. "Lou

can' hardly walk, e's so old an' weak, yet e can jump an' shout hard as a young gal when Gawd puts de sperit in em. Many a time I look fo Lou to pop e gizzard-string right in de middle o de meetin floor. But God takes care o His chillen whilst deys a-shoutin. Don' fret. Not 'bout Doll. Doll is a deacon's wife now, an' e has to shout harder'n de other womens."

Andrew led off again, singing,

> "Drinkin' wine and wine and wine
> Drinkin' wine, wine, my Lord,
> I'll sit in Heaven ten thousand years
> A-drinkin wine."

"Let me hold Unex, honey, an' you go git in de ring. A lil shoutin'll straighten out you back an' make you feel a lot better. I'd be on de floor myself if de misery in my crippled knee would let go a minute. But it's got me hamstrung. I can' hardly lift my right hand foot off de ground."

Mary shook her head no. She was too sad to rejoice.

The low-burning fire gave out less light than heat. Andrew's wet face shone, his eyes glowed, his whole body shook as his long arms, held now high, now low, hammered his hard palms together with terrible claps, beating time for the words of the spiritual which told about the joys of Heaven, the fearsome horrors of Hell. As his square jaws tightened, his strong white teeth bit the words into short cries which sprang out between his heavy lips. His heart was on fire, and its flame was spreading through the cabin. The women joined the singers, their high, thin, wailing notes shrill and fierce. "A-drinkin wine!" Children with bright wide-open eyes stood closer to the walls so as not to be in the way and get their bare feet tramped on by the frenzied shouters. Hot breaths heaved in and out, painfully praising God, praying to Him. "Glory to His name!" "A-men!" "Praise Him, sisters!" "Seek Jesus, sinners!" "A-drinkin wine!"

Maum Lou hopped higher and higher, out-shouting them all. Only Mary sat still, her eyes wandering now and then toward the door, look-ing, watching, hoping for July still. The happi-ness of the others drove her sad thoughts into a deeper gloom. She would have left the shouting except that her own home was too lonely to bear. She sat listless, heedless of everything but her own dark thoughts, until the exhausted singers and the shouters stopped for good.

CHAPTER XIV

MEETING was over. The cabin was dim, the fire almost dead, the dim lamp sputtered out. Most of the crowd hurried out into the cool night.

A few of them lingered outside around the door-step, the men smoking, the women talking low. The street was full of happiness. Some of the people hummed snatches of hymn tunes as they walked home. Some of the sinners were whistling.

A thin yellow moon had risen above the trees that rimmed the fields, and its light fell clear on the earth as Mary stepped carefully down the rickety steps out into the yard. Andrew greeted her kindly, "You baby sho is growin nice, . Si May-e. E'll soon be too heavy for you to tote, enty?"

"Gawd sends strength wid every load," Maum Hannah answered as she grunted and hobbled down the steps. "Wait! honey, wait on me! I want to walk a piece wid you. Stretchin my leg will help to run some o de misery out o my knee, den I can rest mo better to-night."

Nothing but Maum Hannah's kindness of

heart made her come along to keep Mary company. Her limping steps were uneven and slow
as the two of them walked slowly down the street
together.

The road lay cool and white in the moonlight.
A breeze sweet with honey from the September
blossoms fanned Mary's face. A late courting
mocking-bird sang in a honeysuckle vine fit to
split his throat. "Summer is over soon, winter
is just round de corner," Maum Hannah called
to him, but the bird sang more blithely than ever.
Crickets chirred and chirred.

Black moon shadows were dancing in Mary's
yard, and their strange antics made her halt.
She hated to step on moon shadows.

"Honey,——" Maum Hannah stopped too.
"You git some clothes fo Unex and come sleep
to my house to-night. I ain' satisfy fo you to
stay home here all by yousef."

Mary shook her head and thanked the kind old
soul. She had better stay home to-night. July
might get a boat and paddle home up de river.
She'd hate for him not to find her at home and the
house locked up.

Maum Hannah caught in her breath. She
started to say something, then changed her mind.
"Do like you think best, honey. Stay home if
you want to. Budda Ben'll come sleep here to

be company for you. July won' mind him, I
know, as cripple as po Budda is. You wouldn'
feel so awful lonesome wid somebody to call on
if you git nervish in de night."

Mary said she had no extra bed, but Maum
Hannah declared that would not matter to
Budda. Mary could make him a pallet out of
some quilts right down on the floor and Budda
would sleep as sweet on them as he could
on a feather-bed. Budda would do anything for
Mary, and the poor creature had little chance
to do much outside of cutting wood.

She waited until Mary had unlatched the door,
and, after laying Unex on the bed, had blown
the half-dead coals into a blaze for light. Then
she called, "Good night, Si May-e, God bless
you," and limped away. Mary fixed the pallet
and sat waiting on the door-step for Budda Ben.
The night became still, the dark fields spread out
in front were silent. Cabins far across them
showed bright spots of firelight where doors flung
wide open to let out the heat matched in size a
great star shining toward sunset side. But they
were dark red while the star in the sky shone
clear blue.

"Si May-e——" a deep voice called her. Her
heart leaped into her throat, it sounded so much
like July. "Dis is me, June. If you needs any-

ting, any time, please call on me. Budda Ben is so crippled, e can' get around, not so fast dese days."

"Tank you kindly, June," she answered huskily.

"Is you got plenty o wood to keep you fire burnin?"

"Plenty. Budda Ben cut em fo me."

June was a sinner and he seldom went to meeting or church, but his heart was soft and kind. "Is dey anyting I can do fo you? I'd be glad to stay."

"No, Budda Ben is gwine to stay wid me, but sit down, till e comes."

As he sat beside her the narrow step creaked with his weight. He rested his arms on his knees with his head hunched low between his big stooping shoulders. Mary couldn't talk, and they sat silent until June cleared his throat and shifted awkwardly.

"I doubt if July is gwine to get away from Cinder anytime soon, Si May-e."

Mary couldn't answer that and presently he went on, "If I was you, I wouldn' fret 'bout em. You don' have to need fo nothin; you got plenty o friends here to help you long."

"I know dat, June."

"I draws wages and rations too, evy Sat'day

Gawd sends, and I ain' got a soul but myself. I been givin dem rations to Doll, but I'd sooner give em to you if you'll take em."

"Tank you kindly, June."

She wanted to cry, to tell June how her heart was pure sick. She wanted him to give her sympathy, but he was so steady, so clear-seeing she strove to be good-mannered. She slipped a hand through his big arm next to her and leaned her cheek against his shoulder, but June turned his face away and moved his body uneasily.

The clear moonlight showed Budda Ben coming down the street, half squatting as he walked, leaning on his stick. June got to his feet. "I'll be gwine now."

"Good night, June.   Tank you fo comin."

"You welcome, Si May-e."

She could feel the powerful muscles in his arms bulging as they both went gently around her.

"Good night," he whispered.

"Good night, June," she whispered back.

When Budda Ben was fixed for the night on his pallet of quilts, Mary went to bed, but she lay awake and sobbed softly so Budda could not hear her and the baby would not waken. Sleep did not come until long after the cock

crowed for midnight, and it left with the first
crowing for dawn.

Budda got up early and had the fire burning,
the kettle boiling, everything ready for Mary to
cook breakfast. He moved softly, but when he
took down the door bar to go she called to him,
"Stay, Budda, eat breakfast wid me. I'll cook
em in no time."

Her limbs were shaky, her hands trembled
weakly, her feet were heavy weights, but she put
on her garments as fast as she could, then she
mixed meal and cold water together, added boiling water and stirred it carefully and let it cook
gently into smooth white mush, while Budda
fried slices of fat meat, and made sweetened
water with molasses. Then they sat down to eat.

Unex was happy. He jumped and crowed
and cooed and tried to hurry Mary who blew on
each spoonful of food to cool it before she put it
into his greedy little mouth. Budda stared at
his pan of food or at the fire, saying almost nothing, and Mary didn't utter a word. She kept at
the mush and milk, feeding Unex but eating almost nothing herself. Then Budda Ben turned
on her, and put a big slice of meat on her pan
and in a gruff ugly voice began scolding her.
She must eat, and not act like a foolish child.
Already her cheeks were hollow and her skin

ashy. What was July that she should grieve
after him so? Nothing but a trifling low-down
scoundrel, a worthless hound, yet she went on
over his leaving, weeping in the night, hardly
sleeping, not even wrapping her hair yesterday
and it a Sunday, as if July were next to Jesus
himself. She was a fool, a silly fool. She was
lucky to be rid of him.

Budda's eyes snapped, his words crackled, but
Mary made no answer. When Budda had
spoken gently to her last night, it made her cry.
She could bear scolding better than pity and
tenderness.

Budda lighted his pipe and hobbled away,
promising to come back to-night after supper.

When he had gone, Mary scoured the pots and
pans, and straightened up the cabin, but every
little while she went to the window and gazed toward the road that lead from the landing,—
maybe July would come.

The days dragged slowly by, their mild sunshine pale to Mary's eyes. The long nights falling out of starry skies were still and well-nigh
endless. People were as kind as could be to her.
There was scarcely any field work to be done,
but she had a gracious plenty to live on, with
milk from her cow, the eggs her hens laid, the

greens from her garden. Haws, chinquapins and persimmons were ripe. Hickory nuts and walnuts were falling. She had laid in a supply of dry field peas and potatoes and rice and corn before July went off, and now she swapped her fattened pig in the pen with Andrew for a fresh piece of meat every week.

The Quarter people came and went, back and forth, to church, to meeting at Maum Hannah's house, to Grab-All for rations, to dances and birth-night suppers, living their lives happily; but Mary stayed alone, sitting by her fire, staring at nothing, creeping like an old woman about the house, or out into the yard, down to the spring for water, then back again, dull, lonely, sorrowful. The cabin was tiresome but she lacked energy and desire to leave it for some more cheerful place.

Balked of what mattered most on earth to her, she grieved and pined until all her strength was drained and misery had her numbed. For a while she met with sympathy and pity. She could hear the other women discussing her trouble, pitying her, wondering what would become of her. Nobody ever came right out and asked her what she would do, but they all sighed with sympathy whenever they came near her. "I too sorry for you, Si May-e," they'd say. "Dat

July is a case. A heavy case to do you such a way."

She was weighted down with sorrow. Day and night, even when July was not in her consciousness her heart lay hard in her breast. Sometimes her dull misery changed to showers of stinging black fury. She'd like to kill Cinder and July too. She'd like to cut their smooth black throats from ear to ear with a razor. She'd like to beat in their skulls with a hatchet. This world was not big enough to hold them and herself. She knew she was a fool, for they were far out of her reach. Maum Hannah and Budda Ben did all they could to help her to peace and yet in their manner, in everybody's manner, in every word spoken to comfort her, she felt a tinge of reproach.

Day after day went by, night after night, all alike. The hot weather had cooled and the sun paled. Mary picked cotton in the field with the other women, but instead of keeping up with the best as she had always done, her cotton weights fell off, and the money she made was scarcely enough for rations, but every Saturday night, after giving her part of his rations, June got her extra things, such as a can of salmon or a loaf of white bread, from Grab-All.

Winter came with a bleak cold wind and a

gray rain, then she made Unex a red flannel petticoat and put one on herself, for her blood was thin and her bones chilly. Budda could not keep warm on a pallet and Mary made him go home to his own bed. She was not afraid, and she might as well get used to staying alone.

Ducks flocked into the rice-fields, quacking and splashing, feeding all night long. Now and then somebody brought Mary one to eat, or some oysters, or a fish. She had food, fire, clothes, shelter; she needed nothing, yet misery gnawed at her heart day and night. When she failed to take up her life again people lost patience with her and became indifferent. Her silence, her tottering walk, her haggard body were unheeded, and she was allowed to weep alone.

The winter was spotted with cold days and hot days, and Unex took a cough and shook his little body day and night. That vexed Maum Hannah. She said that Mary was to blame. Unex was poisoned with bad breast milk. Mary was wicked to fret while her baby was depending on her for food.

Day after day she sat gazing at nothing, her eyes on the blue hills over the river. There was nothing to see, nothing to hope. The tide came and went, noons followed mornings, night fol-

lowed day. She was young in years, but her
youth was gone. Her heart sobbed in her breast.

On New Year's morning, Maum Hannah
came in for a talk. Jesus was the onliest one
who could help Mary now. Nobody else could.
Nobody else.

"A devil spirit is got you, honey. It's more'n
likely Cinder put a conjure on you an' July all
two. But try prayin. It'll do you all de good.
Jedus'll show you how to live wid you sorrow.
Jedus is de main man, honey, de best one what
ever lived. He had a heap more trouble'n you.
Dem mean Jews hung em on a cross an' e ain'
done em a wrong ting, either. Jedus axed Gawd
to have mussy on em de same as you got to ax
Gawd to have mussy on Cinder what done you
wrong. Jedus'll make you strong, gal. Make
you well, too. Gawd is his Pa, an' Gawd made
de sun an' de moon an' de world an' all o we.
You ax Jedus to help you to forgive Cinder.
He might would send July back home."

Mary said she hated Cinder. She did not
want to forgive her.

"Gawd laid a heavy hand on you, fo-true, gal,
but you better be careful. E might knock you
harder next time. Gawd is a strange Gawd.
You better pray to Him instead o frettin so hard
fo July. 'Stead o lookin down, you better look

up. Git out and work. Sweat some evy day. It'll help you to shed a lot o misery."

Mary asked if she knew what love is.

"Love?" she repeated. "Is I know love? Honey, I knew em fo-true. A 'oman wha live long as me is bound to know em." She smoked silently, then she added:

"Dey is two diffunt kinds o love, Si May-e. Two; eye-love an' heart-love. Eye-love is tricky. E will fool you. E done fool plenty o people. Two people'll meet an' tink dey have love. It seem so. De 'oman look good to de man; de man look good to de 'oman. Evy time dey meet dey talk pleasant talk. Den dey gone an' married togedder. But soon, all-two'll wish to Gawd dey ain' never see one annudder.

"Heart-love is diffunt. Diffunt from eye-love as day is from night. Sometimes joy walk long wid em, but e go much wid sorrow. Heart-love and sorrow is one mudder's chillen. When you meets wid heart-love, peace'll leave you. But heart-love is brave. E kin pure smile in de face . o deat', honey. E pure shames deat'."

Maum Hannah leaned and mended the fire and mumbled on, but Mary thought about July and heart-love.

"It's a diffunce between flesh chillen an' heart chillun too. Plenty o lawful chillen is po pitiful

flesh chillen. A heart child is always a blossom.
I dunno how-come-so, but it's so. Unex is a
heart child, honey, and dat ought to make you
glad, instead o sad."

Unex, who had become a thin, tall, solemn-
faced baby, sat in a box near the fire, listening
and sucking at a rind of bacon, watching Maum
Hannah and Mary with big, round, unwinking
eyes.

"Poor creeter," Maum Hannah pitied him.
"E is hungry as e only can be. Looka how e
strives to get a lil meat off dat skin. I declare
to Gawd, it pure hurts me to my heart to see
how dat child is gone back. E come into de
world as fine as anybody. Now look at em; po as
a snake; hands no bigger'n a possum paw.
I'm gwine to tell you de Gawd's truth, Si May-e;
it might sound hard to say so, but if you let
dat child dead, Gawd'll hold it against you.
You nurses you troubles more'n you child. If
you'd quit cherishin sorrow so much an' give all
dat time to Unex, you would be better off."

Maum Hannah grunted and got up, then
limped to the door to go, when a sudden thought
struck her. "May-e, gal," she called out, "I
know what would help you a lot; you ought to
smoke. A pipe is good to help people when dey
is worried in dey mind."

Mary shook her head. She had tried a pipe once or twice in her life and always got sick as a dog. She was not strong enough to stand tobacco smoke.

"But you mustn' mind gettin a lil sick at de start. You'll get over it. An' when you get so you can stand it, you'll crave to smoke, same as you crave victuals an' water." Maum Hannah felt in her apron pocket and took out a small clay pipe, stained brown with use.

"My pipe is broke in good. I'm gwine to leave em here wid you to-night. You try em. It'll do you all de good. I'd a been in my grave too long if I didn't smoke. My pipe is one o de best friends I ever had. Dat is de Gawd's truth. Soon as you learn on my-own, you get you a pipe bowl from Grab-All an' Budda Ben'll cut you a nice fig stem. A quarter's worth o tobacco a week'll make you a new 'oman. You try em an' you'll see."

Maum Hannah's heart was set on Mary's smoking and there was nothing to do but take the pipe and promise to try it.

"How'll you smoke to-night if I keep you pipe, Auntie?"

"I got another pipe yonder home, honey. It's a twin to dis one, just as sweet an' good. I couldn't live widout em."

Before first dark fell Budda Ben came in. He was vexed, and he began talking at once. "Looka here, Si May-e, you done fretted long enough. You got to stop or I'm pure done wid you. I come here to tell you how I feel about de way you's a-actin."

Budda did not hold back his words in bitter blame of her grief, but, although he had come to scold her, she knew she had no better friend in the world.

"Budda, do light you pipe an' don' talk hard at me to-night. Talk some pleasant talk, instead o such stiff words."

"I come to talk stiff words, gal. You ain' got a soul but me an' Ma to tell you to you face what is pleasin to Jedus: de Gawd's truth. Ma is too good-hearted to hurt you feelins, so I'm gwine to do so."

"No, Budda, you's wrong. Auntie has just been here a-hurtin my feelins awful bad."

"I'm glad to hear it. I'm gwine to hurt em some more. You may as well set still an' listen till I get done. Anybody to see you would think you was a diffunt breed from we. You got so you act like a don'-care, triflin Dinka nigger; or a puny, sickly no-manners Guinea. You must be forgot who you come from, enty? You garden is all growed up in weeds; you ain' set a hen in Gawd knows when; you don' half tend to you cow. If you nanny goat didn' scuffle for rations, Unex wouldn't have a Gawd's drop o milk."

Budda's face looked drawn, his eyes were sorrowful, his breath was quick and short, but his words fell stern and firm.

"Why, gal, you done fretted so you is pure old an' ugly."

"I wish I was dead," Mary faltered.

"No, you don't, neither. You don' wish no such a thing. It's a sin to say so, too. Sposen you was to die, who'd raise Unex? Cinder? Is dat what you want?" Budda stuck his pipe between his teeth and his eyes glared fiercely at her.

"Le me tell you dis, Si May-e; you may as well not wish to die. Nobody can' die not till de times comes. I know. One time when I was so mizzable I couldn't stand to live no longer, I dressed mysef up in my Sunday clothes an' went away down yonder in dem thickest pine woods. I stretched my length on de ground an' I folded my hands across my breast an' I tried to die. I held my breat'. I tried to hinder my heart from beatin. But I couldn' die. I looked straight up at de sun an' I begged Gawd to strike me dead. Den I wallowed all over de ground, an' I prayed to Jedus to take me. I pure sweated, but it didn' do me no good. I couldn' die. I got

up an' come on back home, an' I been here ever
since. It ain' no use to be a-tryin to die. We
got to stay here till our time is out. An' whilst
we are a-stayin we may as well try to act man-
nersable, enty?"

Mary tried to nod her head. Budda Ben was
right. She knew that.

"You hold up you head, gal, an' quit a-drag-
gin you feet. Fo Gawd's sake wash you face an'
wrap you hair nice an' put on a clean dress an'
apron. Yesterday's sun is set, Si May-e. Last
year's rain is dry. It's better to let old sorrows
sleep an' tink on what's a-comin to-morrow.
Plenty o to-morrows is ahead o you. Plenty o
good to-morrows too, if you'll listen at what I'm
a-tellin you."

Budda declared that nobody could help her but
herself. Nobody. She was wasting her life, los-
ing her friends and her health and everything else
she had left. Even if July had tricked her and
broken her heart, she was not the first woman to
have her heart broken by a low-down man. She
would not be the last, either. The best thing she
could do was to put July clean out of her mind,
to forget him. Yes, forget him.

Budda looked straight at her, without flinching, and when the tears flowed out of her
eyes, he did not soften his voice one whit. When

he had finished, he smiled a one-sided smile and said very kindly, "Now, Si May-e, I'm a done-talk man. I hope I ain' wasted my breath."

Mary tried to smile and to sound brave as she answered, "No, Budda you ain' wasted em. I know good an' well all you say is de Gawd's truth. I know I ain' doin right. I'm gwine to learn to smoke. Auntie left her pipe here for me to learn how to smoke on. E said smokin would help me to stop bein so nervish an' down-hearted."

"Sho e will, if you learn how to smoke right an' not careless an' wrong," Budda declared heartily. "Le me fill you pipe now, an' show you how."

A draft from the door took the smoke from Budda's pipe and swept it up the chimney as he filled his mother's for Mary, packing moist plug-cut tobacco into its small bowl, pinch by pinch. He laid a tiny coal on it and putting the stem in his mouth, pulled until the crumbs of tobacco glowed and he puffed out a mouthful of strong sweet smoke. He explained that most people burn up tobacco in a pipe and call it smoking. Smoking a pipe is not child's play. There is a right way and a wrong way to do it. His old grandfather, Daddy Champagne, dead long years ago, taught him how to smoke. Young people used to listen at what the old people tried to teach them. He had listened and learned how to smoke. Puffing fast or drawing hard burns the tobacco and gives little comfort. Mary must pull with a steady slow breath and puff the smoke out gently. That's the way. One good pipeful of plug-cut tobacco ought to last the best part of an hour. Maybe more.

Mary sat on the cabin door-step to breathe some fresh air and steady her dizzy head long after Budda Ben had hobbled away. The sun had set and the dusk lay deep around her. The great, dark red field was blurred and the cabins far across it showed bright spots of firelight from doors flung wide open to let out the heat, for the night was warm and within them the big chimneys held hot-blazing fires that cooked supper.

The air was filled with the cool scent of the frosty earth. Most of the day sounds were stilled, and night voices took their places. A partridge lost from its covey whistled anxiously, and its mates called back swift heartening notes. Little Nan, the mother of two new-born kids, bleated low warning baas to her children who had skipped away from where she was tethered to the crape-myrtle tree for the night. A screech owl began a mournful song. A

bad-luck sound. Mary got up quickly and
put the shovel in the fire to stop it. People
have to rule owls. She would learn to rule herself and her feelings, too. She would not let
another tear fall out of her eyes.

CHAPTER XV

By the time spring came, the big field was plowed and ready for planting. Time was passing, the years were hastening by. One short year ago, Unex was not in the world, and now he could crawl all over the room and go wherever he chose, pulling up to chairs and standing alone. Some day Unex would be as old as Budda Ben. Then a day would come when he must pass on, and other people would live in this old house, while she and Unex would be lying yonder in the graveyard where the pines rose tall and dark over graves that sheltered so many homeless bones.

A soft blue haze covered everything. When the wind blew in sharp gusts, old dead leaves, heaped in low places or caught in dead grasses, crackled and shivered then whirled out into open spaces. Tree branches moaned and shook their swollen buds as the air swished through them.

Only the haze lay quiet and still over the land. The wind couldn't move it at all.

Maum Hannah said that God is a spirit; a hard thing to understand; God in the sky,

God up in Heaven, God everywhere in the world.

A man and a mule crossing the field looked like two black specks creeping along no bigger than ants. Maybe to God up there all people look like ants crawling around on the earth.

Maum Hannah said that God is the life of everything. Every grass-blade is His child, every grain of sand is in His care, the same as the sun and moon and clouds are. The trees and flowers and birds and beasts have spirits the same as people; they can do wrong or right. Every field has a spirit that will make generous crops for the people who work well and wisely. The careless and ignorant invite misfortune and even the dumb earth will work evil things against the wicked.

Maum Hannah walked up and found Mary sitting alone in the dusk. "Git up off de steps, gal," she cautioned. "You ain' to set still when de whippoorwill's a-cryin. De whippoorwill's a bad-luck bird, Si May-e. When you hear em, you must go inside de house. Night air ain' good nohow. Night air, or neither studyin. An' honey," the old woman went on, "dis is Wednesday night. Meetin night. I want you to come go to meetin. Meetin don' last long. Do come go, honey. I want to see you pray, so bad."

Maum Hannah's hands were so small, so somehow pitiful as they held fast to each other. Mary looked at them and gave in. Their simple clasping and unclasping made her humble and pitying. Maum Hannah wanted her to go to meeting. To pray. To be a Christian again. To join the church and be saved from sin. She'd have to seek. That meant praying night and day until Jesus sent her a sign that her sins were forgiven.

"Auntie——" Mary hesitated. "Please, Auntie, le me wait a while. I ain' gwine dead, not soon. I don' want to pray, not yet. Please le me wait until Unex is bigger."

Maum Hannah turned away with a sigh and went to stand in the door. The stars were bright in the sky and a full moon hung right over the crape-myrtle tree. She stood looking up, and praying to God.

Maum Hannah had been praying for Mary to seek. In the sky a few stars glittered clear. Could God, so far away up there, hear what people down here said to Him?

"Honey," she began in a sorrowful voice, "Hell ain' no hole. E couldn' be a hole." Maum Hannah was usually cheerful, but to-night she sounded low-spirited, down-hearted. "Hell ain' no hole I tell you!" she repeated. "A hole would

a been full long time ago. A hole couldn'
hold all de sinners! No! I tink Hell must be a
lake!"

She groaned mournfully at the doleful-sound-
ing words.

"Hell is a lake. A lake of fire. It is full of
sinners strugglin an' burnin now. Right now.
Right down under us in the ground."

Hell is a lake!

Mary had never seen a real lake, but she had
heard July tell about lakes in the swamp that lay
still and stagnant, breeding snakes and alliga-
tors. Slime covered them over, fever lived
wherever they tarried.

Hell is a lake.

The singing at meeting had begun. The words
rose and swelled and filled the dusk.

> "I'm gwine to see my Jedus,
> Set right by His side,
> Set right by His side——"

It was beautiful singing and Mary's heart
beat with the rhythm. Singing always stirred
something inside her, and now she shut her eyes
to listen better.

> "I'm gwine to see my Jedus,
> Set right by His side,
> Set right by His side——"

Maum Hannah hobbled away singing.

"Set right by His side." Mary had seen pictures of Jesus. Why would Maum Hannah want to sit always right by His side?

A warm strong hand closed over one of Mary's, and June sang softly, "Set right by His side, set right by His side," then he sat beside Mary and whispered that the night was too shiny and beautiful to waste. Mary laughed but her heart began pounding in her breast in a funny sort of way.

The cabin door was open, and all inside was still. Unex was sound asleep. As they sat on the steps an earth-scented breeze rose from the fresh-plowed field and floated over them.

White gardenias thick on the bush by the door made spots of clean dim light; June picked one and smelled it, then handed it to Mary. It was sweet, too heavy sweet, but Mary said nothing for her fast, beating heart held her breathless.

CHAPTER XVI

WITH each morning the sun rose earlier, a great shining blossom that moved across the sky, making the day warmer and brighter. All the cabin doors and windows were flung wide open at dawn to let in the light and air. The men laughed and talked on their way to work. As soon as the women finished their household tasks, they sat on the door-steps in the sunshine, sewing, gossiping, their eyes taking account of everything, their tongues scattering truthful news along with bits of scandal. Sunshine is good for everything and even the tiny babies were brought out to enjoy it as soon as the early morning chill was out of the air.

When Mary finished her work she went outside too, and sat on her door-step, sewing pieces of cloth into a frock for Unex who had outgrown every garment he had. With the spring he had taken on new life, and he never could get enough goat's milk and pot-liquor. His cheeks were rounding out and his legs were getting strong, thank God! He could run a little and he never tired of playing with the children who gathered every day at Maum Hannah's house.

The oats were heading out. The water boy starting out on his lazy way to the spring to get water for the plowmen cut a buck and wing step, then beat thudding measures on the bottom of his empty bucket.

A tiny wren perched on a twig of the crape-myrtle tree sang a few blithe notes that were so full, so beautiful, that Mary's heart thrilled to its happiness.

She turned her head slowly and sat hardly breathing so as not to frighten the shy thing away as she watched its small brown throat swell and throb with the song. Its round, beady, black eyes shone and sparkled with joy as they cast quickly this way and that, looking for the knot-hole in the tree where it built its nest last year. When a blue-darter hawk, with a shrill cry and a flight like a thin gray shadow, hid in some of the trees near by, the wren quickly fluttered away for safety. All the little chickens scattered as the hens in the yard began cackling out terrified warnings; but the red rooster walked boldly up to the door-step and facing Mary crowed fit to split his throat. Somebody was coming.

There was not a bite to eat in the house. Mary put down her sewing and, taking some eggs from the basket on the safe, began mixing a sweetened bread. She put it into the three-legged oven on the hearth to bake, then she took the empty eggshells and strung them and hung them up beside the chimney in the place of the old ones which she threw into the fire.

"You time is out," she told the old shells. "But you done you work good. De hens is a-layin fine. I'm much obliged to you." She stood watching the bread rise and brown, and her eyes fell on her love-charm lying on the mantel. She had never worn it although Daddy Cudjoe had made it strong so that it could not fail. Good old Daddy Cudjoe. He was a kind old man even if he did work black magic.

The red rooster would not stop crowing. Somebody was coming. Sure enough, yonder was June, dressed in his best clothes, coming on the path across the field. When he came in Mary saw that his face was as long and solemn as Brer Dee's.

"What de matter ail you, June?" she asked. "How-come you look so mournful?"

"I is mournful."

"How-come you is all dressed up in you Sunday clothes an' it in de middle of de week?"

He sat down on the steps in the sunshine and, taking out his plug of tobacco, cut himself a chew. June would take his time, in face of a house afire. Presently he spat far out to one side, then he answered her question; he was tired of living here in the Quarters; he had no home of his own; Doll fed him well and washed his clothes and patched them, and did all she could to make him contented; but he was not satisfied in his mind; he was going away and find work, yonder in town, or somewhere.

Two slim young girls passed by, going to the field to set out sweet-potato slips. Their skirts were tied high around their hips, old floppy straw hats shaded their eyes, and their low words were followed by laughter as they glanced at June.

"How you do, Si May-e? How you do, June," they called out, then walked on with long easy-swinging steps, their bare feet making hardly a sound.

How happy they were. They were young and strong and well. Field work was easy to their sinewy bodies. Stooping, bending over hour after hour, was nothing at all to them. They were as busy with life as the bees with spring blossoms. They could work all day, then dance and sing all night, for their hearts were light and their bodies full of hot red blood. June's eyes followed them, out of sight.

"Plenty o willin gals in de Quarters, June. Whyn' you marry one an' settle down an' have a home o you own, stead o livin with Doll?"

June chewed on, then he turned and looked full in Mary's eyes.

"I'd been a-married an' settled down long time ago if I could a had my way. But July got my gal." He spat and sighed deep. "What is done is done. Nobody can' change em. I'm gwine off on de boat dis evenin. I'm gwine to some far country where I don' know nobody."

"You must be ain' well, June. You must a eat someting heavy fo you breakfast to talk such a sad talk."

"I ain' hardly eat no breakfast. I ain' had a bit o appetite, here lately."

"How about tastin a piece o hot sweetened bread? E's just ready to come out de oven."

She hurried to the hearth and broke him a piece of the bread, then she reached up on the mantel and took down the love-charm. She could not let June go off and leave her.

Should she touch him with it, or hold it in her hand? To be certain she would do both. Holding the tiny bag tight, she rested her fingers on his shoulder.

"June," she said in a voice that was husky and

low, "please don' go. Seems like if you was to leave home, I couldn' hardly stand it."

June turned and looked at her. His mouth was too full to speak, the yellow crumbs were all over his lips, but as soon as he could swallow he burst out.

"Why, Si May-e, I didn' know you would take it so hard. Fo Christ's sake, looka de pure water in you eyes."

Mary smiled and shook her head.

"No, you don' see no water in my eyes. I'm done quit a-cryin. But I sho would wallow all over de ground and bawl like a stuck hog if you was to go off an' leave me an' Unex."

"Den, I'll stay, Si May-e. I didn' know you'd feel so bad about my gwinen."

That was all. June showed no sign that he had been conjured, but she had done it with her eyes wide open, knowing June, knowing what it all might come to. He showed that the conjure rag had laid its heavy spell on him without tarrying.

The red rooster stepped out in front of the steps and called the hens to make haste and come see some fine tasty thing he had found. Mary knew he was fooling them, playing a trick on them.

Did June mean all the things he was saying to her now? Did she look as young as a single girl? Did he think as much of her as he said? Her heart seemed to stop beating. Her breath was cut off. She could not answer him a single word.

CHAPTER XVII

THE next Christmas Day found Mary with
Seraphine, a tiny baby girl, in her arms. Mary
herself was a new creature. Her heart was
light, her eyes sparkled and her laughter rang
out as gaily as anybody's. She had learned again
how to enjoy waking up to see the sky and to
work all day long without slackening her speed.
Her blood was warm with new life. It was
pleasant to walk along the roads, to go to the
forest for fire-wood, to swing her ax like a man,
driving its keen bright edge into the clean white
wood of the trees. She could never be the same
free-hearted girl she had been, for trouble had
left a scar somewhere deep down in her breast.

But sin and Seraphine had agreed with her.
She would have been completely happy except
for Budda. He would not speak to her, so cross
was he that she had brought a child into the world
after her lawful husband had left her. Instead
of coming to see her Christmas Day, he sat on
the wood-pile cutting splinters, frowning and
being as surly as he was on all the other days of
the year. When she called a cheerful "Christmas

gift" to him, he glowered at her and turned his
face away with an ugly snort that cut her to
the very quick. Budda was too hard on her, too
unforgiving.

He tried to make her marry June, then he
tried to make her quit grieving over July but
now, when she had proved to the world by means
of Seraphine that July was out of her mind, and
June in his place, Budda was cross and mean
and would not speak to her even on Christmas
Day. It didn't seem right. He was so vexed
with her, he hated a little innocent baby.

Mary thought and thought until the long
shadows began closing in on the sunshine. She
must do something. If Christmas passed and
Budda still stayed angry she would never be able
to win him back.

The sun had set and the clear first dark had
grown keen and chilly, but she wrapped a warm
woolen shawl carefully around Seraphine and,
hurrying to the wood-pile, laid the child in
Budda's lap, calling out, "Here's a Christmas gift for you, Budda." She ran away as
fast as she could, stopping behind a tree to hide
so she could peep out and see what happened.
Budda was ready to go home, but now he was
trapped. He dropped his stick and snatched the
baby up as if he would throw her away.

Mary's heart stood still. "May-e! May-e!" he bawled. "You better quit you crazy doins. Come back here an' git dis child!" A dead silence made Seraphine's faint "Goo-goo" sound very sweet.

"May-e! Come git dis chile."

"Goo-goo," Seraphine cooed.

Budda Ben must have been stunned for it was several minutes before he moved again. He carefully laid the child down on the wood-pile among the chips and sticks and reached for his walking stick. But he could not get himself up and balanced on his feet without running a risk of stumbling over Seraphine.

"May-e!" he shouted, and Mary laughed to herself. At last she had made him not only speak to her, but made him call her to come to him.

Seraphine began a little fretful whimpering which suddenly shifted into a furious wailing. The sticks of wood were hurting her soft little bones. She wanted to be taken up.

"May-e, you fool, come get dis baby befo e catch e death o cold on dis wood-pile."

Mary's mirth changed to anxiety, but she must not give in yet. Budda would hate to be caught with a crying baby at his feet. He might try to hush it before anybody saw his plight.

"Sh-sh-sh," he began softly, but it did no good. "Shut you mouth, fo Gawd's sake," he growled, then he leaned and scooped Seraphine up into his arms again.

Maum Hannah heard the disturbance, and came to her door and called out, "Who dat duh cry so pitiful, Ben?"

"Come here, Ma!" Ben growled, and soon Maum Hannah had Seraphine, carrying her into the house while Ben hobbled along beside them, muttering what Mary knew were curses of herself.

When Mary went to get Seraphine, the baby lay quiet in Budda Ben's arms, her small head close against his heart. Maum Hannah had some butter and brown sugar and was tying it into a cloth, making a sugar rag for Seraphine to suck. One of the baby's hands clutched the end of the red kerchief tie around Budda's neck, and the other was closed fast around his thumb.

"You tink you is smart, enty?" he asked Mary savagely. "You counted on havin some sport out o me. Well, you can go on home by yousef. Me an' Ma can take care o dis baby." His under lip was thrust out and his voice was grim, but Mary's heart sang for joy for the trick she played on him had worked.

Disregarding his struggles to pull away from her, Mary knelt down and squeezed his arm.

"Budda, Budda," she whispered, "please don'
be vexed wid me no more. It's Christmas. I gi
you a nice Christmas gift, enty? I wasn' makin
sport o you. No. I want you to love me an'
po lil Seraphine too. Budda, I missed you too
bad. I know I done wrong, but I ain' gwine
never do wrong, not no more. Not long as I
live, Budda."

"You is a low-down gal, May-e. Low-down as
you only can be. If it wasn' fo dis po lil stray
baby, I wouldn' never speak to you again,
long as I live. Dat's de Gawd's truth." In spite
of his contempt which burned her clear through,
Mary felt a smile tugging at her lips.

"Now, Budda——"

"I mean it." His tone was harsh, and his eyes
were blazing. Yet she caught a glimmer of the
old kindliness she had known all her life.

"Budda—smile at me one time, just by it's
Christmas Day." Budda turned his face away
and gazed into the fire that glowed scarlet as
her sin. But from that minute on when nobody
else could hush Seraphine's crying, Budda could.

CHAPTER XVIII

Fifteen years passed and although everything on the plantation looked much the same, many changes had crept in. The pots on Mary's hearth were always full, the pig-pen always kept a shoat fattening on the scraps of food that were left; a flock of hens with red ripe combs clucked and cackled around her door and greens kept her vegetable garden lively; food was plentiful and everybody in her house had plenty to eat. But the old house itself needed help, and June was not there to fix it. The old rock pillars were crumbling and they let the solid weight of the building's square body lean to one side. The front door sagged and scraped on the floor; the board window-blinds drooped on their hinges, one-sided and out of shape. Thank God, the old clay chimney was still firm on its foundations, able to breathe out smoke day after day; and the green moss on the roof held the frayed shingles together from the warped ridge-pole to the edge of the rotting eaves.

Food was plentfiul but money was scarce, for the cotton-fields which had always provided enough for outside needs were cursed with the most terrible pest the plantation had ever known. The cotton stalks grew taller than they ever had done, their leaves stayed green through the worst droughts, but they made no fruit for they fed multitudes of boll-weevils from the first warm days of the spring until a killing frost came. Then the moss on the old oak trees made warm pleasant beds to keep the pests safe through the winter.

Some people called the creatures boll-weevils, others called them boll-evils, some people thought God made them to turn the thought of people to Him, others thought Satan had sent them; but no matter who was right, the wicked things destroyed every lock of cotton year after year and no man or charm or conjure could rule them.

The white landowners sent poison machines to scatter poison dust over the fields. Night after night the strange things droned and whined spreading their poison clouds, but the rain always came and washed the fields clean and fresh again. It must have been that the weevils could eat poison and thrive. The stuff that was meant to kill them seemed to make them grow fatter and stronger than ever. Cotton's time was out. In the fall, competition had always been keen and people had asked each other, "How many

bales did you make this year?" They now sighed
and asked, "Where will we get seed enough to
plant a crop next year?"

In the spring they no longer asked, "Is your
cotton up to a stand yet?" but, "Is your field as
thick with boll-wevils as mine?"

For a few years June struggled on trying to
fight weevils and make a crop but fall after fall
came and found him with nothing to show for his
whole year's work. He got discouraged and gave
up and went away to find something else to do.
He could not write so no letter ever came to tell
Mary where he went or what he was doing.

Unex had grown up tall like July. His eyes
glittered with the same boldness and his white
teeth pierced the blackness of his face when he
boasted that he knew how to work, that his back
would never bend under a load. But at last he
gave up too and left to find better work and
easier money somewhere out in the world. He
went with a laugh in his mouth, he took nothing
but a little bundle of clothes and his father's old
battered guitar (they were all he wanted in
the world); but he had never learned to write
and no word ever came from him. Only God
knew if he was alive or not. Mary had reared
every child she had brought into the world, for
she knew how to start them off right. Her

house was full of them, little and big, but
Unex was her only lawful child. Now he
had gone away and forgotten her the same as
his father had done, although she loved him with
every hair of her head, every drop of her blood,
every beat of her heart, not because he was lawful
or because he was her first-born, but because he
was the child of her heart-love, while all the others
were the children of the flesh.

Seraphine was almost a woman in spite of her
smallness and childishness, and Budda Ben had
worshiped her ever since that Christmas Day
when Mary left her on the wood-pile alone with
him. Budda never saw anything wrong with her
for she never laughed at his infirmities and queer
ways, but took his part whether he was right or
wrong. When she wanted things Mary refused to let her have, Budda gave them to her.
Last year when she craved to go off to town to
school Budda sent her, although he had to dig up
every cent he had saved and buried to keep, just
as he had when Mary wanted a wedding-dress.
But Mary had children enough left to look after
her and take care of her when old age came to
make her weak and helpless. Without them, she
might fare poorly, for she had no husband or
father or brother to depend on.

She was able to laugh and dance and sing

again, her flesh had got back its old smoothness, her old sadness and weariness and bitterness were left behind. Thank God, she knew men at last, and she knew that not one of them is worth a drop of water that drains out of a woman's eye. Once, long ago, she used to think that Cinder was a mean, low-down hussy, but now she knew Cinder was not to blame for July's sins. Cinder's heart got broken too, for July left her to run off with another woman. As likely as not he had been taking women and leaving them all through the years since he went away. God made July a devil. Cinder was not to blame for that.

Last summer Mary went to town on an excursion to see Cinder, a poor pitiful soul, living in a broken-down shack filled with wharf-rats and water bugs. Her black skin was ashy and dried up on her bones, not a decent tooth was in her head, yet she still grieved for July. Deep down in Mary's heart she thanked God for all the other strong men that were in the world. July was not the only one. And June was not either.

The first real spring morning of the year had come and the sun blossomed in the east as bright and yellow as the jonquils and daffodils and butter-and-eggs around Mary's door, dropping floods of warm light over the Quarters. Opening the creaky, dragging door of her cabin as soon as she woke, Mary peered outside to see what was going on.

She had overslept, but so had everybody else, that was plain enough. She looked up at the sky, which promised a fair day, although a slight chilliness, brought by the night, lingered in shady places. Winter was loath to go. But spring had come, with its round of work. Quilts must be washed and sunned and put away, summer things hunted up and mended.

Then she and the children could go fishing for the trout and bream were biting fast. She cared no more about the water-snakes coiled up on the tree limbs along the river-bank and the alligator eyes peeping slyly up out of the water at her children than she did for the yellow-bellied terrapins that sunned themselves on every log. She had learned not to meddle with such creatures and not to fear them.

Thank God, winter had not lasted long, and the few sharp spells of bitter cold which made everybody hug the big smoke-blackened fireplaces, were short and soon forgotten. Summer would soon be here with blazing hot days and still hot nights. Field work would soon keep the clear salty sweat dripping off her hot face, and every thread of her clothing drenched from the skin out, for times had changed. Boll-weevils had come and would eat up the cotton unless it was worked fast. But sweating is good. Out-of-doors is good.

The old moss-hung oaks, towering and spreading with full-bodied strength, were so full of new life that drops of sap were falling like rain from their tasseled, new-leaved branches, and wasting on the ground. Life runs so thick inside them they become wasteful and careless and extravagant. The moss on them sheltered the boll-weevils all winter, giving warmth to the plantation's worst enemy.

The wide-spread fields waiting to be plowed and planted held grass and weed seeds that would sprout and grow among the planted crops. Plows and hoes would have to work from dawn until dusk to keep them from binding their strong roots around the cotton and corn and choking the life out of the crops. Plants have sap, boll-weevils and people have blood. Summer makes both run hot and free. Winter makes them run slow and cold, but, thank God, winter's time was out.

A free school opened a week ago. Another new thing. It began at nine, and if Keepsie wanted to go, she must hurry up breakfast

and let him start, for the walk was long now that
he had only one leg to go on.

A great fire soon leaped joyously up the chimney. The ashes roasted the potatoes, the skillet
fryed the breakfast meat, the three-legged spider
baked the bread, then Mary woke up the children and put them to work, from Keepsie, the
oldest one at home, to the yearling baby who
strove to put on his one lone garment without
help.

Two of them ran to the spring for water, two
went to the wood-pile for wood, one went
with Mary to the cow pen to mind the calf and
hold the cow's tail while she milked and keep it
from switching her face when it strove to brush
the stinging flies away.

Her sinewy hands squeezed two swift streams
of milk into her pail and the foam rose high.
Inside the cabin, pots and pans and dishes clattered, water splashed, children laughed. Thank
God, they were able to help themselves. She had
trained Unex and Seraphine, her two oldest,
and they had trained the others. Even the baby
could dress himself.

She missed Unex and Seraphine more than
ever now that Keepsie had only one leg. But
Keepsie faced his trouble without complaining
although he was only a shoulder-high boy.

People were trying to change the world, letting new ways creep in every day. Except for that newfangled hay-press, Keepsie would have his two good legs to-day. But the poor little fellow had so much curiosity about everything, instead of keeping his distance while the old mule pulled the long pole round and round, packing the hay into tight little bales, he went close to the machine to see how it tightened down on the wire bands before it clipped them off. Somehow, only God knows how, before Keepsie could get out of the way, it caught his leg and held it fast, and clipped it off the same as a wire around a hay bale. The people screamed and cried, but Keepsie made no sound. He knew he had done wrong. He knew Big Boy had warned him about going close to that hay-press. Big Boy told him it was a blind contraption made by white men and it would cut off a boy's arm or leg as quickly as wire.

God must have sent that white doctor from town to go deer hunting. Maum Hannah said so.

Big Boy got him to come and fix Keepsie's leg. Keepsie's eyes got big and shiny, but he held himself still and did not flinch when the white doctor took scissors and trimmed his ragged meat and sewed his skin with a needle and thread the same as cloth.

Keepsie was a brave-hearted boy. He could have died, but he strove to live and now he was as well as ever. He could play around as spry as any of the other children, hopping like a sparrow, doing almost anything the others could do until he decided to go to that free school.

Mary didn't want him to go. She had never learned to read. There were no printed words in the Quarters except in Brer Dee's Bible and on the newspapers pasted on the house walls to hinder the wind from gushing too fast through the cracks. The same white people who made that hay-press made newspapers and books. Such things were dangerous. Keepsie ought not to tamper with them. Who could tell what book-reading might do to him.

Spoken words are safer. If Keepsie would keep his ears open he could hear plenty of good wise talk. Spoken words can cut and sting and beat down almost any enemy. They can bring tears or make people split their sides with laughter. Instead of reading all the time out of books and papers covered with printed words, he would do better to learn how to read other things: sunrises, moons, sunsets, clouds and stars, faces and eyes. Everything has its way of speaking and telling things worth knowing. Even the little grass-blades have their way of saying things as plain as words when human lips let them fall. Book-learning takes people's minds off more important things. The faithful old superstitions, the choice bits of wisdom passed down by word of mouth ever since the first slaves were brought here to live were never written down in any books.

Big Boy and Budda Ben sided with Keepsie. They told Mary to let him learn to read and write too, for Keepsie could never farm. A one-legged boy can not hop along and hold a plow straight to the row in soft ground. Keepsie would have to follow some other kind of business to make himself a living.

Last Monday morning Keepsie got up before day was clean and did all his tasks before breakfast, then he washed and dressed and hopped off to the schoolhouse. Mary hardly thought he could get so far, but she was mistaken. The next morning he started out just as brave as ever, hopping off gaily and laughing with happiness to be going. The children could not leave him then. He hopped too high and too fast. But he came home in the evening hopping slowly, wearily. Hopping up two long hills was a hard task for his one little leg. The hills fagged him out on the way home. He couldn't hop high enough to make any progress up them. Poor little faithful Keepsie. Money was scarce and crutches would cost cold hard dollars, but Keepsie must have a pair. Brer Dee could make heavy crutches for grown men or for old slow-moving people, but Keepsie needed a light pair that would help push him up the hill and not weight him down, or hold him back and hamper him. Big Boy's father, Andrew, had sharp tools and a good head. He might make Keepsie crutches that would fetch him home as joyful in the evening as he was when he started off in the morning. But she hated to ask any favor of Andrew, for he was the deacon who was hardest on her, always the main one to say she was pure scarlet and not fit ever to have been a member of the church.

CHAPTER XIX

PEACH buds were swelling, trees were in bloom, birds chirped around them, but Mary and crippled Budda Ben sat on the wood-pile talking so earnestly she completely forgot to enjoy the morning's bright sunshine. Misery filled his dull red-rimmed eyes. His high-pitched outbursts of fury were pitiful. Mary begged him to be quiet, not to make himself sick. Ranting could do no good in the world; what was done was done.

Ben was raving against all the preachers and church deacons in the whole world, cursing them, hoping they would have to hop in Perdition's hottest flames until that fire itself froze stiff. They did a low-down trick when they turned him out of the church yesterday. He would never forgive them. Never. They were a dirty bunch of rascals.

When they called that meeting Friday night to examine all the members of the church and see if they were living right enough to take the Lord's Supper on Sunday, he knew they were up to something.

One by one they passed every single member

and said all were in good standing until his name was brought up. Then Andrew, the blacksmith, stood up and rebuked him before the whole congregation for cursing little children and blaspheming God's name. Andrew did not tell the people that the children were his and Doll's no-mannered bunch, or how those children tormented him every day God sent. Budda never meddled the pesky black devils. He never meddled anybody. He spent his days sitting here on the wood-pile cutting tough pine stumps into light wood splinters for everybody in the Quarters who needed them. No day passed without one of those same children coming for some of his nice, fat, pine splinters. When he half-soled shoes for Andrew or Doll, he always took extra pains because Andrew was a deacon in the church. Yet those children discounted him and plagued him, and laughed at him because he couldn't run them down and catch them and beat hell out of them. Andrew had no right to be unmannerable to him. Not a bit. He told Andrew right to his big black face what he was, too. Then all the other deacons sided with Andrew against him and said he was too sinful to be a church-member. Sunday, yesterday, right before the whole congregation at Heaven's Gate Church, Andrew

read his name out and the damned fat black
pastor stood up in the pulpit and told him to
get on his knees and pray until he got forgiveness. It was a sin and a shame. A piece of low-
down meanness. Maum Hannah had broken
down and cried.

He could hear her crying in the night last
night, crying all by herself, begging God to
forgive him and have mercy on him, when he had
not done a thing but tell what God himself loves,
the truth. Those children were devils. Everybody in the Quarters knew it. Andrew and Doll
knew it too.

"But I hear-say you got so vexed you cussed
all de deacons right in de Friday night meetin,
Budda." Mary said it kindly, gently, but Ben
was struck all but dumb with fresh rage.

"No, I ain' cussed em nuttin. Whoever say I
cussed all de deacons Friday night—whoever say
sich a ting is a—a——"

Ben's voice was too hoarse to be shrill, and it
broke into a fierce squeak. Mary put her hand
on his shoulder and patted it. "Hush, Budda—
hush! You ain' hurtin a soul but yousef now.
Not a soul. You has talked enough ugly talk dis
mornin to send you to Hell. Fo Gawd's sake
stop it. You's a fallen member now, but don'
fret about it. Abusin de deacons ain' gwine put

you back whe you was. Do keep quiet. When you git ready, you can pray an' seek an' find peace an' jine de church again. If I was you I wouldn' let my mind run on Andrew no more. You leave em to Gawd an' Doll. Dey'll keep em humble enough."

Poor pitiful Budda. Mary felt like crying herself to see how hurt he was, yet his curses were funny enough to make a dog laugh.

"But I ain' been to blame, Si May-e," Ben heaved. "Andrew's an' Doll's chillen makes game o me all de time. Dey don' never stop. De very next time dey does it I'm gwine to brain em wid dis same ax." His brawny fingers twisted around the ax handle and squeezed it viciously, but Mary laughed cheerfully.

"Hush, Budda. You wouldn' hurt a flea, much less brain Andrew's chillen. You know dat. Nobody ain' got a better heart dan you, Budda, even if you does cuss awful bad sometimes. But you must quit a-frettin 'bout what you can' help. Looka how nice de sun is a-shinin up yonder in de sky, a-makin de day most as warm as summer. Be tanksful, Budda. Tank Gawd for life. Dat's de way to do. Quit you gwinen on, a-frettin so till you's all but fool in de head. I don' see how Auntie stands to put up wid you."

"Ma ain' slept none, not since Friday night," Ben said. "An' I—I ain' slept none neither. All 'cause dem devil deacons is a bunch o fools— dey ain' nuttin but a lot o dirty—low-down———"

"If you don' shut you mout', I gwine to leave you. I come all de way out here to make some nice pleasant talk an' cheer you up an' all, but I see you ain' gwine to listen to me. I got too much to do yonder home to waste my good time a-wranglin wid a crazy man like you. I'm done weary a-listenin at blaspheme. Sometimes Gawd strikes people dead for blaspheme. If death was to hit you now, Budda, an' catch you wid dat turrible talk in you mout', Jedus! You'd go as straight to Hell as a martin to his gourd. You must be forgot how awful Hell is. I'm glad de deacons got dat picture o Satan an' all down below a-comin here next Friday night, so you can see good how bad Hell is."

Ben's being turned out of the church was not anything new, but for him to take it so hard certainly was. He had never been so upset before. He was more upset than he ought to be, as many times as he had experienced falling from grace. He must be worried because the picture that was going to be shown Friday night at the church was a picture of Hell, real Hell, just as it was in truth. Mary had not gone to church yesterday, but everybody who went was full of the news; a picture of Hell was coming up on Friday's boat so all the people could see what sinners had to meet when they died.

Reverend Duncan said nobody living could understand how hot Hell really is, but this picture would give them some kind of idea. Although Mary had not gone inside Heaven's Gate Church for years, she was going to stand outside and look through a window and get some idea of how Hell looked.

"Budda," she said, "I come here to say, le's me an' you go look at de picture o Hell."

"I don' want to see em," Ben growled, "I ain' got no money to spend on no picture o Hell. I'll see Hell soon enough."

"I got money, I'll pay you way. Dey ain' gwine charge much if we stand outside an' look at em through de window."

Ben shook his head. His eyes were hard, his mouth was tortured and bitter.

Mary turned her eyes from his unhappy face to the quiet sky where a cloudless spring sun shone white, casting a bright sheen on Budda's black skin and deepening the lines of his haggard face. God's throne was somewhere beyond that dazzling light.

Mary's keen eyes searched the brightness and

the blue sky all around it, but no sign of the Great I Am or His angels could be seen anywhere at all. Only a lone buzzard borne on rigid wings sailed slowly about between the earth and Heaven. As Mary watched him, his shadow floated silently down the Quarter street, then veered toward the wood-pile. She got hurriedly to her feet. That shadow must not come too near to her now. Lord, no!

"Look out, Budda! A buzzard shadow is a-comin," she cried, and the pieces of wood slipped about under his feet as he stumbled away from the dreaded thing.

Her words had startled him. "Whe e dey, May-e?" he asked anxiously, as he shivered with nervous terror.

But the fearsome thing had moved on, and Mary laughed with honest relief.

"You can set still now. E's gone. I b'lieve e was aimin at me, an' not you, but I was too smart for em dat time. Too smart, tank Gawd. I sho hates to see a buzzard shadow. I ruther be close to a buzzard sef, wouldn' you?"

Budda reflected and shook his head gloomily. Either one was poor company for people.

She took a long deep breath and stretched, then yawned as her bare feet sought a firmer footing on the wood-pile. "I got to go, Budda. Soon as

I cook a pot o peas an' rice for de chillen's dinner, I'm gwine to see Andrew and ax em to make some crutches for Keepsie."

"Andrew? You wouldn' let Keepsie walk wid crutches Andrew made, Si May-e? I can' stand for Andrew to make em. You go get Brer Dee to make em, not Andrew——"

"Brer Dee can make crutches for old people, but dey would be too heavy for a lil boy. I want to get Keepsie some light ones so e can hop along to school fast as de other chillen can walk an' hop along joyful too."

Budda pulled his ragged old hat farther down over his eyes. "I been crippled all my life, but I rather drag myself on my belly like a snake and eat dirt, dan to walk on any crutches Andrew ever made. Gawd, how I hate em." And he spat far to show how much.

"Fo Gawd's sake, hush, Budda. Looka Auntie a-comin. Auntie can' stand people to talk ugly talk. Specially about Andrew. Auntie thinks Andrew comes next to Jedus' own sef."

When his breast began making a queer husky sound and heaving in jerks, Mary thought such hard talking had shut off his wind, for he was weakened down with worry and vexation. But when a big round bright drop of water fell through the air, she knew he was crying. Budda

Ben, of all people in the whole world! She had never seen him shed a tear before.

"Budda! Budda!"—she shook his arm,—"if you cry here on dis wood-pile to-day I'll lay down on de ground an' holler same like a dog. Fo Gawd's sake, stop. Cuss all you want to, be mean much as you please, but don' cry. I can' stand to see you cry."

For a minute, Ben could not control his sobbing. Then Mary whispered that all the church-members would be peeping out of their doors at him, and they would be so glad to see his sorrow they would jump up and crack their heels together with joy. Ben dropped the ax and glared at her.

"I ain' cryin about bein a fallen member. No," he bawled, "I'm a-cryin because you don' mind de way Andrew done me."

CHAPTER XX

MAUM HANNAH was coming out of her door and, after closing it behind her, she hobbled painfully down the steps. Her clean white apron was starched stiff and her wide-brimmed, black sailor hat, which she wore only to church or on important occasions, was perched uncertainly on top of the fresh white bandanna that bound her head.

"Auntie is a faithful Christian in dis world. E sho is. We ought not to fret em if we can help it. Neither me, neither you."

"Ma is done too old to be all de time gwine round a-catchin chillen for people. E ought to let somebody else do em now." Ben sniffled and wiped his eyes and nose on his ragged coat sleeve.

Mary laughed. "Nobody ain' gwine have none now. Auntie is gwine to school to-day."

"School? Fo Gawd's sake, shut you mout', May-e. You talk too much crazy talk to be a grown 'oman. You know Ma ain' gwine to no school." Ben's short patience had given out, for he thought Mary was joking.

"I'm tellin you de Gawd's truth," Mary

208

declared seriously. "Auntie is gwine to school.
E ain' told you?" Mary could not help grinning
in spite of the black frown on Ben's face. "You
ain' heard about a new law de white folks is
made?"

Ben had not heard, and Mary tried to explain
to him that the new law said people must no
longer birth children like they used to. The
white folks had a new way to do it now, and
Maum Hannah and all the plantation midwives
had to go to the midwife class at Heaven's Gate
Church for ten Monday mornings while a lady
from up-north tried to make them understand all
about the new style. "Great Gawd, ain' it de
funniest ting you ever did hear?" Mary laughed
so that the thick piece of wood she sat on suddenly slipped.

"Do Jedus," she cried out in alarm, "don' le
me fall an' broke my leg to-day. I got some
birthin to do my own sef before long."

Budda Ben did not turn his head. He sat
glum and down-hearted and silent while she
chattered on trying to cheer him up. White
people are curious things. They pass laws
no matter how fool the laws are, and put
people in jail if those laws are not kept. People
had come into the world over the same old road
ever since Eve birthed Cain and Abel, and now,

everybody had to learn how to birth children a new way. It was enough to upset the whole world.

White people try to be too smart. If they keep on messing in God's business and trying to change things from the way He meant them to be, the first thing they knew, He would get cross and make Judgment Day wipe the whole world clean of them. It would be too late then for them to cry and holler and be sorry. They ought to be careful with their laws and projects. The old way to birth children has its drawbacks, but it is plenty good enough. They had better leave it alone.

"How you b'lieve chillen'll get into de world dis new way, Budda?" she asked presently.

Ben didn't know. He didn't care. All the children in the world could die and go to Hell so far as he was concerned. These damned children of Andrew were the cause of all his troubles, the cause of his getting turned out of the church yesterday. They teased him, tormented him, made their dogs nip at his heels, the dirty, low-down, pot-bellied—— Budda Ben spluttered with such fury Mary laid her hand on his arm. "Hush, Budda. Don' cuss now. Auntie'll hear you, and it hurts her awful bad when you have sin. Look at em. Poor old soul, hoppin along. I don' see how e can walk all de way to Heaven's Gate Church wid dat cripple knee painin em so."

"What you chillen duh talk 'bout?" Maum Hannah called cheerfully to them. "I hear-ed Mary's mout' a-runnin all de way down de street, and I said to mysef, dat gal sho must be a-feelin good dis mornin."

"I been tryin to cheer Budda Ben up some, but I can' do em so save my life. You better take em wid you to de school at Heaven's Gate an' train em to be a midwife. Ben would make such a fine one. E would scare de women so bad dey couldn' crack dey teeth, to holler."

Before Ben could retort Maum Hannah held up her stick and shook it at Mary. "Shut you mout', gal. Dat ain' no decent talk for you to talk. You make me feel pure shame o you."

Mary's boisterous laughter faded. "I was just a-playin, Auntie. I wouldn' hurt Budda's feelins, not for gold. E knows I'm just a-plaguin him."

"I know, honey, but you must have respect for midwifin too. Dat is Jedus' business. You ain' to make sport of it. I b'lieve you'd crack a joke 'bout death, Si May-e. You ain' sensible. You better quit you wicked ways. You joke about birthin when you got to face em yousef, soon as dis same moon changes."

Mary became serious. "I'm sorry, Auntie, I ain' gwine joke bout em no more. I was just a-talkin fool tryin to make Budda laugh. E was lookin so awful doleful."

Maum Hannah shook her head sadly. "Budda ought to look doleful. E don' need to laugh. E needs to pray an' ask God to give em long patience, den e wouldn' be so quick to get vexed an' cuss. Short patience'll make anybody have sin. But, gal, if I was wicked as you an' as sho fo Hell as you is, I wouldn' stop prayin day or night. Not me."

This stern talk hurt, for Mary loved Maum Hannah dearly and liked to win her praise.

"You is too hard on me, Auntie. You makes me feel awful down-hearted."

"Honey," Maum Hannah changed to a gentle tone, "I don' aim to talk hard at you, but when I look at you so, I feel dat sorry fo you I could cry."

"Sorry for me, Auntie? How-come so? I'm heavy fo-true, but I'm well. I don' mean to brag, but birthin a baby ain' no trouble to me. It don' even gi me a backache. My chillen has plenty to eat an' wear; Budda cuts wood to keep my fire goin day an' night. Why be sorry fo me?"

"Honey, sinners is all pitiful. As nigh as you is to gwinen down, you ought to be prayin to Gawd to forgive all dat sin you been havin. Ask Him to help you thu you trouble. E would do it. Gawd is a merciful Gawd."

"Gwinen down don' worry me none 't all," Mary boasted. "I can birth a child easy as I can pop my finger. You know dat, Auntie. How-come you tryin to scare me so dis mornin?"

"I ain' tryin to scare you, gal, but nobody, ex-cusin Gawd, knows what's ahead o you. Nobody. An' when a 'oman turns e back on Gawd an' Jedus like you done, who you gwine to pray to when you needs help? Gawd's got de power to turn dat same child upside down right now. Den you would be in trouble, fo-true. An' who'd you pray to? Don' brag too fast, gal."

A shadow passed over Mary's heart as Maum Hannah spoke, but she smiled in spite of it. "I'm gwine to settle down, Auntie, soon as I birth dis same child."

"I hope so, honey. I hope so. But you ought to settle down befo de time comes to birth dat child. You stays too wild an' wicked. If you keep on a-settin such a bad pattern to live by, befo you know it, one o you gals will walk straight in you tracks."

"I'd lick de hide off em too," Mary burst out. "My gals ain' to do like I do, but do like I say. Enty, Budda?"

Her effort to get gay met with a dead silence. Ben frowned, and Maum Hannah's eyes were filled with distress.

"May-e, honey, de way you do pure hurts me to my heart. I ain' got much longer to live in dis world an' I know it, but I couldn' rest easy in Heaven if you an' Ben was to miss an' lose you souls. Hell is a awful place."

When she took up a corner of her apron to wipe the water out of her eyes, Mary got up quickly and went to her and, putting her arms around the old woman's shoulders, began trying to soothe her as she soothed little troubled children.

"Don' fret, Auntie, please don' fret. Me an' Ben ain' gwine to be lost. No. We is gwine to seek an' pray in plenty o time. All-two o we is gwine to set right beside you in Heaven some o these days. You'll see. Ben is gwine to stop sayin so much-a sinful words, an' I'm a-gwine to pray, myself, sometime soon. I ain' gwine to wait so much longer to repent—not so much longer, Auntie——"

The sight of Maum Hannah's sorrow made Mary feel sad enough to get down on her knees and start praying right then. She could not bear to see suffering, and Maum Hannah's tears would make her promise anything on earth. It had always been so. She never could argue or disagree with the kind old soul. She always wanted to say whatever was the best-mannered thing. Even when she was a little motherless child running around, living from house to house in the Quarters, petted, spoiled, loved by every one there, Maum Hannah's disapproval cut her to the very quick.

"You is a sweet-talkin sinner, Si May-e, but I know how much you promises mean. Promisin talk don' cook rice."

"I'm gwine to change," Mary spoke earnestly.

"Please, honey, change. Try to 'scape Hell if you can."

Mary met the old eyes bravely, and her voice was steady as she declared solemnly, "I'm gwine to change, Auntie. Satan ain' gwine never put his hands on me. Not never." Her words were eager with kindness for she loved Maum Hannah dearly.

"I wouldn' pester you, May-e, if I didn' love you."

"You is right to pester me, an' I tank you fo it. Soon as you learn de new way to birth chillen, you come practise em on me de first one. No matter how bad it is, I'll do anyting you say, Auntie. Anyting in Gawd's world."

"Except leavin off sin. But you wait: Gawd'll

whip you an' plague you till you quit, some o dese days. You'll see. Gawd's done let dat hay-press cut off Keepsie's leg. Dat's one plague E sent on you. Unex is gone an' left you; dat's two plagues. You cotton patch ain' made a lock o cotton in Gawd knows when; dat's three plagues."

"You b'lieve Gawd would cut off Keepsie's leg, Auntie."

"Sho E would, if it would save you soul from Hell. Keepsie better go to Heaven wid one leg dan for you to go to Hell with two. You better pray before Gawd plagues you again. De next plaguin might be de worst one ever was." Maum Hannah sighed. She was so crippled she could hardly put one foot before the other one, but she did not complain for she believed God knew what was best for her.

CHAPTER XXI

As THE years passed life seemed to divide most of the people Mary knew into two groups: men and women; and the women were all her rivals and competitors, except Maum Hannah. Even her oldest girl child, Seraphine, was pitted against her for the first place in the heart of Budda Ben, although maybe Budda Ben could hardly be counted a man. Certainly Maum Hannah was so old she could hardly be counted a woman. For she lived in another world, seeking only the love of God and Jesus, craving only to do what was pleasing in Their sight. To her, human men were no more than children who needed to be fed and encouraged and warned and pitied.

She had been like a mother to Mary all through the years and the love between them was natural, but what bound Mary to Budda Ben was not so much his kindness to her nor her pity and affection for him, but another thing altogether.

The rest of the Quarter people lived and moved and thought in droves and flocks like

217

chickens or sheep. They could not be happy or help themselves except in crowds or groups. They had societies, bury-leagues, sick benefit circles, lodges.

They all belonged to Heaven's Gate Church, whose strict rules tried to curb their conduct. They allowed no ground between sinners and Christians. Church-members were all Christians, saved from sin. They, only, were the children of God and brothers and sisters of little kind Jesus. Everybody else would be damned in Hell.

Budda argued that the Christians often turned right into wrong, justice into injustice. They denied some of the plainest, simplest facts of life, and thought they could run God's business; they laid strict rules for each other because they were too timid, too coward-hearted to come out in the open and live as they wanted to live.

He lashed out against their pretenses. Sometimes they were right, but not always. Nobody is always right. Nobody always knows what right is. The wisest people in the world are ignorant about many things. The most free-handed have to be stingy sometimes and the kindest, mean. If he could only hold out to live his own life without flinching, that would be enough to ask of himself.

With all Budda Ben's bitterness and sadness
he was never humble. He said whatever came
into his head without caring what anybody
thought. He was an unforgiving enemy and
a faithful friend. When he loved or hated, he
let the world know it.

He was wretched over being out of the church
now, not because it cut him off from his neighbors, but because he had respect for God and
Satan. Every man with sense must fear his
Maker, no matter how bold he may be. He had
joined the church over and over, but he could
not stay a member. Every time he joined he
got turned out again. His short patience and
hot words would more than likely send him to
Hell along with Mary. For to save Mary's life
she could not keep her mind fixed on the joys
of Heaven, but sought her pleasure right here in
this world, where pleasures are in such easy reach.
She believed in God and Satan and Heaven and
Hell too, and she had no doubt that sinners fed
Hell's fires, but the rules of Heaven's Gate
Church made the Christian life very difficult for
a young, strong, healthy woman. She and Budda
Ben would probably spend eternity in torment
together and that bound them to each other here
on earth.

She was straight and strong and able, and he

was weighed down by powerless sinews and a painful misery that clogged his joints. She was supple and lithe, and her body seldom knew weariness, while Ben stayed weary all the time. Her feet stepped lightly through the years and Budda's legs had to walk, half-squatting, slowly, following the long stout stick his hands used to guide them. But both of them resented many of the ways and customs of the plantation people who never stopped to think about things, and accepted ideas and beliefs which were handed down to them, the same as they accepted the old houses where they were born and worked in the same old fields which their parents and grandparents had salted with sweat.

When Mary first began sinning openly, Budda Ben tried his best to stop her, then when he found that nothing he said made her change her ways, he began defending her and holding that whatever people crave to do is good for them to do. If Mary fed her children and clothed them and trained them to be brave-hearted, to work, and to have manners, that was enough to expect of her. She was not a member of any lodge or society or church, and she had a right to live her own life as she liked. He defended everything she did. He declared that except for his own mother, Mary was the best woman on

the plantation. She understood folks. She had
sympathy for them. She knew their needs and
sufferings and forgave their mistakes because
she knew that blunders are easy to make. Budda
said she was like a garden where flowers blossom
the whole year through, and, although she had
little money now, one so rich in kindness could
never be poor. Her children were not full kin,
but they grew up together in peace as brothers
and sisters of one family, working, pleasuring,
growing up strong and more able than any lawful children in the Quarters.

Mary was different from the other women. She
had been so all her life. In her childhood among
her playmates, or working in the field with her
blood-kin thick around her, she always seemed
different. She had married July and he left her
to fend for herself, but if she wanted a house
full of children that was nobody's business but
her own.

The Quarter women muttered dark things
about Mary and prophesied dark things for her.
They feared the power she had over their men,
so they had no faith in her kindness.

The passing years made no difference to the
spirit of her youth. The Quarter women could
dream their bad dreams and talk of good and
evil as much as they liked; they made no differ-

ence to Mary. Hard work had kept her lean and hard-muscled. She was still keen-eyed and erect while they were paunchy in the middle and saggy in the cheeks. Their faces were lined and their hair streaked with white, and fear of Mary's charm made their tongues bitter. They had more pleasure in her misery than in her happiness. Her sorrow pleased them more than her joy.

So Mary valued Budda Ben's smiles and dreaded his frown. Nobody could say before her that he was only a cripple who walked half squatting with a stick; nobody could hint at his debasement. She loved him and she was as kind to him as if he stood tall and perfect in grace and bearing. Perhaps she clung closer to him because he was not whole. Maybe if he had been a strong man, she would have treated him as she did the others, whom she lured boldly and without shame, using the love-charm Daddy Cudjoe gave her to get July back.

That charm, old and worn as it was now, still stood by her faithfully. It had never failed her. She prized it and cherished it as if it were God's best gift instead of something that would send her to the bottomless pits of perdition.

When she first tried it, she was stunned to see how it worked on June. She was ugly then with her blood turned to water, and her flesh all

withered and shriveled. For months her eyes
had poured tears, sometimes down her cheeks,
sometimes through her heart. Her breast was
sunken with misery, and her arms were weak
and bony.

She was very cautious with it at first, afraid
of it, uncertain of what it might do, but wicked
as the charm undoubtedly was it had given back
her lost youth, and brought her a strange satisfaction and happiness. Her flesh got back all its
old smoothness, her body its old supple grace.
She could laugh and sing while she worked. All
her weariness left her, all her sadness and bitterness were gone, sorrow was far behind her.

Men are all alike when spring comes and
the sunshine works its charm on them, whether
they are people or beasts or bugs or fowls.
The men grasshoppers fight to the death for a
green six-legged lady, the men fish kill each other
for the sake of a cold-blooded scaly length of
meat, the cocks use spurs and beaks and claws
to possess hens that are nothing but a bundle of
warm cackling feathers. Human men are worse;
they will risk Hell itself for a woman, not only
in the spring when all things mate, but all
through the year. They risk death to drink without being thirsty, and deal death to eat when
they are not driven by real hunger.

Her charm did nothing but draw the men she liked to her, and hold them as long as she wanted them, no more than that.

Her mind was full of two things, and both of them were important: she wanted Andrew to make the crutches for Keepsie and she wanted to know the new way to birth children. The morning was long. She would finish her work, go to see Andrew, then come home by Heaven's Gate Church where the midwife school was held.

Instead of going straight down the road, she took a path through the woods. Everything seemed silent and still, but little by little many sounds fell on her ears. Water trickled, leaves rustled, birds chirruped over their nest-building. A lizard slipped under a root to hide, a snake writhed swiftly across her path then out of sight.

The forest was the oldest thing on the plantation except the earth itself. The trees were mighty and tall, and the long gray moss almost hid the new leaf buds which pushed the old leaves off. Poplars flamed with new yellow leaves and green flower petals. Scarlet bells were falling off the supple Jack vines which had climbed high to get clear of the dark damp shade. Jessamine vines covered naked bushes and treetops under masses of yellow mist and the shadowy undergrowth was splotched with red-bud and dogwood

and crimson buckeye blooms. Nothing changed
here. The same old banks of shiny-leaved laurel
sloped down to patches of blue and white violets
and beds of white lilies. Birds sang everywhere,
and the tall pines sighed as they dropped brown
needles over their feet.

When a flock of mosquitoes hummed in front
of Mary's eyes, she brushed them away with a
smile and told them to go suck some juice out
of the tender leaves and let her blood alone. In
the distance a wild turkey hen was yelping, boldly calling for a mate. All the gobblers went
off by themselves in the winter, leaving their
women alone, but the first spring yelp sent them
flying to begin their courting in earnest.
Gobblers that had been good friends all winter
would fall out and fight, the strongest ones
taking the hens from the others. That same hen's
calling would start trouble.

Turkeys have strange ways, but perhaps no
stranger than people. Men are the queerest of
all God's creatures. Poor fools, not one of them
worth a headache, or a tear-drop, and yet, worthless as they are, by means of them her own life
had become full and her heart had grown warm
and glad again.

She was even with July at last, no matter
where he was, or what he was doing. Her heart

clutched a little when she thought of him, but a woman's heart is a foolish thing.

She stepped carefully across a narrow log that bridged the sluice between the road and the blacksmith shop, a small, black, dilapidated house whose sloping, broken roof let the evil-smelling smoke inside trickle through. A wild plum thicket that straggled up close to one corner made a bold white splash of fragrant blooms right in the face of the smoky shop-door. A crape-myrtle's new leaves were scarlet and tender. Squirrels played in a tall hickory whose bright yellow tassels made a thin screen above the old shop's ugliness, and whenever a sudden light stir of wind freed some of the pretty bits they flitted airily down. Poor things. Their time was out.

Andrew, the blacksmith, was smoking, and his pipe smelled pleasant beside the stench of the coal which floated out through the door.

Mary tapped on the outside and called timidly, "Good mawnin, Cun [Cousin] Andrew."

"Who dat?" came a quick answer, followed by a surprised and polite, "Why, how you do, Si May-e?"

Mary saw how his black eyes deepened as they fell on her with a hard fixed gaze trying to make out why she had come.

His grimy woolen shirt was open across his broad breast, and his sleeves were rolled up high, showing his powerful, brawny arms. But he looked weary. His face was lined, his lips droopy, and the hand that held his pipe was a bit unsteady. He looked different from himself, somehow.

"How you do to-day?" he asked her coldly, his eyes still taking account of her.

She met his question boldly and with a smile.

"Fine, Cun Andrew, fine. Same like a lamb a-jumpin."

More than once those same keen searching eyes had embarrassed her miserably and shamed her until she could not hold up her head, for Andrew was the deacon next in power to Brer Dee, and when they turned her out of the church, he scolded her before all the people at meeting. His reproof had cut her deeply and ever since then she had kept out of his way.

But she was older now and more experienced. She could face him easily without batting an eyelash, and she smiled pleasantly as she inquired, "How do you do yousef, Cousin? You ain' lookin so spry to-day. How-come so?"

Almost unconsciously her fingers began toying with the tiny soiled rag tied on a string around her neck, for such polite indifference as An-

drew's was something she seldom met. He was
not exactly young in years, but he still stood
tall and lean and straight, his muscles were hard,
his teeth strong and his eyes keen.

In many ways he looked better now than he
had ever looked in his whole life. The years had
added flesh to his long, lanky frame, his great
strong double joints were less gaunt and with
worry-ation softening his bright eyes, they became almost gentle. Trouble does most people
good. If they are too weak to bear it, they get
crushed but if they can stand up against it, it
makes them better, in the end. Strange how
Andrew stuck to that stupid fat Doll when
there were so many better-looking, willing
women in the world. Of course, he was a deacon,
and he had always been so severe with sinners
that he had to walk straight himself. But a little
crooked walking might do him good.

"What de matter ail you, Cousin?" she asked
him pleasantly. "You don' have to depend on
cotton for a livin and I hear-say you's got more
money dan you know what to do wid. You
ought to be happy and smilin, enty?" She said
it as softly, as gently as she could, smiling as
woman smiles when she knows her power.

He shook his head gloomily. "I has a lot o
trouble, Si May-e."

Mary laughed out, "Trouble? You has trouble? Gawd have mussy on you, Cousin. If I didn' have no more trouble'n you, I'd jump up an' crack my heels togedder wid joy. Yes, Jedus. What kinder trouble is gnawin on you to-day?"

As Andrew took up his heavy hammer and fingered it, the brawny muscles slid back and forth under the smooth black skin of his powerful arms. It was strange to see this big, strapping fellow down-hearted, for as a rule he strutted around vain as a turkey cock. Nobody was ever more sure of himself or more certain that all he did was right, nobody else had such sharp tools or such skilful, well-trained hands; but he seemed not to know just how to start telling her what his trouble was. "I declare to Gawd, Si May-e, when I think on Doll and de foolish way e done me, I git pure povoked. I ain' never had a long patience, no-how."

"Doll? Fo Gawd's sake, Cousin. You make me surprise. You an' Doll ain' lovin as two turtle doves? I didn' thought butter would much as melt in Doll's mouth, e talks so mild an' pleasant all de time."

"E didn' talk mild an' pleasant, not dis mawnin. Great Gawd, no. E like to a choked esef a-workin e tongue. All 'bout nothin, too."

Mary sighed and murmured that it was a pity for a nice useful man like himself to be worried and fretted. But some women are silly like children, and get spoiled to death if you pet them or treat them anyways soft and easy.

"You got sense, Si May-e, sense like a man." Andrew looked at her with brightening eyes, and his hands tightened their grip on the hammer's handle.

Andrew was a good housekeeper. The shop was crammed with wagon wheels in need of spokes or rims, but they stood in neat rows, one against the other.

The solid block which held the anvil had a band around its middle where punches and cold chisels and other tools stood in the pockets, where his hands could reach them without trouble or waste of time. The oak shavings were free of smut. But, Lord, the shop had an evil smell— the breath of that smoky black coal constantly. To stand near the forge was a terrible thing when Andrew turned the handle of the bellows and fanned the black coals red. If cedar smoke could cause miscarriage, what would this coal smoke do?

"Great Gawd, Cun Andrew, how-come you don' burn hickory or ash or some kind o sweet-smellin wood like you used to? How can you stand a coal fire? It stinks worse'n a blunt tail moccasin to me."

Andrew's eyes twinkled but his voice was grave. "You better smoke you pipe whilst you's here, Si May-e. Le me fill em fo you." And she handed him her pipe, making a wry face.

"I ruther smell a pole-cat, Cun Andrew."

"Me too, but don' blame me, gal. Big Boy is de one fetched coal to de shop. E will try new tings and newfangled ways. Big Boy knows more'n me or anybody to hear him talk."

"Shucks," Mary answered, as she took a tiny ember off the forge and lighted her pipe. "Big Boy'll find out some o dese days dat all de sense his skull ever will hold ain' much as you got in one lil toe-nail."

The iron in the forge slowly turned red, then white with heat as Andrew blew the bellows.

"I dunno. Big Boy is gwine to be a fine man too, Si May-e. I see plenty o signs o dat, but e's been mighty down-hearted lately. E's so raven about Seraphine, e can' rest. I keep tellin' em to wait an' see what kind o 'oman Seraphine'll be. A contrary 'oman is a hard thing to stand."

"Dat's de Gawd's truth, Cousin, but what you know bout a contrary 'oman?"

"When Doll gets e head set e gits mighty contrary," Andrew complained.

Mary puffed her pipe in silence. Her eyes were fixed on the red-hot coals, and Andrew, now fairly started, talked on and on in a vexed, aggrieved tone. He had never mistreated Doll in his life. Every year God sent when all the crops were gathered he sent her to town on the boat and let her get herself and all the children, his and hers, some clothes. She always had shoes to wear on Sundays. She always had a nice hat. He never had stinted her. He made money, but she spent it as freely as water. He had never been hard on her in any way. He provided well for her and encouraged her to pleasure herself as much as any Christian woman ought to do. He never said a word when she stayed all day at a quilting or when she marched around the fire half the night at birth-night suppers.

Andrew paused for breath and Mary put in, "You sho has been a good husband, Cousin. Everybody on de whole plantation knows dat. I ever did say Doll is de luckiest 'oman I ever seen. E got de finest man ever was for a husband, a lot o nice chillen, a good home, an' clothes, an' plenty to eat. What more could heart wish? Doll must be gone out e head if e ain' satisfy wid all dat."

Andrew's eyes narrowed at the last words and he shook his head. Doll was not satisfied. That was the whole trouble. Nobody could please her. The angel Gabriel could not please her. Instead of being satisfied with being a high-up church-member and a deacon's wife, Doll was raven to join the Bury-league. She talked about it day and night.

"Doll is spoiled. You done too much for em, Cousin. Too much. It don' pay to let a woman run over you. If you do, before long Doll will stop an' wipe e feet on you."

Andrew nodded slowly. Mary was right. She knew Doll, but he was going to teach Doll a lesson. She'd find out he was no feeble fool to run after her and be a slave for her. She could stay right where she was the rest of her days before he'd ever go one step to fetch her home.

"Whe e is, Cousin? Whe Doll dey? Fo Gawd's sake, you don' mean dat fool 'oman is gone an' left you! How-come so?"

Andrew tilted his hat a bit farther back and squared himself with his feet farther apart to tell Mary about the whole thing. Doll never could understand that men and women are different creatures. God made them different at the very start. He did not make men to sit down at home and patch and sew and quilt. Mary smiled. Of course, God didn't make men so, and she for one was glad of it. She never could stand to have a man hanging around the house. Men had business to be out working and doing what men were meant to do.

Andrew said Doll couldn't see it that way, not that he ever craved running around day or night. When the crops were growing and the grass growing with them, he stayed right in the field behind his plow keeping them clean. But when his potatoes were all dug and banked, his peas picked, his corn gathered and put in the barn, his cane ground and made into molasses, he got tired sitting at home every night from first dark until time to go to bed with nobody to talk to but Doll and the children. The nights were too long. One winter night was as long as three June nights.

Doll could sleep from first dark until sunrise, but if he went to bed early he couldn't sleep until daybreak to save his life. He twisted and turned like a worm in hot ashes and his bones pure hurt from lying in bed so long. Sometimes he walked out at night and visited the neighbors, but here lately Doll began sticking out her mouth and complaining of being lonesome. Last night she got so vexed she wouldn't talk to him at all. She just swelled up like a toad-fish and sat and looked at the fire without cracking her teeth.

This morning she looked so mean and cross he asked her what ailed her. At first she would not answer him, but after a while she said she was tired of the way he ran around at night. What she said was not so bad as the way she said it. Doll knew he did not run around at night. She was vexed because he would not go buy her an auto-mobile. She rode in one last summer when she went to town on the excursion and she had not given him any peace since then. The ugly, old, worn-out, second-hand thing would cost as much as his whole share-crop of cotton would make in five years. It was fit for nothing but to run into the first ditch it saw and break her neck or her insides.

Money burned Doll. With her, it was easy come, easy go, as if his field still made a bale of cotton to the acre. Doll wanted to spend every cent instead of burying some in the ground to keep for hard times.

Mary listened thoughtfully. Doll was wrong. God did not intend for people to act so. He gave them feet and the ground to walk on. If they get in a hurry or have a long distance to go, He has provided mules and oxen to hitch to wagons and buggies. People ought to stand still and think.

"And pray, too," Andrew added solemnly.

"Fo times is changed, an' de change ain' fo de better. Looka de Bury-league. De plantation ain' de same since it come here."

"You right, Cousin?"

Andrew drew a deep sigh. Friends used to look after one another on the plantation. If you got sick your friends came and sat up with you and rubbed you; Daddy Cudjoe made root tea and dosed you and got you well. If you died they closed your eyes and shrouded you and nailed clean new boards into a box to hold you. When they dug your grave they let the sun set in it before they laid you away in the earth.

If sickness seizes a person now, unless he belongs to a Bury-league society, he is not counted for a thing. He can die and get buried the best way he can. He may be a member of the church, in good standing, or even a deacon or a deacon's wife, but unless he joins the Bury-league and keeps his dues all paid up, he gets no attention. The Bury-league sisters and brothers sit up with the worst sinners now and pray over them and listen to all their last words, the same as if they were Christian people. When sinners drop off into their last sleep, they have a store-bought shroud and lie in a fine store-bought box varnished up and painted like a bureau with a glass window in it to show their wicked faces. The

'Bury-league members don't care how much the preacher preaches sinners to Hell. They are too brazen to care.

They think about nothing but marching and speaking and singing, and wearing white gloves. Women who are hardly decent put on white waists and black skirts and black sailor hats, and journey round and round people's graves, saying words that are written in a book. Strange words instead of the words Jesus told people to say. Before the dust settles they put up a fifteen-dollar tombstone with your name on it. And the dues are high. Every time somebody dies you pay an extra tax of fifty cents. People die fast these days too. They don't wait for plain sickness to cut them down. They run around and find ways to meet sudden death.

He had told Doll all these things as plain as he could. He told her again this morning but instead of listening to him she stuck out her mouth. The way she did made him hot all over and he all but slapped her then, but he didn't. He just told her to pull in her lip and keep it pulled in. Then, Doll jumped up and said he had better pull in his own. He, Andrew, her lawful husband, and a deacon in the church, too, had to take such slack talk as that from Doll.

Mary turned aside to smile, but she made her

voice sound as kind as she could. "It must a been hard for you to take it, Cousin. Mighty hard. All dis you tell me sho makes me surprise. Doll ain' got de sense I thought e had. Not by a long shot."

But wait; he hadn't told her all yet. Doll got so vexed with him she bawled out loud enough for everybody a mile off to hear, and she the wife of a deacon in Heaven's Gate Church. Then, and he hated to tell this—but Doll cursed him for a stingy old fool.

The words didn't have a chance to get cold off her tongue before he hauled off and slapped her dumb. No woman has a right to call a man such a thing, even if she is married to him. No woman could call him so and not get her face slapped good and hard, free-handed as he was.

But, Lord, the devil was turned loose then. Words ran out of Doll's mouth faster than water runs down the gully after rain. She screamed and hollered and carried on until she was too hoarse to whisper. Nobody could stop her or do a thing with her. The more she talked, the more she said.

When she ran into the shed room he paid no heed to her until he heard a strange fuss. He got there just in time to see Doll grab up every bit of the rations and throw them out of the win-

dow into the yard. All the grits and meal and
bacon, all the rice and sugar and coffee. Every
God's thing he had bought to feed her and the
children and himself for a whole week. He had
taken some corn all the way down to the end
of the Neck to get it ground on a water mill because Doll liked water-ground meal more than
meal ground by a steam-engine. God knew he
ever had tried to please the woman.

When she finished throwing away all the rations, he thought she would cool down some, but
she wasn't satisfied yet. She ran out in the yard
and before he could hinder her, she chopped
down all the potato banks with a hoe. Chopped
every single bank right in the top where the corn-
stalks stuck out to let the air in. Then she flew
to the wood-pile and got the ax and gave the big
iron wash-pot one awful lick. The poor thing
pure bellowed when the ax hit it, for a great hole
broke in its side.

Mary was shocked sure enough now. "De best
wash-pot on dis whole place, Cousin. I declare
to Gawd I too hate it myself. I was aimin to
borrow dat pot de next time I kill a hog. How's
Doll gwine to boil clothes now? How's e gwine
to try out lard?"

Andrew grunted. Doll would never wash any
more clothes for him in this world or kill another

hog out of his pen, for when she had done all that devilment she left and only God knew where she went. But she could stay right there until Gabriel blew his trumpet for all he cared. He'd never ask her to come back. Never as long as he was in his right mind.

Mary listened, puffing at her pipe now and then, thinking the matter over. Andrew was wrong.

"Mens is different from womens, Cousin, but all o we has two minds, enty?"

Andrew agreed it was so.

"I got two, you got two, an' Doll's got two, enty?" Andrew started to speak but she stopped him, "Wait a minute, Cousin; you's willin to own Doll's got two minds de same as you, enty?"

He was.

"One o Doll's minds is good an' sensible, de other is mischeevous, enty?"

Perhaps so.

"All whilst you was talkin to me, a-tellin me 'bout Doll, all two o my minds was speakin. One mind say, 'Doll is a mean 'oman;' de other mind say, 'Doll is a po pitiful creeter. E can' stand for Andrew to go off to see anybody else after dark.' My first mind say, 'Tell Andrew to don' never fool wid Doll, not no more,' but my second mind say, 'Tell Andrew fo Gawd's sake

go hitch up a mule an' wagon an' fetch Doll back
home.' Doll's a-lookin down the road fo you
right dis minute, Cousin. Evy time Doll sees a
dust a-risin e heart jumps inside e breast a-hopin
dat dust is you."

Andrew's eyes widened and he stopped quite
still to think it over. "Si May-e, you's a good
'oman. You got a good heart, even if you is
de wickedest sinner Gawd ever made."

Mary grinned. "I ain' so wicked, Cousin,
neither so good. You's a man an' I's a 'oman.
You want to have all de pleasure, an' don' leave
me an' Doll none. Dat ain' right, church or no
church. Gawd ain' gwine be too hard on people
what misses an' makes mistakes sometimes.
You'll see. But you better go fetch Doll home.
An', Cousin,"—Mary laughed, smiled right up
into Andrew's eyes,—"if I was you, you know
what I'd do?"

"What, gal?"

"I'd go beg Doll's pardon."

"Beg em pardon?"

"Dat is what I say."

"But I ain' done Doll no wrong."

"It don' matter who done right or wrong. If
you would go humble like to Doll an' beg em
pardon, it would do em an' you all-two good."

Andrew wasn't convinced, but Mary persisted.

"What's done is done. You can' change em. You may as well make de best o em."

Andrew stayed dumb as a clam.

"You must be forgot how you licked Doll on you weddin-night, enty, Cousin?"

"I didn't lick em so much. I was just lettin em know I was gwine to rule em. Dat was all."

"Den why don' you rule em, if you know how?"

"Times is changed, Si May-e. Womens is changed too. Nobody can' rule a 'oman by switchin em dese days. Dey hides is pure tough. A leather strap can' sweeten em now."

Andrew did not see that Mary covered up a smile under her hand, for he was making her a comfortable seat by turning upside down a broken wash-tub which was waiting to have a new band put around it.

He began bending a steel rod into a smooth strong link and Mary drew her skirts to one side for the sparks flew wildly about under the beating of the heavy hammer.

She liked to watch Andrew's big hands ruling the hot metal and molding it into a pattern. The rumbling boom of his deep voice was pleasant. His skin was as smooth and black as her own and in spite of his height and bulk he moved as easily as a cat. Suddenly his eyes lifted and looked straight at her.

"How-come you named you cripple boy Keepsie, Si May-e? Dat's a new name to me."

The smoke from Mary's pipe curled into a
curious shape which broke and faded as she drew
in a sudden breath. She hated to answer the
question truthfully, yet if she lied, Andrew
would know it.

"You ever did hear of a town named Pough-
keepsie?"

Andrew had not.

"Well, it's a town up-north."

Andrew nodded, then waited for her to go on.

"Keepsie's daddy come from Pough-keepsie."

"Who e is?"

"When I went to town on de excursion long
time ago, I met em."

"You ain' seen em since?"

"Not since."

Andrew reflected and nodded his head. Since
Keepsie had no daddy to provide crutches for
him, he would be glad to make them. He would
put all his other work aside and start them as
soon as he got Keepsie's measure. Big Boy
would go to the swamp and get the right kind
of ash wood, so the crutches would be both stout
and light. Together, they would soon get them
made. And maybe after this Seraphine would
treat Big Boy with more manners.

"When did Seraphine ever mistreat Big Boy?"

"Last Sat'day when e went all de way to town to see em."

"What Seraphine done, Cousin?"

"Seraphine wouldn' much as come out an' speak to em."

The morning was warm and the air in the shop was hot from the fire in the forge, but cold sweat broke out on Mary and chilled her the same as if Andrew poured a bucket of spring water over her. Fear stabbed her to the heart. Seraphine was always so glad to see anybody from home, why would she not come out and speak to Big Boy?

"How-come Big Boy ain' told me how Seraphine done?"

"Big Boy ain' had de heart to tell you." Andrew's eyes shot a swift look at Mary's face then went back to the hot white rod which shed scales of red-hot skin every time that it was given a twist.

"Big Boy is wrong, somehow, Cousin. Seraphine wouldn' miss seein em, not fo gold. Seraphine is a good manners-able gal, an' e ever was raven over Big Boy."

"So much book readin might be changed Seraphine from how e was, Si May-e."

Mary could not answer that. Book reading

is an unnatural thing, and it might have gone to
Seraphine's head fo-true.

Andrew plunged the piece of steel into a tub
of water and the sigh he made was almost as deep
as its hissing. Women have got to be strange
things these days. They don't need book
reading to make them act crazy. All they
want is enough money to buy themselves cake
and candy and bottle-drinks and stuff to sweeten
their mouths and rot out their teeth. They were
not satisfied to ruin their feet wearing shoes
every day, but they wanted irons to straighten
their hair and grease to lighten their skins.

"Seraphine ain' like dat, Cousin. Seraphine
is a sensible gal. E do wear shoes lately fo-true,
by e got such a awful splinter in e heel de last
time e danced barefeeted. But e skin is black
an' e teeth is solid as my own. Soon as e gits a
depluma e's comin straight home to stay."

"Wha dat you call a depluma, Si May-e?"

"Gawd knows what e is, Cousin. I ain' never
see one in my life, but Seraphine craves to get
one, I know dat."

"If dat is what Seraphine craves, I hope e
won' be disappoint."

The big boat was coming up the river, bellow-
ing and splashing water like a great vexed alligator. The day was passing. Mary must go.

And yet the news about Seraphine had rooted her feet to the ground so she could hardly pull them up and move them.

"De day is young, Si May-e. It ain' middle-day, not yet. What's you hurry?"

"I'm gwine by Heaven's Gate road, Cousin. Dat's a long ways home."

"Is you comin to Heaven's Gate Friday night?"

"I might. I ain' certain."

"You better come see de place whe you is gwine some o dese days."

"Who? Me?" Mary laughed. "Lawd, Cousin, when you gets to Heaven I'm gwine to be waitin for you, ready to set right by you side."

"I hope so. I hope you will, gal."

The cool air outside was full of delicious scents which were all the more pleasant after the horrid smell of Andrew's shop with its black coal smoke. Mary sniffed it, then breathed it in deep before she started walking swiftly on the road leading toward Heaven's Gate Church.

New leaves, fragrant weeds and grasses were reaching up to catch all they could of the day's yellow sunshine. A light breeze full of summer softness floated in from the rice-fields and, snatching at the strong sweet smoke Mary pulled out of her pipe, swept it away, then climbed up

and whirled some of the yellow tassels down
from the trees.

Mary was worried. What in God's world
ailed Seraphine? Big Boy was a fine-looking
fellow. When he got on his Sunday clothes
and tilted his hat over on one side, any girl would
be glad to get him for a husband. She must try
to straighten Seraphine out somehow. She would
go to Daddy Cudjoe and get a love-charm for
Big Boy to use on Seraphine and cure her of
any foolish notions book reading had put into
her head.

Meantime, she might try her own hand at
working a spell on Big Boy's daddy. Andrew
was a fine-looking fellow. Such a proudful fellow too. She would like to see him humble just
once. One time would not do him any harm.

She would have to be careful, for he was fiery-
tempered and headstrong, and if she displeased
him he would make her rue the day she ever
crossed his path. He had the name of being a
good friend but a mean and heartless enemy.
He liked to think he set an example which ought
to be followed by every other man on the plantation, but the strongest men were weak before
her little cloth conjure rag. If it failed to put a
hand on Andrew it would be because he was such
a faithful Christian man, always praying and

singing holy hymns and abusing sinners and sin. If she did fail to get a spell laid on him, it made no difference. Plenty of other men were in the world, and the difference between one man and another does not amount to a very great deal. There had been a few men she preferred to all the rest for a day or a week; some as long as a year, because they were kinder or stronger or maybe weaker and more in need of what she had to give, but not one of them had ever satisfied her long at a time. Not one, although she had always picked the best.

Men are too much alike, with ways too much the same. None is worth keeping, none worth a tear; and still each one is a little different from the rest; just different enough to make him worth finding out. Everybody has a selfness that makes the root of his life and being.

If getting men, taking them from their rightful owners, had been hard work, she would never have bothered about it; but it was such an easy thing. All she had to do was call them with a look, or a smile, or the wave of a hand. Sometimes with no more than a glance. Whichever man she wanted came running, whether he was old or young, sinner or church-member. All she had to do was to wear that little charm on a string around her neck as it was to-day.

Most of the women who had grown up in the

Quarters with her were fat and logy or skinny
and sharp. Thank God, she had kept supple
and young. The years had been easy on the
others and hard on her, but toil and carrying
heavy loads had hardened her sinews and length-
ened her wind and kept her body lean and slim.
She could swing an ax and cut the toughest wood
for hours at a time without a taint of weariness.
She could jerk a hoe day after day through the
hottest sunshine. She could pick cotton with
the best and come home at night as cheerful and
fresh as when she waked at dawn. Thank God!

Instead of going straight into the Big Road,
she chose to leave that at one side for a narrow
path which made a short-cut through the neigh-
boring woods, where everything was silent and
still. Hardly a leaf or blade of grass trembled as
they reached up to catch the light, and forest
shadows made a dark veil across the damp earth.

Mary walked on, fast at first, then more
slowly, for she had two heavy loads to carry this
morning, her unborn child, and her heart full of
fear that something had gone wrong with Seraphine. Poor little girl. How little she knew now
of life, of people, of her own self for that matter.
The tall old trees let no sunshine fall on the path,
and only a narrow strip of sky showed overhead.
The earth smelled moldy under the trees.

The road gave a narrow white glimpse of the

Big House at the end of the long avenue. Whenever she wanted to be by herself a while, in
some quiet place so she could think, she went
and sat on one of the old stone benches in the
weed-grown flower garden; nobody would disturb her.

The great silent house looked grand and
solemn, with its high gray roof and tall red chimneys. She had a timid feeling when she walked
near it or sat alone in the garden, lest a ghost of
somebody who once lived there, a servant or one
of the fine white ladies, should call out to her and
ask her what she wanted.

The plantation owners, had lived there many
a year, ruling the land and the tides in the rice-
fields as firmly as they ruled the black people
whom they bought and sold as freely as they
did the mules which slept in the great open
stables and ate out of long wooden troughs.
Black people used to make up a part of the plantation's wealth the same as the carriage and sad-
dle horses with their well-rubbed, shining hides.

They were valued according to their strength
and sense. The weak and stupid were sold.
Only the best were kept. A good thing. Mary
could see it now. The white people were gone.
The forest had taken back many of their fields,

the river had swallowed their rice-fields, but the
black people were used to hardship and they lived
on here and throve. Her mother had been born
here and her grandmother and all the other
women before them right on back to the first ones
who were brought long ago up the river from the
town where a slave market gave them and other
black people to the rice- and cotton-fields. She
had got her health and strength and vigor from
them.

The same old cabins housed them. The same
old fields had taken their days. Sunshine and
work, darkness and rest, that was all they had,
and there would be nothing else in the world to-
day if a body did not stop to pleasure a little now
and then. Yet, work is good, and sunshine is
good, even when its scorching heat burns backs
and the soles of bare feet. It freshens weakness
and brings back strength, and the field which
takes time and labor gives back pay enough to
make life pleasant.

A crooked old rose-tree had covered its knotted
black limbs with red blossoms which were sweet
with honey. Bees hummed eagerly over them,
then settled on them, searching them, walking
through them with bold brown legs, shattering
them and scattering them on the ground. Bees

don't mind if they hurt rose-blossoms, for when
those blossoms fell they'd go somewhere else to
find honey.

Mary sighed. She loved the sunshine. Its
warmth and brightness lulled her, soothed her,
but the bees—they buzzed so. They might sting
her. She'd go.

CHAPTER XXII

THE last time Mary was turned out of the church, she swore she would never darken the door of Heaven's Gate again, but now as the old building came in sight and a cloud of dust rose right in front of it, and a great booming and buzzing and puffing made the day quiver, curiosity filled her. An automobile was moving away from the church, swerving and rolling into the big road taking along with it a cloud of smoke. The birthing lesson was over, the teacher was going away. The midwives—Mary counted twelve of them—stood out in the churchyard watching. They all stood motionless until scarcely a sound was left, then they turned about and went back inside the church.

The cool morning wind fluttered their wide white aprons and their long full skirts, and tugged at the broad-brimmed hats they all wore perched uncertainly on top of their bandanna covered heads. They moved slowly as if they were in a trance. No wonder. That new birthing law was enough to addle their brains.

Through the open church door, Mary could

see them all chattering at once, bobbing their heads until their hats threatened to topple off into their laps. Only Maum Hannah sat still and silent with her old head bowed. She shook it slowly now and then as the others discussed something earnestly. They were arguing with her, that was plain, but she was holding out firm.

Mary was no midwife and she had no intention of ever being one, but the church is a public place and if the door is left wide open anybody has a right to walk in and sit down to rest. And if there is a new and easy way to birth children, surely nobody had a better right than she to find out how it was done, whether she practised it or not.

Twelve women were already in the church, she made thirteen. It was a risk to go in. Mary stepped silently inside the door, then halted a minute to let her heart slow down a little, for a delicious suspense which was almost like fear had it thumping hard in her breast. Her wind was short, her breathing hurried, and her blood running fast and hot. The midwives were so engrossed in their talk that nobody saw her as she walked slowly up the aisle, between the long rows of empty brown benches, to where they all sat huddled in a group near the pulpit. Doll was there too, and when her sharp eyes glanced around and saw Mary she cried out, "Fo Gawd's sake, looka who's come!" The talk hushed. Maum Hannah must have been crying, for she took an apron-string and wiped her eyes so she could see. Something bad had happened, for more tears ran out to take the place of those that were wiped away.

Maum Hannah couldn't talk and the others seemed all excited, but no sooner had their astonished eyes turned on her than Mary felt herself suddenly strengthened. Face to face with that group of failing black women, some of them fat, some of them shriveled, she felt young, firm-bodied, a part of the fresh outside day. The church was cold with a damp chilly smell, but the blood in her veins rippled warm now. Life burned bright within her, making her feel young, strong, and light on her feet in spite of the troublesome burden she carried.

"How yunnuh all do dis mornin?" she asked politely, and a shower of answers greeted her.

"Come in, honey. I too glad to see you." Maum Hannah said over and over. "Too glad! Too glad."

"I'm too sorry you didn' got here sooner."

"Sooner! Great Gawd, I'm glad e didn'," Doll cried out. "If Si May-e had a walked in dis church befo dat fine lady from up-north, a-lookin like e looks, I would a been so shame I couldn' a held up my head to hear what e was a-sayin."

Maum Hannah made room on the bench and beckoned to Mary to come sit beside her.

"Come set down, Si May-e, I'm glad to see you. I need you to walk home wid me dis mawnin. I'm dat weakened down, I couldn' go dat far by mysef."

The old voice quivered pitifully and a lump came in Mary's own throat as she saw how the drops trickled out from under the shriveled eyelids and rolled down the wrinkled old cheeks.

"What de matter ail you, Auntie? Who dat hurted you feelins so you got to cry? You don' like de new way you got to catch chillen?"

As she sat down beside Maum Hannah the narrow bench creaked sharply with the added weight. Mary jumped with a startled laugh, in which all the others but Doll joined. "Do Jedus! Don' let dis bench fall down wid me to-day!" she cried out.

"Fo Gawd's sake, don' make no mistake in dis church to-day, Si May-e. Dis is Gawd's house," Doll warned, but Mary declared there was no danger.

"Dat bench don' like to hold up sich a heavy load o sin, Si May-e," Doll suggested sourly, but Mary gave Doll a pleasant smile and told her that the bench would not have to hold its load very long. She had just happened to be passing by and when she saw that the church door was wide open, she stopped in to rest herself a minute.

"You sho look like you would need some rest. You better had go home an' hide."

"Dis child is a load fo-true, de heaviest one I ever carried yet." Mary still kept her temper although Doll's talk rasped her.

"You is gwine to have twins, enty," Doll suggested, but even this met with a polite answer.

"If you say so, Sister Doll. You knows a awful lot. Nothing couldn' please me better. I ever did wish my chillen could come in a litter. Havin' em one at a time is awful slow; it takes so long to get a house full. I been at it gwine on mighty nigh twenty years now."

Doll stared at her trying to shame her, but Mary talked on pleasantly.

Birthing children was not so bad. It was as easy for her as to pop her fingers, but she wanted to have some gal sleep once more. Good, sweet, quiet sleep. It had been many a long year since she had had one single night of it.

"When you gwine to stop a-sinnin, Si May-e?" Doll asked with a hiss on the edge of her words.

"When I get tired seein pleasure. A lot o mighty fine men round here ain' so awful satisfied wid dey wives. I might try one more round befo I stop fo good."

"Shut you mout', May-e. You can' talk such brazen talk in de house o Gawd. You must be forgot, enty?" Doll's tubby body, her husky, breathy voice, her little sharp eyes all made Mary feel suddenly cross.

"When did Gawd appint you to run His house, Doll?" she snapped out before she knew it.

Doll answered that she would rather live without a drop of bacon grease for her bread or a speck of molasses for sweetened water than to be like Mary with a pack of men for ever at her heels and bringing a poor little fatherless child into the world every other year God sent. Hatred for Doll scraped against Mary's heart.

She felt like slapping her. "Don' fret about me, Doll. You don' have but one man when I has a plenty, but dat don' make you so much better'n me. I couldn' stand to have de same man a-snorin in my face evy night Gawd sends. No Lawd. I rather change. I like to shoot down de ducks as dey rise. But I don' forget my manners like some women I know. I treats my men fine. When I sees em a-feelin down-hearted I cheers em up and sends em off a-struttin wid dey hats pure cocked on one side. You don' treat dat one man you got half-way decent. You got em all worried in his mind an' fretted half to death right now. Is you call dat bein a Christian?"

"What you got to say 'bout dem poor nameless chillen you got?"

Mary leaned back and laughed.

"Do fo Gawd's sake, Doll, don' talk so fool. My chillen come into dis world by de same road as you own. You know dat good as me. You own don' travel a bit easier road 'n my own either. Not a bit."

"Well, I can say dis much, Si May-e, July done right when e left you. You is pure slippery as okra."

"Ki, Doll," Mary said scornfully, "you's a fool." She sucked her teeth and all the women straightened up.

Maum Hannah took her hand. "You ain' to talk such a talk, Si May-e. De Book say if we call nobody a fool, Gawd would burn we in Hell-fire. *Fool* is a awful sinful word. Honey, do don' say em no more."

The women began murmuring, nodding their heads.

"Dat's de Gawd's truth, Auntie."

"You's right to talk to Si May-e."

"Si May-e is a heavy case in dis world."

"A heavy case fo-true."

Mary raised her arms and tightened her head-kerchief. "You have to excuse me, Auntie. Doll got me vexed an' befo I knew it de word slipped out my mouth. But if Doll had any manners e wouldn' be throwin up July's name to me, an' blowin at me like a porpoise."

"You must be forgot July's my own brother, enty?" Doll snapped out.

"No, I ain' forgot, Doll. An' I ain' forgot July used to be my own lawful husband too. Reverend Duncan read out o de Book over me an' July, but July didn' count dat readin no more'n air. Not July. E went off wid Cinder just de same as if e was a single man. Just de same. An' Cinder was my own second cousin, too. But July left Cinder de same way." Mary laughed carelessly. "No 'oman livin couldn' keep a some-time man like July."

"De Lawd have mussy," Maum Hannah sighed, and the other women stirred uneasily.

Mary loosened the string which held her full skirts tied up short, then she straightened up.

"Let me tell yunnuh someting. July's been gone a long time. I don' know whe e is, an' I don' care. But if de boat yonder on de river would fetch em home to-day, cold an' stiff in a

box, I could look at em same as if e was a
stranger. Not a drop o water wouldn' drean out
my eyes."

Maum Hannah jumped.

"Jedus, gal, you pure scare me when you talk
such a talk. Gawd'll make you eat dem same
words yet. No matter whe you is, or whe July
is, yunnuh two is man an' wife. You can' change
dat. When Gawd joins people togedder nothin
can' put em apart. Nothin. Not even sin."

"How long is July been gone, Si May-e?" one
of the midwives asked.

Mary reflected. She could not remember
exactly. Seraphine was in her sixteenth year
now, so July must have been gone over sixteen
years.

"How much chillen you had since July went?"
asked another one.

"Plenty, sister, an' all of em is a-livin an'
a-growin fine. Most of em big enough to work
evy day. We has plenty to eat, plenty to wear,
plenty to pleasure wid too."

"Mind how you brag, Si May-e," Maum Hannah warned.

"I ain' braggin, Auntie. All dis I'm tellin is
de Gawd's truth. Me an' my chillen don' need
no man. We can git on better widout em. I
can easy pick three hundred pound o cotton in a

day. I can hoe a acre clean o grass quick as any 'oman on de whole plantation. I done birthed all my chillen de old way an' I ain' never had a backache in my life."

Nobody answered this, and Mary looked Doll in the eyes.

"I know yunnuh talks about me behind my back, but I don' mind. Talk all you want to. I ain' no member o de church. I been baptized an' I been a member four different times in my life. A member, de same as you. When I git old an' tired seein pleasure, I'm gwine to seek and pray an' be a member again."

She looked around and smiled.

"If I was fat or either old, I might would settle down, but, tank Gawd, I ain' neither one. Not yet."

Maum Hannah got stiffly to her feet.

"Come on, gal," she said, taking Mary by the arm, "le's go home. Gawd's house ain' no place fo sinful talk."

"Befo I go I want to hear how to birth chillen de new lawful way, Auntie."

"Don' let's talk dat talk now, not till we get out o Gawd's house. It ain' decent. No. It ain' fitten to hear. I declare to Gawd, it made me have sin to hear about em."

"You had sin, Auntie? I bet you ain' sinned, not in forty years."

Mary could not help laughing, but Maum
Hannah looked very sad. "You's wrong, honey,
I sins all de time. Every breath I breathe, every
word I say is a sin. Dat's how-come I have to
pray so much an' ask Him up yonder to help me
be faithful an' hold out to de end." She wiped
her eyes and got to her feet. Mary took her arm,
and together they went down the aisle and down
the steps of Heaven's Gate Church.

The misery in Maum Hannah's knee was
much worse since she heard the indecent things
the white people wanted the midwives to do when
they caught children.

"You ought to sit down, at home, Auntie, an'
let de misery rest."

Maum Hannah shook her head. Sitting still
was the worst thing for it. She needed to stir
around. A bed or a chair will trick you if you
stay still on them long at a time. They will
draw out your strength and leave you weak as
water. A hot earthworm poultice would help her
to shed the misery. It always helped her. When
she got home she would brew some green walnut
tea and get Keepsie to pour it on the ground
near Ben's wood-pile where the worms were
thick. They'd rise up and he could get her a
plenty for a poultice. Earthworms are fine
things to run out pains and miseries. Thank
God for making plenty of them.

"Tell me what de lady said, Auntie."

"I can' talk dat talk, honey. No. But I'll tell you dis much; de lady had a razor wid em. E took em out an' showed em right in de house o Gawd. E say all de midwives must carry razors. Great Gawd. Dat is one sinful 'oman in dis world. Honey, I hate to say a harm word, but dat 'oman ain' decent to come in a church."

CHAPTER XXIII

On Friday Mary was washing clothes at the spring. The tubs were set close beside a tree whose shade was thick that morning, but the sun had crept around and was shining hot and bright on her back. She was wet through with sweat, but she made up her mind not to stop until she was through. She might not get to wash for herself again soon. Her time was getting short. The next change in the moon might be the time. Surely she could not go much longer.

This was the heaviest child she had ever carried—somehow the strongest one, too. She raised herself from bending over the tubs, straightened her back, and with a smile patted her distended body and said gently, "You gittin tired, enty? I tired too. Me most ready though. Po creeter! I gittin dese same tings ready fo you. You don' know dat, but it's so. Po ting, shut up in de dark—you soon gwine git you work finished, too—soon, same as me."

With a heavy sigh, she rolled her sleeves a little higher and bent over the tubs again.

She did not hear steps behind her and when

Big Boy spoke to her, she turned with a start.

"Gawd! How you scared me!" she said with a laugh. "How you do, son?"

"Oh, I'm well, considerin, Si May-e. Pa sent me to ax if you didn' want to go to Heaven's Gate Church to-night?"

Mary straightened up and looked at him with a grin. "How-come Andrew sent me a answer like dat. E knows I'm gwine. I pure want to see de picture o Hell. I'm raven to see Hell."

"Well, Pa tell me to say we got a automobile now so you could have de buggy to ride in if Budda Ben would go long wid you to drive de mule. Pa say it might do you good to ride out."

Mary looked at Big Boy and smiled. "Tell you Daddy I'm much obliged. I b'lieve I will ride, I b'lieve I will," she said slowly. "But how-come you's in such a hurry, son. Stay a while an' talk wid me an' tell me what you see in town."

But Big Boy hurried away.

When the buggy with Mary and Budda Ben reached the church, a large crowd was already gathered there. People were thick in the church-yard, and all the doors and windows were jammed. The Bury-league had turned out, and the members were marching and singing until the picture was ready to show. Solemn black faces dripping with sweat were wiped with sleeves to keep from soiling the white gloves that covered the awkward unaccustomed hands.

A dark cloud looming in the west, hiding the sky, was cleft at frequent intervals by sharp zigzag lightning.

"Lawd, it's gwine to storm," Mary murmured nervously, and Budda whispered that he ever had heard when a Christian was buried, rain always fell in the grave. Maybe all this marching and singing by the Bury-league was stirring up the clouds and making them think somebody was dead. "No, Budda, no," Mary replied scornfully, "I seen rain fall plenty o time in a sinner grave when nobody wasn' makin a sound. Clouds can' see an' hear like people."

Budda did not argue the question.

"Le's hitch de mule, Budda," she said. "Le's hitch em to dis saplin. De lightnin's too close to hitch em to a big tree. Le's get out."

"Mind, 'oman! Don' trip. I don't want nothin to happen here dis night. Great Gawd! what you would do!"

Both of them laughed behind their hands at the thought of Mary's tripping as they joined a crowd near a window. "How you all dis evenin?" they asked.

"I well, how you?" came many answers.

The Bury-league marchers were moving toward the church door.

"Dey better hurry," Mary whispered as she watched the black, swift-moving cloud. As she spoke a blinding flash of lightning was followed by a deafening crash of thunder. The singing marchers moved faster. Reverend Duncan walked bareheaded at the head of them, and his hymn book was open, ready to begin the service.

Mary was glad to see Andrew coming toward them with his hand reaching out to shake theirs and a pleasant smile on his face.

"I'm glad to see yunnuh is come out to-night. Mighty glad. I saved two good places for you to sit. Come right on inside de church. Big Boy is a-sittin on all two until you get dere."

Andrew went in first, Mary next, and Budda followed them down the aisle right to the Amen corner where their seats were.

Mary could see that the whole congregation was amazed. The Bury-league people who were marching in stared so hard at her that they almost forgot to sing. Some of them tripped and stumbled, so surprised were they to see Budda Ben and herself, the two toughest sinners in the whole country, escorted in by Andrew.

A great white cloth was stretched in front of

the pulpit, and Reverend Duncan took his place in front of that to read out of the Book how scarlet sins could be made white as snow. It was a beautiful reading, and with the lightning flashing and the thunder crashing outside it sounded so solemn it reached clear down to the bottom of Mary's heart. "Though you sins be as scarlet, they shall be as white as snow." Reverend Duncan said nobody living could know how hot Hell was. He said that if all the stumps in the world, not only the stumps on this plantation, but all in the whole world, were dug up and put in a pile; and all the coal down in the bowels of the earth taken out and piled on top those stumps; then all the kerosene and gasoline and gun-powder in the world poured over the pile and set on fire; a sinner who had been in Hell no longer than three short weeks would freeze to death in ten minutes in a fire so cool as that.

The picture of Hell began with clouds of smoke coming out of a bottomless pit; smoke that was far blacker than the smoke from the river boat, and God knew that was black enough. Mary could smell it, and the stench of it was like coal-smoke mixed with burned feathers. It all but choked her. She had to cough to get her breath. Then, Satan's black head, with two horns like a bull, and grinning tusks like a boar hog, rose up out of the smoke which gradually cleared away until the awful fire from which it came could be seen.

Hundreds of devils smaller than Satan, and all of them with horns and long forked tails, danced around in front of the fire waving their pitchforks and making horrible faces at each other. Mary was almost afraid to look at them for fear she might mark her child on them, and yet she could not pull her eyes away.

As the poor pitiful sinners were dropped down, one at a time, through the mouth of Hell, the devils took them up on their pitchforks and stuck them down in the fire and burned them until they turned to little black creatures no bigger than hop-toads. They hopped and hopped around in the fire until Mary was so sorry for them she wanted to cry. All her life she had heard that sinners had to hop in hell, but she had never understood how awful it was until now.

When the people in the church saw all those terrible things the women began screaming. Some of them fainted and some of them went off into trances. The men were kept busy holding them and trying to comfort them. Mary was scared half to death herself, and she might have

fainted too, but Doll who had a seat not very far
from her began carrying on so, jumping up and
down and shouting for help, that Mary felt she
must help Big Boy try to keep the woman from
dying, for Andrew paid her no attention at all.

If the Hell part of the picture had not been cut
off then, to show a picture of Jesus, only God
himself knows what might have happened. As
likely as not the church would have been
full of corpses, but Jesus, a kind-looking white
gentleman with a beard and long hair like a
lady, all dressed in a long baptizing robe, looked
so harmless that everybody felt better at once.

Then Reverend Duncan got up and read out
of the Book how Jesus said, "Come unto me, all
ye that labor and are heavy laden, and I will
give you rest. Take my yoke upon you, and
learn of me; for I am meek and lowly in heart."

Before he finished reading, the people were
falling over themselves running up to the
mourners' bench, yelling and crying, calling on
Jesus to have mercy on them, and forgive them
their sins. Not only women and children, but
big, broad-shouldered men, the toughest boldest
sinners, got down on their knees and begged
Jesus to save them from torment. Their words
fell thick as the heavy rain-drops on the church
roof, but their prayers and weeping were feeble

things beside the great peals of thunder that
crashed down from the sky.

God was talking. Each terrible roar shook
the church. The glass windows shivered and
rattled, and the wind whirled and lashed the
trees. Budda Ben turned and twisted and
groaned, and kept looking behind him at the
glass windows which let the glares of lightning
shine right in on his back.

"I have hear-say glass draws lightnin, Si
May-e."

Mary shook her head. She didn't know. She
had never been around glass in her life. So much
glass did look dangerous.

Then she thought of the Big House with glass
windows all over it and all kinds of glass inside;
looking-glasses and chandeliers hung with hundreds of pieces of glass. Lightning had never
struck it, and it had stood there a hundred years.
"No use to fret, Budda."

Just as she said it a pain hit her so hard she
groaned, "Do, Jedus, have mercy." She sat still
for it to pass off, but a trembling seized her. She
could not keep still.

"I got to go home, Budda——" Budda did
not understand her. "Home, I tell you—I got
to go home." She tried to stand up, but Budda
pulled her back.

"Pray right here, Si May-e. You'll get trompled on sho as you try to get to dat mourner's bench. De people's gone crazy."

"I ain' gwine to no mourner's bench, Budda, I gwine home. Is you deef?"

"You can' go home in dis storm, Si May-e. Sit down an' try to keep still, fo Gawd's sake."

"Don't talk to me bout keepin still. Oh, Lawd! Oh, Lawd! Do help me go home, Lawd! Oh, Lawd! What am I gwine do?"

Reverend Duncan was bending over the sinners urging them to pray harder, to be like Jacob and wrestle with God until He forgave them and put His sweet peace in their hearts. The whole congregation was in a stir, singing, wailing and weeping.

Mary called Big Boy to come help her get out. She yelled at the top of her voice but she could not make him hear her.

Thank God, Andrew heard. "You want to go up to de mourner's bench, Si May-e?"

"No, Jedus! I want to go home! Fo Gawd's sake, take me home, Andrew. Budda ain' able to make dat slow old mule hurry. Somebody's got to go long wid me."

Budda held to his stick, ready to follow in the path which Andrew cleared through the jam. Budda had forgotten his hatred for Andrew, and

the strong man was very gentle as he helped the
crippled sinner down the aisle, then down the
church steps into the black wet night.

Mary did not wait for them, but ran through
the rain, to the buggy which the flashes of
lightning helped her to find in the confusion
of vehicles around it.

"Do yunnah hurry, fo Lawd's sake," she
called to the two men who were coming behind
her as fast as Budda's feet could possibly shuffle
along.

The mule's head was finally turned toward
home, and the buggy wheels rolled in the water-
filled road. Mary tried not to moan, not to
rock her body back and forth.

"Beat de mule, Andrew, make em step more
pearter."

Andrew frailed the mule's haunches as hard as
he could, but the beast's feet were hampered
by floods of water and his eyes blinded by sheets
of rain.

"Don' fret bout de mule, Si May-e, you hold
on to dat child till we get you home. It ain' so
far now," Andrew spoke kindly, but Budda was
wretched.

"Great Gawd, Si May-e," he cried, "you
can' turn em loose in dis buggy."

Mary had to laugh with Andrew at Budda's terror.

"I tried to get you to go wid Auntie to de midwife class last Monday mornin, Budda, an' you wouldn't do it. You better had. Den you wouldn' be so scared now."

CHAPTER XXIV

"Lawd, we had a time!" Mary said to Maum Hannah when all was over. Then she looked at her two new-born sons and said gently, "Dat picture o' Hell scared me so bad I couldn' wait for de moon to change, enty? An' de pain hit me so hard, I couldn' pray not to save my life! No, Jedus!"

Maum Hannah did not go to bed, but sat by the fire and smoked. She never slept in any bed but her own. Whenever she stayed from home at night she sat by the fire and nodded and smoked without even taking off her shoes.

Mary and the new-born babies were in the big room bed. Mary was too tired even to talk to Seraphine who had unexpectedly come to the landing on the boat that afternoon but could not get home until after the storm. Maum Hannah was mortified for the girl to find Mary like this. She had been away with fine town people trying to make something of herself, while her mother lived in sin. Mary ought to quit her ways. She had a daughter almost grown now. Maum Hannah talked until the storm had passed and the night was still. She sat close to the hearth, for the rain had chilled the air and the flickering fire gave out a grateful warmth. Mary was glad to see her rest, for hurrying around so fast must have made her tired. She smoked a pipeful and laid her pipe on the hearth and settled herself with folded arms to sleep a little. She had hardly dozed when something roused Mary. She opened her eyes and peered through the dim light at her two babies. They were sound asleep. They did not move the slightest bit. Yet she heard a baby's faint cry. She called Maum Hannah, who hurried to the bed and leaned over and looked. Both the babies were asleep. Sound asleep. But she certainly had heard a baby's voice. One had waked her.

A dream maybe.

Maum Hannah laughed and went back to her chair by the fire. Mary was getting foolish. Waking herself up with dreams.

Maum Hannah sighed, then turned in her chair suddenly. She heard a baby too and she was not dreaming. She hobbled to the bed. No sound came from there. What was it she heard? Where did that cry come from? Not from Mary's boys. Both of them slept. What could it be?

The room was almost dark for the fire burned low. Maum Hannah said she felt nervish. A ghost must be walking around under the house. Mary was too brazen. Something was bound to happen to her. Maybe a plat-eye was outside, screech owls and whippoorwills had both been crying. She had put the shovel in the fire to stop them.

She added a light wood knot to the fire and a blaze flared up bright. At the same time a feeble wail sounded. Mary was sure it was in the room, but Maum Hannah waited to hear it again. Maybe a little goat had gone under the house out of the storm. There it was again. What was it? The old woman went to the corner; the sound seemed there, behind the organ. She didn't feel comfortable close to that organ. Why did Mary have it? Organs were tools of the devil. The idea of Reverend Duncan wanting one in the church.

Could that sound like a baby crying come out of the organ? Satan might be playing it. Mary had talked a lot of impudent talk lately. It made her uneasy.

"Open you eye, Auntie. Wake up, good," Mary called out sharply.

Something strange was in that corner by the shed-room door. What in God's world was it? Where did it come from?

"Open you eyes an' look good, Auntie."

Maum Hannah leaned and picked up something, then she hurried to the fire with it. She broke into a laugh.

"Great Gawd! What is dis? Whe you come f'om, gal? You most scare Aun' Hannah to deat'! Gawd bless you! Lemme wrop you up an' git you warm. Po lil ting! You mos' froze, enty?"

Mary jumped up out of the bed herself.

"Fo Gawd's sake, Auntie, who had dat baby?"

"Gawd knows, gal, I found em in de corner behind de organ. E's most freeze too——"

Mary took the child in her hands. The two women looked at each other. Both were perplexed. Whose child was this girl-child?

"May-e—you reckon you could-a had dis chile an' didn' know?" Maum Hannah suggested.

"Do, Auntie!" Mary laughed. "Now how could dat be?"

"Den who dat fetch em here? I been catchin' chillen all dese years. I know I ain' never caught one off de naked flo' befo in my life. Who dat put em on de flo'? Must be somebody."

"I know e ain' me. No, Jedus. When I birth chillen, I know it. Mebbe you had em, Auntie."

"Shut you mout', Si May-e, don' gi' me none o you' slack talk! No! Whose baby is dis? Whose?"

"I declare to Gawd, Auntie, e ain' my own. I wouldn' be shame to own em, if e was. Jedus, no! Three ain' no worse dan two. E's a fine child, Auntie. Better put em close to my own an' get em warm.—Git someting to wrop em up in."

Mary lay back down, and Maum Hannah covered her up with the three babies! Mary never had seen three babies but once before, and one of those was a little runty thing. All three of these were fine big children.

"Auntie, go in de shed room an' see if Seraphine is wake," Mary whispered.

"Lawd—I been forgot bout em," Maum Hannah said with a wise smile.

She opened the shed-room door. It was too dark to see much, but she called, "Is yunnuh all sleep in here?"

There was no answer.

"Wake em up," Mary said.

"You Ma say you must wake up, Seraphine," Maum Hannah called, but nobody stirred or answered.

Everybody was sound asleep, Seraphine and all of the rest.

"Try Seraphine one mo' time," Mary directed. "If e don' make answer, I'm gwine to get out of dis bed an' gi' em a lickin' e won' never forget, whilst e lives. When I say, 'Git up,' I mean, 'Git up!'"

"You hear you Mammy say e gwine lick you, enty? Wake up, Seraphine! Wake up!"

There were three beds in the shed room and the covers on all of them moved. Mary's threat was effective.

"All yunnuh get up an' come in dis room. I want to look in all you face," Mary called to them.

"Don' make dem lil chillen come, May-e, not dem boy-chillen. Dey so sleepy," Maum Hannah interceded.

Mary reflected a moment, then called sternly:

"Evy one got to come! Evy one! Seraphine, you an' Keepsie come stand close to dis bed! Right now, too! Dis minute! You low-down no-manners gal. You gone an' had a gal-child right here in my house, an' den lay down in de bed an' make out it my own! I good mind to lick you till I scorch you gown-tail."

Seraphine and Keepsie were two awkward figures standing there by Mary's bed, both of them denying most positively any knowledge of the extra child.

"E ain' my own," Seraphine declared over and over, and Keepsie echoed, "I know e ain' my own."

Finally Mary got tired of questioning them.

"Git on back to bed. I too vexed to fool wid yunnuh. To-morrow I'm gwine to get up an' lick all-two. I ain' gwine let you get away wid any such-a doins in my house. No. I'm gwine lick you haf to death. You wait!"

A good long sleep calmed Mary's anger, and the morning light showed that the girl-child was the prettiest one of the babies. Mary began feeling as proud of it as she was of her boys.

"I'd as soon take care of three as two. Gal-chillen ain' de trouble boy-chillen is, nohow."

Seraphine woke with a fearful toothache. Her throat was sore too, and Mary made her stay in the house while the ground was so wet.

When Doll came to inquire about Mary, Maum Hannah was sitting on the door-step in the sunshine smoking her pipe. She still had the white cloth on her head and the strange wooden beads around her neck that were the signs of her night's occupation.

"You look faded, Auntie," Doll said with sympathy.

"I is, gal. I is," Maum Hannah affirmed. "I been catchin chillen all night."

"How much you catch, Auntie?"

Maum Hannah held up both hands to the sky. "Three. Mary had triplets."

"Three? Si May-e had three? Great Gawd! Dat's a litter, enty?"

"No, e ain' no litter. E is triplets. Plenty o people has triplets. I used to wish I could have em myself."

"Can I look at em, Auntie?"

"Not to-day, honey, Si May-e is sleepin' now. E's weary by e had a long hard task last night."

CHAPTER XXV

MARY mended fast and before long she was her old strong able self, out in the field, doing a regular field hand's work. Every morning she thanked God that she was well again, and that the babies were all three thriving.

The patches she had planted all around her house were growing well. Cabbages were heading, watermelons and figs and peaches were ripening. Okra and tomatoes were bearing fruit enough to keep a big pot filled with soup. The hens laid and hatched well, and the red rooster strutted about helping them find worms and grass seed for themselves and their children. Portulacas blossomed by the front door-step, a morning-glory vine had climbed clear up over the shed-room door and held it fast with curly green fingers. Everything went well except Seraphine, who stayed weary and thin and down in the heart.

Mary tried to cheer her up, to make her eat, but all her coaxing and cooking did the girl little good, until Mary took her away off in the woods one morning and talked seriously to her. As they sat on the ground under the tall pines, Mary said that fretting was worse than sickness to thin your blood and dry up your flesh. If she had missed and made a mistake one time, that was not so bad; everybody makes mistakes, that is no disgrace. Not a soul in the whole world but Maum Hannah knew that the nice little girl-baby was not Mary's own. It was a nice little child. Seraphine ought to be proud of it. It was a good child to have around, because it had never looked on its daddy's face. That very thing gave it the power to cure sickness, not only things like fevers and rheumatism and thrash in babies' mouths, but all kinds of bad ailments like swelling and breaking-outs on your skin.

Seraphine listened with a solemn face, tears began pouring out of her eyes, then she bent over and crumpled up no bigger than a little child. Mary put both arms around her and drew her up close.

"Now, honey, don' cry so hard. Si May-e loves you just de same as e ever did. Evybody loves you. Budda Ben's eyes ain' big enough to see you. Big Boy is most dead e loves you so much." Instead of helping, this kind of talk made Seraphine cry more. It was doing harm instead of good. So she tried different talk.

She drew her arms away and stood Seraphine on her feet. "Look at me, gal. You think I don' know what ails you? I do. You ain' frettin because you done wrong. No. You's frettin because one o dem town mens tricked you and dropped you. You is a fool. As much mens as Gawd put in his world, any 'oman what would shed a tear over one man ain' got good sense. You make me pure shame. Shame. Me an' de chillen an' Budda Ben all has been a-pinchin an' savin an' doin on half-rations so you could stay yonder to school until you got a depluma. Gawd knows what a depluma is, but I know I rather have dat lil gal-child yonder home den all de deplumas in de world. You got to stop dis behavishness or I'm gwine to tell evybody on you. Budda Ben and Big Boy an' evybody else."

"No, Si May-e—don' tell Budda——"

"If you don' eat more victuals so some can stick to you ribs, I'm gwine to tell em sho as you live. None o my chillen ain' never been weakly before now. I can' stand to see a weakly 'oman, creepin around a-lookin doleful. Nobody can stand em. If you want people to hate de sight o you, stay weakly." Mary smiled and softened her voice. "Listen, gal, if you wants de mens to be raven 'bout you, don' never gi em a

chance to feel sorry fo you. You better listen
to me; an' eat a plenty and get fat an' sassy
again. Soon as cotton-pickin time comes an' I
get some money ahead, I'll buy you a hat an' a
dress an' some shoes an' pay you way on de boat
to town. You go let dat man what fooled you
see how you forgot em. You go look em
straight in de eye, suck you teeth at em, den
walk off an' leave em. Walk off proudful. Strut.
Dat is de way to treat big-doins town men. Let
em see you ain' noways down-hearted.

"I wasn' no older'n you when July done me
de same way. My Unex was just 'bout de same
age as you lil baby when I found out how July
was a-runnin roun.—It like to kill me at first. I
fretted haf to death—I couldn' sleep—neither
eat—I got po as a snake. I sure did love dat
low-down July. I did. Same like you love some
strange man yonder to town."

Seraphine looked up, and a pitiful smile flitted
over her lips.

"It don' pay to love mens too much, gal.
When a man finds out fo-true a 'oman is crazy
bout em, he don' crave dat 'oman no mo. Dat's
de very time e gwine crave some new 'oman alto-
gedder. Gawd made mens so. It don' pay to
love no one man too much. It's all right to
like em. But don' never let yousef tink on one

man all de time. It'll run you crazy if it don'
kill you."

Seraphine's face was thoughtful. It had a far-
away look. She stood with her arms akimbo.
Her full skirts, tied up short with a string around
her hips, were wet with dew. Her plain homespun waist, buttoned straight down the front,
was open at the neck where swift beats showed
how fast her heart was running, but her bare
feet, brown as the dirt they stood on, held her
weight up firmly.

She was almost crying, yet ready to smile
again, as she gave Mary a hug around the neck.
"Si May-e, you's de best ting ever was, yes, you
is. I love you too good, Si May-e."

"I'm glad, honey, I need a lot o lovin. Now,
le's go home and milk de cow an' de goat an'
give all dem babies a good supper."

"I hungry myself. I'm gwine cook some fried
corn-cakes to eat wid dem peas I left in de pot
dis mawnin."

CHAPTER XXVI

As THEY walked home a bright afterglow tinged the fields and Mary hummed happily. At last, thank God, everything in the world was right. She talked of how she'd cook the bread for supper that night; she'd mix the meal thick and pat it into little flat cakes and fry them. She hadn't made corn-cakes that way in a long time, and the children would be glad for the change. They'd taste fine with the new wild honey Keepsie had robbed from a tree.

For some reason, July came into her mind, maybe because July liked fried corn-cakes better than any other kind of bread or maybe talking to Seraphine about fretting brought July back to her mind. Where was he—gone so long—where? How did he look—after all these years? Had he forgotten her too?

She heaved a sigh as she poured water into the basin on the shelf and washed her hands to mix the meal and water together. The children would all soon be coming in hungry. Already she heard steps outside and a soft tiptoeing right up to the doorway.

Mary smiled. One of the children was tipping up the steps, getting ready to jump at her and scare her; an old game of July's. She'd be ready.

She put the pan on the table and crept softly along the wall till she reached the door, then she eased behind it and stood waiting——

Somebody was outside, right at the door. She could hear the quick breathing. She could almost hear the heart-beats as she waited, too, breathless. It was a game she and the children often played. But now the wait became too long. She would jump first, and turn the tables to-night. How the children did love to play!

In the soft twilight Mary stood behind the door—waiting—ready for the shrieks of laughter that would come with the quick-shouted, "I got you!"

She smiled and drew in the cool air stealthily through her nostrils. A strange smell came with it. It was not one of the children who stood there in the door. No! Mary tried to lean a little and see without being seen.

It was a stranger. A man.

"Who dat?" Mary called out sternly, moving out from her hiding-place. For some reason the words shook in her throat as she stepped forward and stood boldly in front of the door.

The strange man stood looking at her, hesitat-

ing, half smiling. Then he held out both hands.
Who was he? He took a step toward her and
stopped, and a familiar voice spoke softly. "Si
May-e? Is dis you, Si May-e?"

Mary's heart leaped at the sound, and her
astonished eyes stared at him.

"You ain' know me—Si May-e? Is you forgot
you July?" he asked gently. He stood waiting
for her to speak, holding his hands out to her—
almost like a child. She looked at his face. At
his hands. They were shaking. July's hands!

What must she do? What?

She could not think straight. She swallowed
hard and put her hand up to her throat, and her
heart thumped crazily as he spoke again.

"May-e—May-e, gal, I come back, honey.
Please say you glad to see me. Don' stand up
a-gazin at me so hard. Dis is you July, Si
May-e."

He took her hands—both of them. She let
him. She was paralyzed with joy and with
misery. Her eyes dimmed and his face was
blurred, but his voice had her heart quivering
just as it used to do in the old days.

She drew her hands slowly out of his, and her
voice sounded hollow and strange as she made it
say, "No, you ain' my July. I ain' had no July
in twenty years."

Her lips stiffened over the words; her tongue felt frozen, but July's old bold laugh answered her as he put a hand on each of her shoulders. "Yes you is, honey. I been gone a long time, fo-true, but I ain' forgot you, an' I ain' never blongst to nobody but you since de day you marked me in de ear wid dat knife. You 'member, enty?"

She nodded her head. She remembered well. She was dizzy with old memories. The old love and the old hurt and the old bitterness had all come back and were making her weak and faint. July took her swiftly in his arms and held her close to him and pressed his hot lips on hers.

That woke her up, wide awake. With the strength of a cyclone, she gave him a backward push which sent him stumbling down the steps. But he laughed pleasantly.

"Great Gawd, you is strong still yet. You got de same old devil in you, too. I don' blame you for pushin me off, honey. I wouldn' say a word if you was to knock me down an' stomp in my face, so long as you take me back."

"Take who back? You. July Pinesett? Befo I'd let you come inside my door, I'd see you rotted in Hell."

"Why, Si May-e! What you mean? You

wouldn' send me away, not after I come all dis
way to see you. I been comin four days to git
here. Stand still and lemme look at you good.
I swear to Gawd, you ain' hardly changed." In
the half-light, his black eyes peered at her.
"You look better'n I ever see you. Yes, you is!"

His hand reached out and touched her shoulder, but Mary drew away and she felt her lips
curling proudly, even if they did tremble.

"I might be ain' changed on de outside, but I
sho is changed on de inside. Yessuh! Dis ain'
de same silly gal you left, July. No. Don' fool
yousef." She looked straight at him. Her
weakness was passing, and the dim light was
helping her hide it. July couldn't see how she
shook from head to foot.

"Ki," she laughed. "I been duh talk 'bout you
no longer'n last month. I told dem people right
yonder at Heaven's Gate Church if you was to
come home cold an' stiff in a box, I could look at
you same as a stranger an' not a water wouldn'
drean out my eye. I mean it, July." She
nodded her head for emphasis. Then she pointed
to the street.

"You may as well go on. I got to cook
supper. I'm hungry. I ain' hardly eat good
since breakfast."

But July persisted. "May-e, you listen.

You don' know 'bout all dem things I fetched in my valise fo you. I got fine presents fo you an' Unex, too. Don' be so rash wid you talk. Wait! Lemme show you——"

He picked up the suitcase from the bottom step. It was heavy. Bulging. He laid it down on the ground to open it. His fingers fumbled with the straps. But Mary stopped him.

"Don' open dat satchel, July! Don' unbuckle a strap in my yard. No! You own sister is a-livin right yonder down de street. Take you foot in you hand an' go to em. I don't want you or anyting you got."

July looked astonished. He took a purse out of his pocket. It was fat and full. He had brought money. Lots of money!

"Looka dis, Si May-e. I fetched all dis for you. All dis." He opened it and smoothed out the bills. Selecting the top one, he held it up.

"Ten dollars fo Unex," he said, then, taking the rest, he held it out to her. "Dis rest is fo you."

The light flickered weak in the sky. The world was dim. It was hard to send July away. Her charm could hold him faithful to her as long as she lived. Her blood raced through her body. The twilight showed that he was the same old July who had broken her heart, whose face

was for ever sealed on her eyelids. He was
dressed differently. He was a town man now.
But he was still slim and straight, and the words
fell from his lips with the same bold laugh she
remembered so well.

It was not the sight of his money that kept her
silent, but July did not understand. "Kiss me,
gal. Say you glad I come home." He stepped
forward with confidence, and Mary felt she must
yield, but she caught herself.

"Don' put you hand on me again, July! Don'
touch me! Take you money an' go. Get out o
my yard. Me an' my chillen don' want not a
brownie you got! Not one."

"Chillen?" July asked. "You got chillen? Si
May-e?"

Mary placed her hands on her hips and held
her head high. "Sho I got chillen." She
laughed. "I got plenty o chillen! Plenty! Dey
ain' none o you-own, July, so it ain' none o you
business how many I got."

In spite of her laugh she shivered as a still tree
shivers under a sudden gust of cold wind. He
must not stay here and break her heart again.
She must send him away, even if it wrung her
flesh in two. Yet the bare thought of letting him
go made the life in her dwindle.

She had taught her lips to laugh and sneer

whenever his name was spoken. She made herself say ugly things about him. She had hoped to God that his body had grown fat and soft and paunchy; that his white teeth had dropped out. But here he was. Tall and straight, lean and keen-eyed. Hardly a gray hair was in his head.

"Whe is Unex, Si May-e? Maybe de boy what you had fo me would like to see his Daddy. E use to love me."

"Unex is gone, July. E went off and left me de same as you done. Gawd knows if e's livin or dead."

The children were coming, trooping up the street, laughing, playing; then they became quiet when they saw the stranger.

July looked at them, then he looked at Mary.

"Good-by, Si May-e."

"Good-by, July."

He picked up his suitcase and walked away.

"Who dat, Si May-e? Who dat?" the children asked curiously as soon as he was out of hearing.

Mary sucked her teeth and grunted.

"Yunnuh ever hear de people talk 'bout July Pinesett? Well, dat's him." And she went on with her cooking

"Whe e come f'om, Si May-e?" another asked.

Mary turned one of the smoking hot cakes over before she answered. "I don' know whe e come f'om, an' I don' know whe e's gwine; what's mo, I don' care." She sounded brave but her heart was beating wildly in her breast and hot tears were stinging her eyes.

As soon as supper was over Mary banked the fire and went to bed. It was early, but her head ached and her heart was fluttering like a bird.

She lay still in the dark, nursing her new grief with burning tears while the street rang with merriment. Everybody was welcoming July, everybody was rejoicing to see him back home again. And she, his lawful wife, was lying alone soaking her pillow with salty tears because she had sent him away.

When the cock crowed for midnight she got up. The house was hot and steamy, the bed was sweltering and the quilt cover stung her like nettles. She must have some fresh air to breathe. Easing the window-blind open she leaned out in the cool black night. Every tree was filled with the talk of crickets and locusts and katydids. Frogs were croaking in the rice-fields. The guineas roused and cackled. A whippoorwill called with every breath. Far down the street a guitar was strumming out chords, keeping time to a man's clear singing. July was picking his box and his song was the old one, "I'm gwine to live on till I die."

Would she see him to-morrow? Would she ever see him again? The stars were high and cold. The night was full of ghosts. She closed the window and drew the blind in tight.

The next morning dawned bright and hot, promising the kind of day Mary liked best, but her head was too heavy to lift off her pillow and her knees were too shaky to hold up her weight. Seraphine and Keepsie had to cook and milk, feed the beasts and fowls and children, and fetch water from the spring. She tried to speak cheerfully and encourage them, but the tears she strove to hold back rose and choked her words.

The tide was going out. The river wind smelled of the mud-flats, steaming and baking in the fire poured down by the sun. The water had gone and left them naked. The poor things were fastened down so they could not move. Like herself. Fastened down tight. She must bear her misery without complaining.

CHAPTER XXVII

Mary spent most of the day lying on the bed except when she heard footsteps on the path in front of the door, then she got up quickly and pretended to be patching clothes.

When she heard Maum Hannah's limping steps across the yard, she went to help her up the steps, for the misery in the old woman's knee seemed worse than usual.

"How-come you duh hop so bad to-day, Auntie, de sun is a-shinin fair."

"Worry-ation, honey. Worry-ation makes a misery worse dan east rain an' wind. But how-come you eyes is red as red flannel?"

Mary hesitated. She had to think quickly or tell the truth. "I been a-thrashin peas an' peas-dust got in my eyes. It like to blinded me."

"Poor creeter," Maum Hannah pitied her. "I didn' know peas-dust was pizen."

They lighted their pipes and sat down to talk, yet the silence stayed on, hard to break. Presently Maum Hannah cleared her throat.

"July told me you wouldn' much as let him darken you door."

A heavy sigh fell from her bosom, and she shook her head mournfully from side to side. Mary was wrong. She could have a house full of children for other men, but she could not change the law of God. Whom God has joined together all the men and all the sin in the world can not part. She was July's wife, July was her husband just the same as the first day Reverend Duncan read out the Book over them and married them together.

"You must be forgot how July done me, Auntie; how July suffered me. I done well to live."

"Is July de first man ever suffered a 'oman?"

"No, Auntie, I don' mean dat."

Maum Hannah grunted. Before she left she wanted Mary to tell her one thing. What had she ever done to make God bless her with a husband that would not suffer her?

Mary shook her head. She had done nothing to win such a blessing. Maum Hannah sighed and said good night.

The dusk dropped deeper. The light was almost gone. The air in the house was hot, and thick with the smell of cooking food. The children crowded around the hearth, laughing, happy, greedy, their black faces glistening in the red firelight. Their mouths chattered with talk, all at one time, nobody listening to anybody else. Bright faces, white teeth, slim bodies, quick-moving hands and feet filled Mary's eyes. These were all her children, the fruit of her body. Healthy, strong younglings, all growing fast.

But her heart had that heavy dull aching, the same old aching of those first years when July left her. Her whole breast hurt, it was hard to catch air enough when she breathed.

She stepped out into the yard and looked toward the evening star. Such a hot bright star, standing in the path of the slim new moon.

"How-come you duh star-gaze, gal?"

Budda Ben was on his wood-pile, so still and black she had not noticed him until he spoke. With the night blotting out his poor body his voice had a different sound. It was a man's voice and his words had warmth and tenderness.

"Budda Ben——" She stumbled over a piece of wood as she went toward him, and sat down beside him heavily.

"Mind, gal," he warned her, "don' fall down an' broke you leg. I ain' able to cook for no house o chillen."

She knew he was trying to boost her, to make her laugh, but she couldn't do it. Not yet.

"Budda Ben, July come——"

"I know, I seen him."

"Now he's gone—— I wouldn't let him come inside my door."

"Enty?"

Silence fell between them. The night closed around them. Budda Ben's stick fell from his hands, as they both reached slowly out and took one of Mary's. What strong sinewy hands they were, although they trembled now.

"Please don' be sorry for me, Budda. I can' stand dat. I made July go. I sent him off. He been want to stay, but I wouldn' let him."

"I know, gal. I know how proudful you ever was. Too proudful."

CHAPTER XXVIII

THE day had been lowering and gray, and before the first dark fell, rain began. Nobody could go out in such weather, so the children ate supper early and went to bed, the three babies in Mary's bed in the big room and Seraphine with the other children in the shed room. They were all sleeping soundly when the boat on the river, due since early in the afternoon, made a hoarse blowing for the landing. Its voice must have reached to the clouds for a fresh downpour of rain beat on the roof and against the side of the house; great gusts of wind swelled and crackled the newspapers pasted over the cracks on the walls; those cut into fringes and decorating the high mantel-shelf shivered and shook with the draft, and the ones tied to barrel hoops and hung on the rafters swung slowly back and forth like bells tolling.

The red rooster, out with his flock of hens in the fig tree, flapped his wings three times and tried to give the boat a brave answer, but the rain and wind cut off the words in his throat. A shiver suddenly ran down Mary's back, and she straightened up and drew her frayed shawl a bit closer around her shoulders. That shiver meant that a rabbit was running over her grave. Jesus have mercy, how she hated to think of a grave on a lonesome black night like this.

The fire spat sharply when raindrops fell down the chimney and dulled its flame. Mary put down her needle and with the long iron poker punched the sticks of wood sharply together to make them brighter.

The top of the pot which hung on a pot hook in the back of the fireplace began clicking and clattering as steam from the stew inside it rose and filled the room with pleasant smell of goat-meat and herbs cooking together. Outside, in the rain, a goat bleated pitifully. Poor little Nan. She must smell the stew which was made out of her own son, a weanling born only last spring. She ought not to take his death so hard. She would have two more kids as soon as next spring came. Fretting would dry up her good sweet milk, make it bitter, and the babies would suffer.

Mary got up and, taking down the door-bar, cracked the door open wide enough to peer out into the thick wet darkness. "Nan—Nan," she called gently, "don' fret so hard, gal."

Nan's quivering answer guided Mary's eyes

to a dim white spot where the little goat was tethered to the fig tree.

"I see you, Nan. Don' be lonesome. I'm here wid my mind a-runnin on a child o my own too. I know how you feel wid you son gone. I know good."

The wind whistled and lashed at the trees. Mary's long skirt whipped at her legs and pulled her back inside the room.

She closed the door tight, put the bar into place and, filling her pipe, sat down to smoke one last pipeful before she went to bed. It was good to be under shelter with all the children well and safe and out of the cold black rain. Lord, what a night!

She looked up at the enlarged picture of Unex hanging on the wall. It was taken from a small one he sent her and it cost a lot, but it was good to have his face there over the mantel-shelf where she could look at it the first thing every morning when she got up and the last thing every night before she went to bed. How much like July he was. The same high bony forehead and full eyes, the same broad mouth. If the picture could talk, it might tell her where he was, how he was; then she could be happy and satisfied. But it could only stare and stay dumb.

A large yellow cat crept in through the cat hole, a notch cut in one corner of the door. Mary chuckled. Tom had come home early to-night. The rain must have run the rats too deep in their holes for him to catch; or maybe he found courting no fun on such a wet night. Tom thought of nothing but pleasure: eating, sleeping, courting, keeping his fur smooth. He had not a trouble in the world, although his yellow kittens were scattered from one end of the plantation to the other. He was like all the other men. Children could come and children could go, but as long as his belly was full of victuals and he had a warm dry place to sleep, he was happy and satisfied. Women are different. Poor little Nan cried and could not sleep for grief because her child, a tall weanling, was gone from her.

Somebody stumbled up the steps and made a loud knock and called, "Si May-e, is you home? Do, fo Gawd's sake, open de door."

"Who dat?" she cried, almost startled out of her wits, for the voice was Unex's own. Spirits trick people on nights like this, she must be careful what she did.

"Who dat, I say?" She called out boldly, and the prompt answer came.

"Dis is me, Unex, Si May-e. Do le me in——"

Mary dropped the door-bar. Her brain felt addled, her knees shook, she could not speak a word.

Unex was soaking wet, laden with luggage, a drenched hat pulled over his face. As he staggered toward the fire, each step he took left a puddle of water on the floor. His wet coat and breeches clung tight to his body and he seemed to have no breath left for speaking.

The door swung wide open, pushed back by the wind, and Mary's hands shook so she could hardly shut and bar it again. She hugged Unex and kissed him with many a sob, and he wept with her, but all the time he held fast to a bundle.

"Unex—honey—whe you come from?" She took off his hat and pushed his head back and stroked his thin cheeks. "Whe in Gawd's world is you come from, son? Put you bundle down an' get off dem wet clothes, dey is plastered wid mud."

Unex held tight to his wet bundle with both his arms.

"Lawd, I'm glad to git here. I mighty nigh give out back yonder in de big road," he sighed, and bending his head over wiped his wet face on his sleeve.

Mary got up and ran to get him a dry towel.

"Wha dat you got wrapped up so tight, in a blanket?"

Unex smiled a slow sad smile. "Dis is a present I brought you, Si May-e! De nicest present ever was, but I liken not to a got here wid em. Look at em and see how you like em."

He began undoing the blanket carefully, awkwardly. His hands were cold, the joints of his fingers stiff; but Mary stood still and watched him. At last the top of the blanket was off, and Unex bent over it saying, "Is you wake, Emma? Looka, Si May-e. E's you gramma, honey."

"Whe in Gawd's world did you get em from, son?"

The baby's bright black eyes stared up from a tiny wrinkled face, both small fists were clenched tight. Unex slipped a finger inside one of them, and it held on tight for dear life. "Emma is my own, Si May-e. I fetched em to you to raise for me."

Mary shifted her weight unsteadily from one knee to the other. "Who had em for you, son?" she whispered.

"E mammy is dead, Si May-e," the boy answered simply. "I couldn' raise em by mysef."

Mary brushed her tears away and patted Unex's shoulder briskly. "Gi me de child, son. How-come you had em out in all dis rain to-

night? You done well not to drown em. Po lil
creeter. Put some wood on de fire. Put de
kettle up close so de water can hotten, den go
wake up Seraphine. I bet dis baby is hungry
as e only can be. When did you feed em last,
Unex?"

Unex opened the wet paper suitcase and took
out a big shining nickel bottle and held it up to
show her. It was a fireless bottle, he said. Milk
would stay hot in it all day and all night. Emma
had been drinking out of it ever since he started
for home, two days and two nights ago.

Then he held up a milk-stained glass bottle
with marks to show how much milk to give Emma, so she would not drink herself to death.
Emma never knew when to stop. Mary
looked and listened in bewilderment. She was
deeply impressed, but when she looked at the
tiny creature in her lap, touched its little cheek,
felt its bony hands, she knew it was hungry and
cold, too weak to cry or complain. The milk in
the fireless bottle must be stale, but she had three
babies of her own to feed and Emma would
have to depend on Nan's milk.

"Wake up Seraphine, son," she ordered.

Seraphine was so dazed it was hard to make
her understand at first, but as she got wide awake,
she began crying with joy.

"Get a cup out de safe an' go milk lil Nan. Stale milk'll gi dis baby de colic. E needs warm milk fresh from de breast. Nan'll have a plenty. E ain' been milked since befo sundown."

Seraphine hesitated. "It's dark outdoors, Si May-e. How can I find Nan?"

Mary laughed, Seraphine ever was afraid of the dark. "Open de door, gal. You can see em; lil Nan shows white on de darkest night."

Seraphine soon had a cup and was gone, and Mary got the baby unwrapped. Poor little thing. Such a tiny mite. Its hands were no bigger than bird claws, its belly was withered up with emptiness, yet its eyes were bright as chinquapins. Emma had a brave little heart.

All the clothes in the paper suitcase were either wet or soiled, so Mary got things belonging to the three babies and dressed Emma in them. When Seraphine had the milk bottle washed clean with soap-suds and rinsed with spring water, Nan's milk was mixed half and half with hot water from the kettle, and Emma's supper was ready.

"Dat is too much," Unex protested when Mary filled the bottle almost full. Emma was not due to have more than up to the first mark on the bottle. Mary laughed.

"Do, fo Gawd's sake, Unex. Emma'll know when e belly gits full. Gawd made chillen wid more sense'n people. If Emma misses and drinks too much, e belly will know, and throw em straight back up, and be shet of em."

Unex gave up. Mary was too positive for any argument.

"Do looka how Emma duh level down on de milk. E's pure a-starvin, po lil creeter," Seraphine sympathized.

And while Emma leveled down, Mary untied the strings of Unex's wet shoes. When he got off his wet clothing, he had no dry ones to put on so he wrapped himself in a quilt and sat by the fire warming, stretching his bare feet out to the fire, while he ate a little cornbread and goat meat. He was not hungry. For two or three days a burning in his belly had killed all his appetite.

When Emma was fed and dozing, Seraphine took her and sat listening, while Unex and Mary talked.

When he left home he went straight up north.

"Wid Yankees?" Mary asked quickly.

"Yes, wid Yankees." But they seemed much like other white people except for their talk. At first he could hardly understand a word they said.

He drifted from one city to another, looking

for better work, bigger wages. Then he met a girl, her name was Emma, and he went no farther. That was last spring. He saw her almost every night and on Sundays, in the week-days both of them were busy, both working. By Thanksgiving she had to stop work, but he worked on at the docks helping load and unload ships that came and went over the ocean. He made her come stay with him, but she didn't seem well. She had to stay in bed most of the time and that was when she made Emma so many clothes. Unex paused and looked sadly at the pile of rumpled things on the floor. It was not little Emma that got her so poorly, but a fever. First a night fever, then an inward fever gnawed steadily at her insides and gave her no rest day or night.

He bought that same fireless bottle for her so she could have something hot to drink any time she wanted it without getting up out of bed and worrying herself to fix it. Thirst troubled her a lot, and cold things gave her a chill. One night, when he came home late from work little Emma was there, but the little mother was gone.

Unex sat silent, looking at the fire. Nobody spoke for a little, then Mary told him that inside fretting is bad for people. It is better to cry and get it out. Unex shook his head. Talking would do more for him than crying. He had tried crying and it made him feel worse. He wanted to tell her all about it, and then he would speak no more of it again.

The people in the house did all they knew to help him, the policeman on the corner came in and said he could have sent Emma to the hospital if somebody had only told him she was so sick. But it was too late then. She was gone. Nobody could bring her back. They took her out on the far edge of the city in a graveyard crowded with other poor people and put her in the ground.

One of the women in the house offered to take the baby and raise her, but babies in cities have a hard time. He wanted Emma's to have a chance to live. So he sold some of his things, gave the rest away and bought a ticket for South Carolina.

On the train everybody was kind, from the engineer to the conductor. They gave him two seats and asked if the baby's milk was hot and sweet. They washed the milk bottle and did everything they could to help him. People are kind all over the world.

When the train reached town, there seemed no way to get home up the river before morning, for the old river boat had its engine broken. By the time it was fixed the tide was right to help push it up the river through the blackest darkness God ever made. They reached the landing in the pouring rain. He would have spent the night there, but Emma's milk was out and she had to have fresh clothes.

Unex looked at Mary with a wistful smile. "You don' mind raisin de baby for me, is you, Si May-e?"

Mary smiled back. Lord no. She was glad to do it.

"I see you ain' forgot how to hold babies yet," he added, then Mary laughed out.

"Who? Me? Great Gawd, I ain' had no chance to forget. I ain' been widout one since I had you, son. I got three right yonder in de bed. Now I'll have four. A full litter, enty?"

Three? How could she have three? Unex was puzzled.

Mary told him how on the night her own twins were born, another baby was found behind the organ. Nobody had ever owned the child yet. Unex looked at Seraphine and growled.

"Who had em, Seraphine?"

But Mary laughed pleasantly, and warned him not to let himself get upset. Seraphine was a good girl. If she had missed and tripped one

time, it must not be held against her, and he
must not hurt her feelins by asking her questions.

Tears filled Unex's eyes. "You is too good,
Si May-e. I bet dey ain' no 'oman in de world
good as you."

"I know so," Seraphine echoed softly.

Mary shook her head and sighed. No, she
was far from good. She loved her children and
she was not going to let anybody hurt their
feelings.

She had a few more questions to ask Unex.
Had he seen July on any of his travels? Unex
shook his head. He had not. He looked for
July but he would not have known him anyway,
for July left home when he was a helpless baby,
less than a year old.

And how did Unex get money to have the
baby's mother buried?

Unex explained that the baby's mother belonged to a burying society which pays sick
people fifty cents a day every day while they
are sick and buries them when they die. Most
city people belong to some society like that.
It's a big help too. City people have some nice
ways.

"We got a Bury-league, now," Seraphine
boasted. "I don' belong to it, but a lot o people

in de street does. De members pays fifty cents
evy time somebody dies; if you lose a child as
much as twelve years old, you get fifteen dollars;
if you lose a baby or a child under twelve, you
get twelve dollars and a half; if a man loses his
wife he gets twenty-five dollars an' a good store-
bought box to bury em, an' a nice tombstone."

"How much does a dead man bring?"

Seraphine looked grave. "A lawful husband
brings sixty dollars, but if e ain' married to you,
you don' get a Gawd's cent."

"Dat don' seem ezactly right," Unex ventured,
but Mary said it didn't matter. She and Seraphine had no husbands and did not belong to the
Bury-league, not yet. It was cheaper for her
and the children to stay well, so they could spend
the money they made on rations and clothes and
pleasure. None of them was likely to die anytime soon. Of course, if one was to show any
sign of getting weakly, she might join then, but
it was not a bit of use now. Not now.

CHAPTER XXIX

A WIDE-SEATED split-bottom chair with a pillow for a mattress, made a fine bed for Emma, who seemed glad enough to sleep and roused only for food or fresh clothes. Then she wailed pitifully and shook her fists and waved her thin legs about. Mary woke at her first whimper and, gathering her up close in her arms, soothed her with low crooning words, fed her with Nan's sweet rich milk, and patted her back to sleep again.

Unex slept beside Emma on a pallet of quilts on the floor with his feet up near the fire, for the night stayed damp and chilly and his blood was hard to warm after that terrible wetting the rain had put on him.

Dawn brought a stiff wind that cleared the clouds out of the sky, and a winter sun came out white and warm, drying off the drenched earth. Before sunrise Mary mended the fire which blazed up bright in spite of the wet wood, but Unex slept on heavily. Poor fellow. How long and narrow he was stretched out there on the floor. His body seemed shrunken, his face dry and ashy, deep black shadows lay under his eyes. Sorrow had left its mark on him. Nothing but time could heal him, but good food and rest and love would help him.

When Unex woke, he said his bones ached, his head felt heavy and a misery had his insides restless, but Seraphine hurried about, waking the children for Mary, helping them dress, laughing and playing with them, stirring a pot, cooking the sausages while Keepsie milked the cow, and the cabin became gay with happiness except for Unex's sadness. He tried hard to seem glad, to meet the children who had come into the world since he went away, but his heart was in none of it; Mary could see that. Maybe he was hurt with her having so many children; maybe he was sick and weary from his long journey, sad that Emma's little mother was dead.

Big Boy came in for breakfast, and ate greedily, a great pile of hominy wet with sausage gravy, great hunks of sausage, one after another; it did Mary's heart good to see such an appetite; but Unex shuddered when he looked at the nice panful of victuals she fixed for him. He wanted nothing but a cupful of sweetened water. He was thirsty, he craved things to drink, yet when he swallowed them down, they burned his insides. A strange thing ailed him.

The news of Unex's arrival spread with speed, and all the Quarter people hastened to greet him and bid him welcome home. Everybody brought something; the cabin table was full of good things, but he ate nothing. By daylight his hands looked bonier than ever, the hollows in his neck deeper. His shoulders were stooped; his feet were heavy and dragged him along slowly, wearily. Once he reeled, then he sat quickly down in a chair and leaned his face forward in his hands. Unex was sick. Still, when the neighbors kept coming with their hands filled with gifts: chickens, eggs, fresh-baked bread, bottles of last spring's sweet blackberry wine, this fall's scuppernong wine, good smooth corn liquor, he sat up straight and talked to them, with a smile on his thin features. He said he was very tired from his long journey and trying to care for Emma, but he had a special word for everybody, the children as well as the grown people.

Maum Hannah was overjoyed to see him and was set on feeding him plenty of nourishing food right at once. He looked starved out to her. Hot meal gruel made with milk would strengthen him. He was too big to go without victuals; he must swallow some down whether he felt like it or not. But Unex craved no food, he wanted cool spring water, not sweetened water or hot table tea. Soups and gruels and smelly high-seasoned food made him retch.

Mary hovered about, feeding her babies and Emma, and watching Unex. She noticed with terror how his hands shook and his lips trembled when he talked, how his eyes had a strange gleam, making them bright like glass, although a shadow lay under them.

She put him a chair outside in the yard where the sun shone warm and bright, and the fresh cool air fell soft from a clear blue sky. He sat there for a short while, but he soon became tired, for the people crowded around him, laughing, talking. The hens were too noisy with their scratching and clucking; Nan's bleating was too sorrowful, the cock's crow too mournful; the flies settled on him, crawling, biting; the squealing of the shoat in the pen made him restless. It was too much for his strength, he would be better off inside, lying down and resting on a bed.

Mary's heart turned cold. Unex was sick. His body was hot, his hands and feet were cold. His eyes burned red, as oil lamps burn just before they go out.

Wagons went creaking past, taking the people to church, and by noon the Quarters were almost silent, then Unex fell into a deep sleep. Seraphine took all the babies to Maum Hannah's house so their cooing and crying would not disturb Unex's rest.

Mary looked at him from time to time, huddled there on the bed, sometimes asleep, sometimes awake, without desire for food or for talk, and, it seemed to her, with little desire to live. Unex was sick, bad sick. She went to the open window and stood looking out so he could not see her tears.

She had gone through a good deal, this fall, without weakening, but now she felt her strength giving away. Unex was her heart-string. If he died she could not, could not bear it.

He lay gazing at her, his big pitiful eyes asking dumbly for help. She must not let him see how sad she felt, that would be against him. She must smile and be cheerful, make him believe he would soon be well.

"Would you drink a lil chicken soup now, if I fetch em to you, son?" she asked cheerfully.

"Not now, Si May-e, le me wait a lil while. You come set by me. Put you hand on my head like you used to when I was a lil boy. Dat's de way. You hand feels so cool an' good. It makes my head feel better a-ready."

Seraphine tiptoed in to say it was time to feed the babies, and Mary whispered to her to milk Nan and the cow and feed them fresh milk and give them a taste of pot-liquor out of the pot of greens on the hearth. Her own breasts had no milk now. They were empty and dry.

"You better eat some victuals yousef, Si May-e. You ain' to starve dem chillen. If Unex ain' gwine to drink dat gruel, whyn' you drink em? It ain' no use to waste em."

Mary swallowed down a cupful of the creamy white soup and asked for a cupful more. It was good and strength-giving. She did need food, all she could hold, to help her keep up a brave heart. She would nurse Unex back to wellness, back to life. Death should not have him. Not Unex.

A hang-dog look came into his eyes. The hot fever that scourged him quenched their brightness and made them milky. His skin was hot and dry. His gaunt bony body groveled and rolled with pain. He groaned and begged for cool water from the spring. Always water. Cool water. The paper suitcase was empty except for a few rags, but he kept calling his dead wife to fetch it to him so he could change the baby's clothes.

His calling and calling for her and for water, made the hair rise on Mary's head. It was his call for Life. The soup she made for him was always too hot or too cold or too luke-warm. Chicken soup, okra soup, pigeon soup, all sick-

ened him. He wanted water. Cool water, fresh
from the spring. If he had strength in his legs
he would take the path down the hill and find a
smooth sandy place in the branch. He would
stretch his full length in the cool water. The
fever had the blood in his veins turned to steam.
He wanted water. Cool spring water. It would
dull the hot thorns in his belly.

People in towns have no cool spring water,
or shade or green woods. Their shade is filth.
Their sunshine is hot sidewalk breath. Last
year's breath. Last year's sickening smell.
Their streets hold the fever that makes thorns
grow in your belly, thorns that never stay still,
that stick clear up into your heart.

Day after day melted into long black nights,
and Unex grew steadily worse. Sometimes he
thought he was falling and cried out for Mary
to catch him. She would hold his hot hand tight
and try to make him understand he was dreaming, but his fear often frightened her too. An
agony of dread chilled her every time she leaned
low to hear his whispered words, for his breath
had the faint sweet smell that always comes
ahead of Death.

The neighbors were kind as could be. Two
of the women stayed with her all the time and
kept the fire burning, the floor scoured, the

house clean, the pots boiling, the water buckets full. But Mary and Maum Hannah scarcely took off their clothes or slept more than an hour at a time.

One night, when Unex seemed to be a little better, Maum Hannah went home to catch a short nap. The women with Mary nodded in their chairs, for she sat beside the bed watching. The tide was coming in, nothing would happen before it turned. God knew what the ebb tide might bring. She could not close her eyes until that was past. When a sudden short shudder ran through Unex from head to foot, terror shook her, but she set her teeth against it and, putting her lips close to his ear, whispered:

"I'm right side you, honey. Go back to sleep. Si May-e ain' gwine leave you."

His eyes had cleared, his senses had come back. He knew what he was saying.

"Hold my hand, Si May-e—I got de rattle— my legs is cold to my knees——" he whispered.

"Is you want me to call de people, son? Does you want em to come an' sing?"

He shook his head. No, he did not want them.

"I want you to hold my hand, Si May-e.—E is gittin dark."

"E ain' dark, son, de lamp is a-burnin." But as she said it she could see by the lamp's dim light how a deeper darkness was clouding his big sad eyes.

"Son—is you f'aid? Tell Si May-e."

"I'm cold, Si May-e——"

"Does you want me to lay aside you on de bed an' warm you, son?"

Without waiting for him to say yes, she eased herself down close to him and put her arms around him. How thin he was, and so weak.

"Now, now," she whispered in his ear, "Si May-e is got you right in e arms. Don' be f'aid, honey.—Death ain' gwine to suffer you—no—all de worst is done over—shut you eyes, sonny, an' go sleep——"

She wanted to sob, to scream out with grief, but she held herself still while his breath grew less and less. Death was wrenching his life out of his body.

"Sonny," she whispered. "Sonny," she called him again with her lips pressed close to his ear. He did not answer although he was warm and yielding. She tried to pray, but it was no use.

She choked back a sob. She must not cry yet. He might not be gone and would hear her. She held him tighter, closer in her arms, as if he were a baby again and sleeping too sound to be wakened.

Death took him. For all her trying and loving and pleading with God to leave him here with her, he was gone. God knew he was the only heart-child she had. The others were the fruit of eye-love, the children of her flesh, yet they were strong and hearty; and her joy-child, her first-born, her jewel, July's son, was gone.

Grief smothered her. Her heart was a rock in her breast. She hurried to the window and opened her mouth wide to catch enough air to breathe. She could hear herself moaning softly, not bawling, not beating her head against the wall as women do when they lose out in a fight with Death. Sorrow had her dumb. It had her body weighted down. Her eyelids were numb. Her eyes were too parched for tears.

She looked up at the sky where her precious child's soul was wandering about seeking its way to Heaven and God. The battered horn of an old red moon hung low above the dawn. The stars were pale and dim, poor lamps to light a lonely soul climbing that steep road trying to find its long way home.

The earth lay still and black. The high sky might have the dead boy's clean soul, but the greedy old ground would get his body, his poor, thin, fever-wasted body, and turn it back into dust.

CHAPTER XXX

THE women woke up, and one of them ran to the doorway screaming and howling. Voices from the other houses answered and people came running down the street and into the room until it was jammed full. Everybody was moaning except Maum Hannah who stood outside in the yard, sending her long death cries out into the dawn so the whole world could know that Unex was gone.

"Oo—Oo—Ooo—Ee—Ee-Eee!

"Oo—Oo—Ooo—Ee—Ee-Eee!"

The cries rose higher and higher breath by breath. Mary felt that if they kept on they would cut the thread of her own life in two, tough and strong as it was.

Her bare feet kept padding across the room as she blundered back and forth from the bed to the window. She strove to think of the things that must be done, but she needed air to keep her from smothering.

Somebody had hung up an old shirt for a curtain and it kept fluttering backward into the room, then outward again, as two strong winds,

327

one from the land, one from the sea, tried to rule the coming day.

The children were huddled in a corner, weeping softly, except Keepsie, who had forgotten his new crutches and went hopping about on his one leg. His face was drawn, his eyes winked fast with fear, now and then Mary felt his hand holding tight to hers. He must have seen her feet totter, for he hopped toward her with a chair. She sat down and held her face in her hands. Her palms could feel the quivering of her mouth and her gaspy breathing, but she held her silence doggedly.

She longed to scream out and butt her head on the wall, so God could see that she knew He had turned against her. But before all these people, these women, she must hold on to herself.

The hours passed slowly. Unex was washed and shrouded and covered over with a sheet. Andrew and Big Boy measured him and went away to make his box. The room was scoured until its cleanness looked bare and cold.

At last the day began shedding its light and heat. The sun was dropping. Mary sat by the window holding little motherless, fatherless Emma asleep in her lap.

Andrew touched her on the shoulder and cleared his throat.

"I reckon we better be gettin ready, Si May-e." He sniffed and fumbled the hat in his hands.

Big Boy stood wiping his red eyes.

"Si-Maye," Maum Hannah hobbled up, "gi Emma to me. You got to go now. De sun'll soon set."

The new pine box stood waiting on two chairs, its cover leaning against the table's legs, waiting to be nailed on. Andrew began turning back the sheet.

"Please, Cun Andrew, don' put Unex on de naked boards. E's so thin—dey is so hard."

She got a quilt which Andrew folded into a long narrow length and laid smooth in the box; then he put a pillow at the head. She stood watching all that was done in silence until Andrew took up the board cover, then she could not help crying out, "Oh, Gawd, why couldn' you le me keep my child a lil bit longer?"

She fell on her knees by the box and bowed her head to the floor. The cover fell out of Andrew's hands and clattered heavily down.

Big Boy picked it up and said brokenly, "Gi me de hammer and nails, Pa, I'll finish em." He called out solemnly to the crowd standing outside in the yard, "All o you-all what wants to look at de body come on in."

A long line of people filed in and then out. And the hammer in Big Boy's hand began falling on the nail-heads with quick telling strokes. Mary gripped her jaws tight together trying to keep her mouth shut, but she couldn't.

"Don' nail de cover down so tight, Big Boy. Seems like it'll smother em.—Oh, Jedus—Master—look down———"

Andrew's mule was hitched to the plum tree, and as Andrew helped Mary climb up into the wagon, to sit on the board seat laid across the coffin, a soft shower of white petals fell over her.

"Tell Auntie to come set by me," Mary whispered, and Andrew lifted the old woman and put her on the seat beside Mary, then he took up the rope reins and the mule drew the creaking wagon down the street. Reverend Duncan came next. He was alone in his buggy, for his huge body so completely filled the buggy seat, there was no room for his big fat wife who drove alone in another buggy right behind him.

A stream of men and women and children on foot followed them. The sun was almost down, it soon would set in the open grave. The treetops glowed red; the people marched and sang.

Mary heard none of the words, but she knew that all these great waves of sound were prayers sent up to God.

Reverend Duncan took his place at the head of the grave and opened his Book, the same Book he used to marry her to July.

Doll yelled at the top of her voice. Andrew and Big Boy hurried to hold her and keep her from hurting herself in her grief. The whole congregation wailed and wept as Reverend Duncan told how Jesus rose from the dead.

Night fell before the service was done. Torches lighted the men who filled in the grave with heavy red earth and patted it smooth. All the medicine bottles were laid on it.

Then Reverend Duncan opened the Book again and read: "De Lawd gave, de Lawd have take em away. Blessed be de name o de Lawd."

CHAPTER XXXI

THE sky was thick with stars, but the earth was black with sadness. Hot grief tore at Mary's heart, almost splitting it in two, yet her eyes stayed dry. Her joints ached, her flesh was sore, but she tried to hold up her head.

Her house had been put in order before she got home. Supper was cooking on the hearth, the bed and chairs were in place, burning rags were trying to drive out the scent of death which still tarried thick in the corners. Doll helped Seraphine feed the babies and put them to sleep. She promised to come back in the morning and have all the bed-clothes washed.

Long after everybody else in the house had gone to sleep, Mary lay awake. The night was full of curious sounds that made her sit up and listen. Some of them made her mouth go dry and the cold sweat pop out all over her. She could hardly keep herself from calling Seraphine and Keepsie to wake up and hear them.

Once, Seraphine's baby cried out, and she hushed it with a few sleepy words. Then the blood-chilling sounds stopped for a minute and started again.

At last dawn rose, the cocks crowed lustily, the cattle lowed, the birds sang. The flies clustering on the wall-papers woke and buzzed and crawled. Mary got up and dressed hurriedly. God had plagued her enough. She would pray until she found peace.

Where could she go and not be seen or heard? The Big House garden held too many ghosts. She hurried down the street, down the hill, toward the thick pine woods. Nobody would find her there. The morning star blazed in the gray east, the night was over. She would spend this day in prayer.

Her misery was not a garment that could be shed. It was mixed in her flesh and blood. Only God could cast it out and heal her.

A deep hush lay at the foot of the pines, but high overhead an early morning breeze moved.

She closed her eyes and fell on her knees and bent her head to the earth. But her tongue and lips and voice had got separated and dumb. Despair threatened her. Misery split the shell of her heart clear in two. She could feel it break and bleed. God's mercy was hardened against her and His hand fell heavy on her; thoughts came into her head, but when she tried to hold to

them and get them to speak they slipped away
from her like dreams.

She held up her arms to the sky and tears
gushed out of her eyes as her lips whispered,
"Do, Jedus, look down, hear my heart a-cryin to
you." Then suddenly a clear silent voice spoke
out of her pain, praying and calling on God.

The bright morning gave place to noon and
the voice in her heart prayed steadily on. When
her body got too weary and heavy to stay on
its knees, she eased it down flat on the ground,
moving quietly so as not to disturb her heart's
praying. Surely, God could not help hearing
and heeding if it kept on calling and calling on
Him like this.

The sun, God's own great shadow, stood
straight overhead, casting down spots of warm
light on her. She raised up and tears fell on
her breast for her head was still bent low.

Unex's soul must have climbed high by this
time for he was young and strong.

To-day he would stand before his Maker.
Unex was not hers any more. Maybe he had
never been hers at all. Maum Hannah was always saying that people's children are not their
children. Nobody belongs to anybody. Everybody belongs to God.

The shadows grew long and her weary, thirsty

body was half asleep. Yet she made it roll and wallow and try to make God look down and hear her cries.

Sleep must have fallen heavily on her for she saw her own soul, walking in and out among the pines trying to find the way home. It was dark and a high wind from the sea lashed the treetops. Unex called her, but when she turned her head to find him she saw an open grave. Her naked soul stepped down into it. Unex spoke:

"Looka dat white cloth on de ground."

There it was, right at her feet.

"You done give your soul for dat." He began weeping. "You see dem stripes on de cloth, enty, Si May-e?"

There they were, ten stripes red like blood across the width of white cloth.

"Dem scarlet stripes is Jedus' blood. Every sin you had laid a open cut on Jedus' back."

Mary counted them again. Ten scarlet stripes were there.

"You had nine chillen, enty, Si May-e?"

She had.

"All was born in sin, enty?"

She bowed her head low. But she had only nine children. Why were there ten stripes?

"Seraphine had a sin child, Si May-e."

She had.

"Gawd holds you responsible for Seraphine's sin. You set de pattern and Seraphine followed em. You is to blame."

Mary knew that Unex spoke the truth.

"Wha' you gwine to do, Si May-e?"

She lay speechless.

"Prayin is all de hope you got so pray widout ceastin until dem stripes come clean and you soul gets white as snow."

The grave melted, Unex was gone. Mary and the bloody white cloth were left alone.

Voices called to her all through the long night, but she did not answer them. She could not as long as that cloth lay there striped with Jesus' blood.

The voice in her heart no longer prayed quietly, it groaned and screamed and cried, hour after hour, begging Jesus to take away all those stripes. In her misery she rolled over and over on the ground, her fists beat on her head and breast, but the stripes stayed pure scarlet.

She must try some other plan or she would die unforgiven.

Maybe if she took them one sin at a time, that would help. She began with Unex, her first scarlet sin and prayed for it until that stripe slowly faded and was finally gone.

Next, Seraphine's stripe was changed into whiteness.

Keepsie's stripe was the deepest of all. It took long hard pleading to get Jesus to wipe it out. But at last a dazzling streak of whiteness shone in its place.

One by one all the stripes were gone and the cloth became shining and beautiful. It was white as snow. Whiter than snow, and so shining her eyes could not face it.

She rubbed them and tried to wake out of her dream for Andrew's voice was close to her calling her to wake up. At last she roused and opened her eyes. A new day was shining bright and Andrew was kneeling down beside her. His face was haggard and drawn, and his eyes were red and sad.

"Si May-e, what de matter ail you? Whe you been all night? Nobody in de street ain' slept for tryin to find you. We thought you was lost. When we couldn' find you, I got f'aid you had jumped in de river an' drowned yousef."

Thank God, although her whole body was shaking like a leaf, and her voice was so hoarse she could hardly talk, she could smile and look him in the eyes and tell him that she had been lost but now she was found. Yes, thank God, she was found. Her sins were gone. She had seen her soul striped with pure scarlet, but God had taken pity on her and made it clean. She saw it with her own eyes. Now her soul was white as snow. Jesus had washed it whiter than snow.

Her head was too dizzy to hold it up and she leaned against Andrew's shoulder. Her heart was throbbing heavily too, but her tears were painless.

"I'm so happy, Cun Andrew, I can' keep from cryin. Unex talked wid me dis mawnin. E talked as plain as you. An', tank Gawd, Jedus washed my soul clean. E's whiter'n snow. Yes, Lawd, whiter'n snow."

Andrew patted her shoulder and lifted her to her feet and made her lean on his arm as he guided her up the slope of the hill toward the Quarters.

CHAPTER XXXII

THE deacons appointed Wednesday night, for Mary to come and give in her experience and they invited all the people to hear them decide if her vision meant that her sins were forgiven, or if Satan had sent a dream to deceive her.

Before first dark she dressed herself carefully in a new black and white checked homespun dress and a large white apron which covered the whole front of her skirt. She bound her head with a fresh white cloth instead of a colored head-kerchief, then put on a wide-brimmed white straw hat. The hat was old, its crown was broken and its brim flopped down at one side, but it was white, and she felt it was better for to-night than her new black sailor.

She had not worn her earrings lately, for the babies liked them and tried to snatch them out of her ears. They were in her trunk wrapped up with her love-charm. She slowly untied the cloth that held them and put the earrings on, then the charm.

Instead of tarnishing, the earrings had got brighter with the years. They glittered as gaily as on the first day she ever saw them. Should she wear her charm? Would it be sinful to wear it to-night? She looked in the glass and asked the question to herself. One of her minds said, "Take it off." The other mind said, "Don't be a fool, keep it on." The earrings shook and twinkled. The deacons were men who needed to be ruled in her favor to-night. She would wear the charm too.

When she reached Maum Hannah's house, the place was packed and jammed with people. The news of her finding peace had traveled fast, the crowd had come to hear her experience and to see how the deacons dealt with her. She held her head high and her eyes straight in front of her as she walked through the crowd and took her seat on the candidate's bench at one side of the fire-place facing the five deacons who sat on the other side. Andrew was dressed in his Sunday clothes and his face had a solemn look; Doll sat high up in front with the members, with her sharp little eyes on her husband.

Doll was nervous. Her hands kept clasping and unclasping, her eyelids batted fast now and then, and she kept whispering to Maum Hannah, who sat with her eyes closed, praying.

Brer Dee whispered to Andrew, who nodded his head and stroked his chin and gazed

around at the assembled crowd. The time had
come. He got up and took the cow-bell off
the mantelpiece and made a few hoarse tinkles,
then he began lining out the hymn to be sung,
two lines at a time:

> "My soul be on thy guard.
> Ten thousand foes arise."

Brer Dee raised it, all the people joined in
singing it; high treble voices mingled with deep
basses, but Mary stood dumb. If she cracked
her teeth and tried to sing she would break down
and cry like a child.

> "The hosts of sin are pressing hard,
> To draw thee from the skies."

Andrew's voice rose high and his eyes stared
at something away above Mary's head.

When the hymn was sung, Brer Dee read out
of the Book how the angels in Heaven rejoice
over one sinner who repents; then he prayed a
short prayer asking God and Jesus to guide the
deacons to-night; to help them know whether
the sister who was a candidate here before them
was truly saved or if she had only been deceived
by a vision from Satan.

Mary felt a vague dread of standing up trying to tell all these people what she had seen; of trying to make them understand how her misery and mourning had been changed to joy. Her knees were shaking and when the prayer was over she sat with downcast eyes, while Andrew announced that on the night after her son was buried, Mary Pinesett, a fallen member, had experienced a deep conviction of sin. She did not wait to seek forgiveness, but started to pray that very night, and had prayed on without a drop of water to drink, without a crumb of bread to eat until a vision had come before her mortal eyes. She was here to-night to tell the deacons this vision.

When she got to her feet to speak, the room grew so quiet she could hear her own quickened breath. She was very hoarse and her first words were low and trembling, but as soon as they cleared the way, others that were steady rushed in and loosened her tongue. She was back in the pine woods, seeking, praying, crying in the night. She could hear Unex speaking again, but now his voice was no voice from the grave but an angel's voice from Heaven.

A strange power seized her and held her and she spoke with a new, quickened tongue. Instead of looking first at one deacon, then at another she hardly took her eyes from Andrew's face and he gazed back at her spellbound, with his eyes as bright as stars.

She could feel how eagerly the people listened, how they leaned forward trying not to miss a word she said. Some of them smiled kindly, others wiped tears away.

Brer Dee listened eagerly too, but when she finished, he got to his feet and said solemnly, "Brudders an' sisters, Si May-e has been a turrible sinner. E has sent many mens to Hell. His soul might be clean but his body ought to be baptized again befo we receives em into Heaven's Gate Church."

Brer Dee's words stung. The blood burned Mary's face. A flutter of whispers ran through the room. Andrew rose and cleared his throat. A frown was on his face, and his rumbling voice was deep as he said that Brer Dee was the head deacon, and besides, Brer Dee was a wise man. But Brer Dee was sometimes so anxious to safeguard the church that it made him fall into mistakes. Andrew had never heard of anybody who was baptized more than once. No matter how much they sinned or how many times they fell, one baptizing was enough.

He sat down, but Brer Dee got up and held his ground. "You ain' never hear-ed of no sinner wicked as Si May-e, Brer Andrew. Evybody in dis house to-night knows as good as me, if Gawd didn't take Si-Maye's son to break em heart, e would be a sinnin right on till yet. I think e needs a new baptizin."

Mary felt bewildered. Brer repeated what he said as if she had not understood him. "I say you needs to be baptized again, Si May-e."

Doll got up and said that Brer Dee was right, exactly right. Another baptizing would do well if it rid Mary of all the sin she had.

Mary's earrings quivered in her ears for all the grudges she had ever felt against Doll rose and rankled in her heart for a bitter second. Then she glanced up and met Andrew's eyes, and her hatred suddenly melted. Pity for poor short-necked, short-waisted, short-winded Doll took its place.

The deacons talked on and on, the members said what they thought. Most of them agreed that Brer Dee was right; Mary should be baptized again.

She stood waiting for the decision, listening, thinking, looking at Doll. Maybe, Doll was not to blame for being fat and mean and deceitful. No woman would be so heavy and ugly and common if she could help it. God made her what she was. He had fixed Doll so she knew nothing of pleasure or sorrow, and spent all her days on foolish tasteless half-baked things. Poor duck-legged Doll.

The discussion was done at last. Mary bowed her head meekly and said she was willing to be baptized again. She felt cool and steady; as she bowed she felt her earrings dangle. They were not down-hearted, but gay and bold and shiny.

Meeting was over and the people came up to welcome Mary back into the fold. They shook her hand until it was numb, her arm ached with weariness, but her heart was warmed through with so much kindliness.

Old Daddy Cudjoe came last, after most of the others had gone and only Andrew waited outside to see Mary home. He took Mary's hand and shook it, then he cut his eyes all around to be certain Maum Hannah could not hear him when he whispered:

"If you gwine to quit wid mens now, Si May-e, do gi me you conjure rag. E's de best charm I ever made."

Mary looked straight into his eyes and smiled as she shook her head.

"I'll lend em to you when you need em, Daddy, but I couldn' gi way my love-charm. E's all I got now to keep me young."

THE END

LaVergne, TN USA
22 December 2009
167775LV00001B/1/A